HOW TO ROPE A SAVAGE COWBOY

SILVER SPRINGS RANCH: BOOK 6

ANYA SUMMERS

Published by S & G Books LLC
P.O. Box 3353
Ballwin, Missouri 63022
USA

How To Rope A Savage Cowboy
Anya Summers

Image By: Furious Fotog/ Golden Czermak

Cover Model: Sebastian James

Print ISBN 979-8-4145014-5-9

Ebook ISBN 978-1-7370605-4-3

ABOUT THE BOOK

Lincoln is floundering. He did something undeniably stupid. On an evening out with his best buddies in Vegas, he hooked up with a smoking hot female for a torrid, all night escapade. It was one of the most carnal experiences of his life, and one he wouldn't be averse to repeating.

Under most circumstances, a one-night stand wouldn't be an issue. Except, the woman is his boss and his best friend's sister. If his buddy discovers their tryst, Lincoln is a dead man. Utter disaster. And yet, there was something about that night that makes him want to risk life and limb to hold her, experience her scorchingly addictive surrender again.

As if that isn't bad enough, after they return home, her ex-boyfriend appears in a bid to win her back, unleashing the territorial beast inside Lincoln. She belongs to him, not some city slicker in a suit.

He plans to prove to her that she belongs in his bed. That he's the only one who should be gifted with her seductive surrender.

Now he's navigating wooing his boss, and falling for her. Can he convince Amber to take a chance on him for more than one night?

1

_____

*E*uphoria infused every part of Amber's being.

Why was she so excited?

Bachelorette party in Vegas, baby!

For the first time in forever, Amber was leaving the ranch for the next day and a half. She was flying to Vegas for a night of frivolity as one of Bianca's bridesmaids. That meant, for the next thirty-six hours, she wouldn't have to consider ornery cowboys, temperamental horses, or any of the problems associated with operating a twenty-four thousand acre working dude ranch in the heart of the Colorado Rockies.

She loved Silver Springs Ranch, truly she did. She had been born on this ranch twenty-six years ago. She had been raised on this ranch. In fact, the only time she had lived anywhere else was when she had gone to college in Boston. And yet, there were times when a woman just had to get away from the cows and the mud, and spend time in a place where the people outnumbered the horses.

While there were a few of the ranch's cowboys heading to Vegas with her, she wasn't counting them in the ornery cowboy category since they were partaking in Maverick's bachelor party. She considered every man journeying with her to Vegas tonight her friend, even if they worked for the ranch, and had been her older brother's friends first.

Well, most of them she considered her friend, anyway. One thing she would never do was categorize her relationship with Lincoln Sinclair as friendly. It was more like they were two feral cats who had just been baptized and tossed in a room alone together to duke it out. The man drove her bananas with his grunted answers and caustic stares.

Did he need something? Grunt. How were the repairs coming along in cabin A17? Grunt. Was he able to repair the tractor, or did they need to buy a new one? Grunt.

The dude absolutely infuriated and irritated her to the nth degree. If he wasn't such an expert with his Mister Fix-It skills, they would have real problems. But the man could fix damn near everything that needed it. His abilities were almost legendary. That didn't excuse the bad attitude and scowls he directed her way, though, even when he thought she wasn't looking.

So of course, she had the hots for him. For the guy who only answered her in monochromatic syllables.

He might be rather pissy with her most days, but his six foot three, broad-shouldered frame always revved her internal combustion engines to meltdown levels. His muscular form gave her wayward, naughty thoughts, like having him bend her over her desk to bang her brains out. While she wasn't entirely sure whether she was submissive or not, Lincoln was a Dominant. There were a few of them on this ranch. When her brother had been the Chief Executive Officer, he and his best buddies, Lincoln included, decided to convert one of the out of the way guest cabins to a member's only sex dungeon on the ranch. Amber knew all about Cabin X even if she had never been invited into its sanctity.

She was totally mental for crushing on a guy with a chip on his shoulder who snapped and snarled when he was in her presence. As in: sign her up for the looney bin with a padded cell crazy. But his pissy attitude toward her was her fault. Lincoln had never moved past the incident between them five years ago.

Not that she had gotten over it and forgiven him either, making them two peas in the same damn uneasy pod.

But today was not for mulling over the past, with all its foibles and mistakes. Today was about the hope and promise for the future. The moment she boarded the plane, every problem would be relegated to the back burner. She could pick them all back up when she returned tomorrow afternoon.

The only things on her agenda were making sure the bride had a good time, drinking enough alcohol to impress a drunken sailor, and maybe finding a guy to spend the night with since her man crush, Lincoln, wanted nothing to do with her.

Which was a damn shame because she wanted to climb that man like a tree. No, really. The thought of Lincoln going all dominant on her in the bedroom was super sexy.

However, being the boss meant making the hard choices. One of the casualties of those choices had been her dating and sex life. Amber had a strict policy of not dating the cowboys or any of the employees who worked for the ranch. Although, Lincoln was the one exception she would make. When a woman lived on a ranch and couldn't date anyone on it, that tended to leave her with no one to date.

And going further afield to date, even into Winter Park? Pft! Like she had the time. She worked from morning until night every day, and easily put in eighty hours a week. Occasionally she took a day off, mainly for her sanity and health. Yet the last thing she wanted to do on those precious few days off was put on her dating armor and head into town. On her days off, she preferred burrowing at home and avoiding people as much as possible. But as CEO, there was always something that needed to be tended to.

Frankly, it had been such a long time since she had gotten horizontal with a guy, she worried the next man who got between her legs would find dust bunnies had accumulated on her girly bits. Fingers crossed that it really was like riding a bike since she felt like she had been re-virginized with the lack of action she had seen over the past few years.

It wasn't that she had intended to never date when she returned home to the ranch after her five-year stint in the accelerated combined bachelor's and master's degree business program at Harvard. But it turned out her dad had antiquated notions about her role on the ranch when she returned. She'd been forced to fight tooth and nail just to make her voice heard. Even though her brother Colt was much better than their dad, and had given Amber loads more responsibilities, it had still been tough. But then her brother had met Avery, and had fallen boots over Stetson for the scientist. In the end, Amber had taken over the ranch, becoming the Chief Executive Officer by default.

And everyone on the ranch knew it.

They never let her forget that she had gotten the job not because her father felt she was qualified, but because there was no one else to run things. Especially when her mom vetoed the idea of her parents moving back to the ranch so her dad could take up the reins again.

In the time since being named CEO, Amber had worked twice as hard as her brother and her dad to be accepted by the ranch employees, some with more success than others. There was an entire swath of what she considered the old guard, with the older cowboys, who were determined to prove that she didn't belong at the helm of the ranch.

It frustrated her to no end. On a daily basis, she still felt like she was trying to prove that she was worthy of the position.

In the dead of night, in the same bedroom she had grown up in, with its peach walls and ivory wooden furniture, she sometimes wondered if they were right, and that she didn't belong here. Not that she knew where she belonged if it wasn't on the ranch.

Jesus.

She was supposed to stop thinking about the ranch for the next two days, not dredge up everything about the place that made her downright miserable.

Focus, girl.

If she was going on the hunt for a man to play with tonight, she had to dress the part. So far, she had narrowed her dress options down to two—a little black number that barely covered her rump, or a fire-engine red number with a plunging neckline and built-in bra that put the girls on display while presenting her legs and other attributes nicely. Hell, she couldn't decide which she would like to show more of, tits or ass. Which was why both dresses made it into her small carryon suitcase, along with the required shoes—one pair for each dress—a pair of patent leather Louboutins in the same red as her dress, and a pair of Jimmy Choo's that were dusted gold, crystal strappy sandal heels. Both would make her legs and respective dresses look fabulous.

She would figure out which to wear tonight once they

made it to their rooms at Caesar's Palace. Plus, she had a replacement if something happened to the other.

She tossed in her pajamas, extra panties, and a casual outfit for the journey home tomorrow. She added her toiletry bag, remembered to grab her makeup bag, and hair straightener. She even snatched the package of condoms she'd picked up at the drug store the other day, and tossed them in her bag. Because when a woman made plans to get her groove on, it was better to do so responsibly.

She could hear the comments from some of the ranch hands now about the CEO who got herself knocked up in Vegas because she had been too stupid to use protection. Even though she was on birth control, accidents did happen. Knowing her luck, she would end up being one of those exceptions to the rules.

Amber was just double checking that she had everything she needed for the trip when her cell phone blared on the bed.

She closed her eyes at the sound.

Please don't be the ranch.

When she glanced at the name that popped up, it brought a huge smile to her face, along with a boatload of relief. She answered on the second ring. "Brecken, how are you? It's been a long time."

"Amber, I'm so glad you answered. I've been thinking about you a lot lately." His cultured baritone resurrected so many fond memories.

"All good things, I hope." She and Brecken had dated starting her junior year of college, and all the way through grad school where she'd earned her MBA in hospitality management. To date, he was her longest romantically inclined relationship. The last she heard, he had been made a Vice President at his father's global investment firm.

"Nothing but the best when it comes to you, I can assure you."

He sounded overzealous. What was he up to? "Not to rush our call, but I'm leaving to catch a flight here in a bit. Maybe we should have a catch-up phone call when I return."

"Going somewhere fun?"

"Yep, Vegas. It's for a bachelorette party for one of my good friends," she explained, zipping up her carryon luggage.

"I'm officially jealous since I'll be working late tonight. Remember when we went to Vegas after undergrad graduation?"

They had both been in the accelerated business program, although Brecken had gone down a different avenue with his eye on running his father's Fortune 500 company one day. Amber chuckled and shook her head at the warm memory. "How could I forget? You kept telling people that I was your wife. I think we were drunk the entire weekend. And we made sure to get all the upgrades because we were on our 'honeymoon.' You even had me wearing your high school class ring like it was a wedding band."

"Looking back, I wish I could have convinced you to marry me. I think I asked you at least a dozen times that weekend."

The recollection made her grin. It had been a spectacular weekend. And there was a part of her that longed for those simpler days when she didn't feel the weight of the world on her shoulders. "You even took me to one of those drive-through chapels with the Elvis impersonators. But I seriously doubt you, Mister Urbanite himself, would have enjoyed living on a ranch. I told you that back then, if you'll recall."

Amber remembered how torn she had been, staring at her responsibilities to her family and the ranch versus how much she cared for Brecken and wanted their relationship to continue past graduation. In the end, she had held herself back, refusing him when he asked her to stay in Boston with him, because she didn't see a future where they could be together.

"Life's strange. The older I get, the more I realize how much I didn't know back then. I miss you, Amber. We were great together."

She almost dropped her phone at his sappy statement. "What? It's been three years since we broke up."

Three years since he had broken up with her because she wouldn't toss away her responsibilities to her family's ranch for him.

"I know. I was arrogant. I thought that it had to be a certain way, that my life had to be a certain way, and I was wrong. I recently relocated to Denver. We're establishing a new office here, and I'm heading up this branch."

Denver was close—really, really close—to Silver Springs Ranch. On a good day with little traffic, it was a two-hour drive. "Oh, really? Congratulations on the promotion!"

"Word through the alumni grapevine tells me that you made CEO before I did. Not that I'm surprised, you've always been smarter than me. But the reason I'm calling is because I'd like to take you out to dinner... on a date. In full disclosure, I'd like you to consider seeing me again. I know this is likely coming out of left field for you, and I don't even know if you're seeing someone..."

"I'm not seeing anyone."

"Then it's a date." He sounded extremely pleased over her single status.

The thing was, she had been crushed when he'd broken things off because she wouldn't stay with him in Boston. "I'm not sure, Brecken. I don't know if we're even the same people we were back then. I know I'm not, with all the responsibilities I have resting on my shoulders."

"Let's be real. We might have grown up a bit since then, but at our core, we're still the same people. I bet you still eat your fries slathered in ketchup, and cry at Hallmark commercials, and tend to be cranky before you've had that first cup of coffee. You're not a morning person but can be bribed out of your funk with coffee and donuts. Your favorite color is blue—not like the mid-afternoon sky, but as it deepens to indigo as the sun sets in the evening. I know you, Amber, and I know me. I've thought about this, about you and me, quite a bit. I *want* to be with you. And I hope you'll give me the chance to convince you how amazing we would be now."

"Oh... um, can I think about it?" she said, because she sort of had an obsessive crush on Lincoln. Not that her crush on him was good for her in the slightest sense of the word. But it was also super sweet how much Brecken remembered after all this time. Like he really had kept a flame burning for her. It knocked her off-kilter.

"Absolutely, take whatever time you need. But Amber, I know we're right for each other. Think about it. Consider it, and me."

Did she want to date him again? Denver was infinitely closer than Boston. It would still be long distance. Uncertainty filled her. It felt like one more problem she had to deal with. Perhaps after the night in Vegas and taking time to get away from it all, she would have a clear idea of her path forward. She checked the time on her watch. "I'll think about it. I promise to give it considerable thought. Look, I wish I could talk longer, but I've got to go meet everyone to drive to the airport. No matter what I decide, I would love the chance to catch up with you."

Maybe they could meet for dinner in Denver somewhere simply as two old friends getting together without the pressure of making it into something more.

"Have fun tonight. We'll talk again soon." There was a wistfulness in his voice.

"I plan on it. Take care." She hung up.

What in the world? Brecken wanted to date her and start their relationship up again? Talk about a blast from the past. She hadn't thought about him in a long time.

Back then, when they were dating, she had loved him. Past tense. When she had refused to stay in Boston because of needing to move back home to work the family business, it had been the demise of her longest, most adult relationship.

But working on the ranch had been expected of her. In her mind, there had been no choice but to move back home.

And yet, he wasn't wrong. They had been great together, compatible both in and out of the bedroom. He treated her like a princess, while respecting her intelligence and drive.

Then again, if she hadn't moved back home, Colt would never have been able to follow the love of his life Avery around the world.

Amber was pleased as punch that they were coming back to the ranch for Maverick and Bianca's wedding next weekend. They weren't arriving until tomorrow. It was something to do with Avery's job, and a speech she was giving tonight at some hoity toity function.

Amber hefted the suitcase and headed down the stairs, flipping off lights as she went.

It would be nice to have her brother home. She'd missed him, and her sister-in-law.

As for the rest, she had no clue what to do about Brecken. Mainly because she had been mooning over Lincoln for so long, it had become a part of her identity on the ranch with her small circle of friends. Her bestie, Noelle, would freak when she told her about Brecken's call.

And there was a part of her, the lonely, exhausted, and overworked part, that wanted to say yes to Brecken. She was just so tired of fighting every day just to keep her head above water. It wasn't that the ranch was too much. It was constantly proving that she had a right to be there, to have the title of CEO.

If she said yes to Brecken and started seeing him again, and the pressure grew too massive for her to handle any more, when she walked away from the ranch, at least she would have a direction of where she should go.

Amber's head told her it would be a smart move on her part, while her heart whispered another tale.

Could she bury her unrequited longing for one guy by dating another man?

*S*ilver Springs Ranch was located near Winter Park, Colorado. The ranch itself was over twenty-four thousand acres, and had been in Amber's family going on five generations, although it was her grandfather who had turned it into a working dude ranch to invite tourists to come play cowboy.

His nugget of an idea had turned into a gold mine. Today they had the main hotel, with an onsite sit-down restaurant, and a newly installed café run by Amber's friends, Morgan and Kate. There were cabins available to rent that had all the amenities including a full kitchen. They hosted cattle drive excursions, had horseback riding, and hiking trails galore. They even offered outdoor survival training and guided backpack camping. Plus, they hosted festivals and events like the upcoming rodeo day the weekend after Maverick and Bianca's wedding.

It was mid-April, and everything was going green. Spring was one of Amber's favorite times of year. She loved watching everything blossom and return to life after winter. On the drive to the hotel, the main hub where her office was located, she schooled her features into a pleasant façade, as if she hadn't just received a world-altering phone call.

The last thing she ever wanted to show around here was weakness. Because then the sharks would scent blood in the water and come for her, proving those good old boys right that she was too emotional, too irrational, to successfully carry out her duties.

One of those cantankerous cowboys would contact her father. She knew it as sure as the sun would always set in the west. It was a fact. And it meant she walked around this place with an invisible ax over her head. One wrong move, and everything she had slaved away on for the past eighteen months would vanish.

Amber rounded a crest on the road and there it was, the jewel of the ranch. The hotel was considered a premier destination in the Colorado Rockies, and had been for the past fifty years. It sat nestled in the valley, surrounded by craggy slate mountain peaks still covered with snow. The rustic hotel stood three stories tall. The exterior was a blend of hickory-colored wood logs and shimmering, clear glass that gleamed in the sunlight. There was a wide veranda, with plenty of pewter Adirondack chairs for guests to relax in and watch all the activity on the ranch.

As she neared the parking lot, she noted the steer off in distant fields, grazing. Cowboys on horses rode around the outskirts of the herd, ensuring every cow's safety despite the sharp increase in predators this past winter.

They had lost half a dozen cows to predators this winter —too many in her book, and in her father's as well. She grimaced at the memory of that lovely phone conversation. Like Amber singlehandedly had a hand in global warming or the increasing spread of construction and deforestation that was causing predators' ecosystems to shrink, making them desperate for food.

She drove her SUV straight to the front where she noticed the group of people standing around with their luggage, waiting on her. Bianca and Maverick, the respective bride and groom, were laughing at each other. They looked good together, like they fit each other. Noah had his arm around Morgan's waist. They had married this past fall in a lovely little ceremony, and were expecting their first child together this summer. Kate, formerly known as Eve, was gesturing to her fiancé, Duncan. Tanner stood beside Lincoln, and they were chatting with Amber's best friend, Noelle. On the stairs leading up to the hotel's front door, she watched Mrs. Gregory stride inside with Emmett and Grace's little boy, Jamie, bundled in her arms, only for Grace to turn into her husband with a dejected look on her face.

"Hey guys. Everything all right?" Amber asked Grace and Emmett as she exited her vehicle.

"Yeah, just some new mom anxiety. Jamie will be all right with Mrs. Gregory," Emmett soothed Grace.

"Matt and Eli aren't coming?" Amber asked Duncan with a raised brow. They were part of the wedding party, even if they were just ushers. Amber thought everyone in the wedding party was heading to Vegas.

"No. I've got them helping out here. We had a last minute camping trip get booked for the weekend that Matt is going to oversee, and Eli is going to stay to help out in the stables," Duncan stated. Matt and Eli had served as Navy Seals in Duncan's unit. Now retired from the military, they had come to work for the ranch last spring, and had slid right into ranch life with ease.

"Then everyone's here. I can fit three people in my vehicle. If the rest of you want to pair up and drive to the airport..." Amber took charge, mainly because that was what she did. Not that she heard any arguments from the troops.

And while everyone else had smiled at her arrival, Lincoln simply stared with his dark, impenetrable, espresso gaze. Amber did her best to ignore the way her body electrified with him near, or the fact that he looked like down and dirty, up against the wall, sex.

Lusting after him would only end one way: with heartbreak and utter ruin.

She redirected her focus away from the broody alpha to the task of getting everyone to the airport in a timely manner. Noelle, Grace, and Emmett ended up in her car. The three vehicles caravanned to the Winter Park airport. It was a tiny little strip of an airport—a blink and you'd miss it kind of deal. But it was where they were catching her family's Lear jet—one of them—to ferry them to Vegas and back again.

One of the perks of being an Anderson, beyond her trust fund and sizable bank accounts, was the ability to travel on a dime. It was why Amber had suggested Vegas to Bianca as the perfect place to go for her bachelorette party. Not to mention, she wanted to watch the cheeky Brit slip dollar bills into a big, muscular, naked guy's G-string at the Australian male review they were attending tonight.

The plan was for the two parties to separate for dinner and their own celebration, like the Australian male review the bride's party was seeing at eight, before meeting back up with the guys at one of the clubs in Caesar's Palace, where Amber had reserved a VIP booth for them. She believed the men were heading to a strip club but that wasn't her area to oversee.

It didn't take long for them to get to the airport and go

through security. Everyone chatted excitedly as they boarded.

Amber had their flight attendant break out the champagne so the festivities could begin on the flight there.

"I just want to say thank you to everyone for coming, and to Amber for setting this amazing night up for us. Maverick and I appreciate it so much." Bianca toasted her with her champagne glass.

"You're welcome."

"It's too bad I can't drink tonight." Morgan rubbed a hand over the slight protrusion of her belly. She and Noah were expecting their first baby together this summer. Noah had a pair of twin boys from his previous marriage whom he had raised on his own after his first wife died.

"It's all right, love. He's going to be just fine, I swear," Emmett consoled Grace, who looked crestfallen.

"I know, but what if he needs me?" Grace stated with a trembling voice. It was Grace's first time away from little Jamie. He had been born at the ranch during a horrible snow storm right before Christmas last year, and was just the sweetest little boy imaginable.

"Just think of it this way, you get to sleep all night long without waking up for a midnight feeding." Noelle squeezed Grace's hand since she was sitting on the other side of her. Those two had become thick as thieves since Noelle moved to Winter Park.

"I know. I just never thought it would be this hard to leave him. Going back to work was hard enough." Grace swiped at her tears.

"Mrs. Gregory watched Colt and me when we were kids. Jamie will be fine, and likely spoiled beyond redemption. And you get a night out in Las Vegas on the ranch's dime with your husband," Amber assured her.

Grace dried her sniffles and looked at her husband. Emmett nodded, casting her a sexy grin full of innuendo. Grace stiffened her spine, and the first hints of a smile appeared. "Right. Sorry. Didn't mean to be a downer before we even take off."

"Being a new mom, a new parent, is tough. I never knew worry until the boys came along, not really, anyway," Noah stated, his arm around Morgan's shoulders.

"And at least you can drink tonight," Morgan said with a wry grin.

"There is that." Grace nodded.

The pilot came on over the speaker, letting them know they were cleared for takeoff. Amber relaxed back in her seat. Or she tried to. It was not easy to do with Lincoln sitting across the way, his unreadable gaze studying her.

He'd barely spoken two words to her, other than a few grunts and nods. But no one thought it was unusual. It was just Lincoln being Lincoln. Although, he did smile at something Tanner said. And he had no issues debating the merits of the coming baseball season with Duncan and Maverick.

Amber wanted to shake Lincoln. Wanted to ask him why he treated her the way he did. He held her at arm's length. He was never cruel. But there was always distance between them.

It smarted because she was desperate for his touch.

And she was a glutton for punishment apparently. Because here she was, on the way to a fabulous night out with her friends, she had an amazing man interested in dating her, and yet she was reaching for something else, for someone else. Her dissatisfaction with her life infiltrated every corner of her being.

Brecken was the smart choice. Wealthy, career-oriented,

intelligent, from a good family that doted on him, kind, handsome, and everything that she *should* want.

But her stubborn girly bits didn't even tingle at the prospect of dating him. And yet, one sneer from Lincoln, and those same girly bits fluttered their lashes and flirted with him.

What she needed to focus on tonight was neither man. Maybe a night off from her life was exactly the ticket required to get her head on straight. This way, she could figure out her path forward with a clear head. It *was* Vegas, after all. There would certainly be loads of hunky guys up for a one-night stand.

Amber finally glanced away from Lincoln, breaking contact with the enigmatic gaze that stirred every molecule in her being, and stared out the window. She was tired of wanting what she couldn't have.

And that man would never want her.

3

*L*incoln sipped at his beer, surveying the club scene. The strippers had been gorgeous, sexy fun. But he had also recognized the avarice in their gazes, which was why he hadn't gotten a lap dance. In fact, the only one in the bunch who had gone that route was Tanner, mainly because he was the only other single guy on their trip besides himself. And that look in those ladies' eyes was something he had seen on faces in the trailer park where he'd grown up.

It left a foul taste in his mouth.

Not that he was going to allow it to ruin his night. However, it zapped his interest from lustful into merely appreciating their beauty. When one of your best friends was getting hitched, you took him to see strippers. Period.

But now they had rejoined the women, which Lincoln didn't mind. The stripper thing had run its course. If you've seen one pair of tits and ass, you've seen most of them.

The nightclub inside Caesar's was packed tonight. Amber had rented one of the large, purple, U-shaped booths that was big enough to seat everyone in their party. The lounge area was elevated enough it gave them a clear view of the black-tiled dance floor.

It was a nice place, if a bit on the flashy side of things. But that was Vegas.

Lincoln didn't want to get piss ass drunk, which was why he was sipping his drinks. Initially, he'd thought about finding a hookup for the night. But that was before he realized the bane of his existence was going to be there.

It was stupid that he hadn't considered that Amber would be at the parties for Maverick and Bianca. She and Bianca were thick as thieves since Bianca had emigrated here from England last summer. And she was a member of the bridal party, along with being the brains behind the idea to have the bachelor and bachelorette parties here in Vegas.

It wasn't that he didn't like Amber. He liked her a bit too much. The woman had starred in far too many of his fantasies over the years. Not that he would ever do anything about it. She was his boss. The money he made helped pay for his sister's college tuition. He wouldn't jeopardize his position simply because his dick acted like a dowsing rod every time Amber strutted in his vicinity in those high heels and tight skirts.

Instead of hooking up with a cocktail waitress, he kept an eye on the women. All the guys were doing that, to be fair.

Maverick was out on the dance floor with his bride to be, looking as happy as a fly on shit. Emmett and Grace were cuddled close together on the opposite side of the table with Grace blushing to high heaven. Considering this was their first night away from the baby, he doubted they would last much longer before heading up to their room. Tanner was attempting to charm Noelle, who seemed uncomfortable with the crowds present in

Caesar's Palace, and while she smiled at Tanner, that smile was tight.

Lincoln couldn't really get a read on Noelle. She was new to the Winter Park area but was close pals with Amber. Morgan and Noah had headed to the casino a while back. Which likely meant those two would be heading up to their room since they didn't have the boys with them.

Duncan and Kate were up at the bar, getting more drinks. Those two were getting married in June. That pair had been through the wringer together. In fact, when Kate first came to the ranch last November, she had used an alias and gone by Eve.

It was too bad Colt and Avery hadn't been able to make it tonight. Lincoln was looking forward to seeing them when they returned to the ranch tomorrow. He had missed his friend while he had been gallivanting all over the globe with his wife.

He was happy for all his buddies and their connubial bliss.

But, as glad as he was for them, he had started to feel like the odd man out quite a bit lately. All his friends were getting hitched and leaving him without a wingman—with Tanner being the exception. Granted, Lincoln had never given much thought to marriage for himself. Yet seeing the satisfied gleam on his friends' faces made him think they might be on to something.

He shot a glance across the club as the music changed to a fast number.

She was fucking stunning.

The woman took his damn breath away. But then, she always had. From the moment they first met at Park Tavern years ago, it was like he had taken one look at her and had been smacked upside the head with a frying pan. His entire being came to life whenever she was around. And it took all his control not to walk around sporting wood when she was in the vicinity.

Amber's jet black hair fell in a waterfall of silken tresses down to her midback. And the dress she had on? It was enough to give a guy a heart attack. It was a slinky, fire engine-red number that hugged every toned curve of her body. On her feet were a pair of skyscraper heels that displayed her killer legs and looked sexy as sin.

He had to fight a hardon every time he looked her way, and he had been hard pressed to keep his eyes off her.

Jealousy gripped him when she laughed up at her dance partner—some random dude with over stylized blond hair that shouted douchebag to him. The guy kept putting his hands on her. Every instinct flared that Lincoln needed to defend Amber. Waves of possessiveness flowed through him. That dude shouldn't be allowed to touch her.

Like Lincoln was the only one who had a right to touch her.

He had no rights to her, no claim on her. In all the years he had known her, they had never ended up in bed together no matter how much he would love to have her in his bed. She was in the forbidden, untouchable category for him. But the green-eyed monster had him clenching his hands around his beer bottle to keep himself from striding over and knocking that guy's lights out for touching her.

And did she do anything about the guy groping her? Nope. Just smiled prettily up at him and stepped closer in invitation.

Watching Amber with him was driving Lincoln nuts.

Dammit. He should be flirting with a cocktail waitress, not obsessing over his boss.

Amber was totally off limits. Not simply because she

was his superior. She was also his friend's younger sister. She was the daughter of the ranch owners. She was satin, lace, and silk, and all the finer things in life. Lincoln was from a trailer park gutter, and would tarnish her with his touch. She was far too good for the likes of Lincoln, and he knew it.

It was why he kept his distance. Even when he spied the invitation in her eyes, he knew there was no future there.

When he looked at her, it was a constant reminder that as far as he had come by his own grit, he would never be good enough for someone like her. It didn't stop the yearning though.

He'd be lying if he said he didn't want her. That he hadn't jacked off more times than he could count thinking about all the dirty things he would love to do to her.

Fuck. He craved her like a dieter did sweets, and who had been dropped unattended in a candy store.

Only in this instance, he was the one who wasn't good for her. But that didn't stop the clawing need, the yearning to have her submit herself body and soul. To have her hand over her power and let him crack her open as he gave her a taste of the purest ecstasy she would ever know.

Watching her in the arms of another man was pure, undiluted torture.

He imbibed another swig of beer as the song ended and changed to a slow number. The douchebag pulled Amber close, his hands all over her body. And Amber simply beamed up at him like he was the greatest thing since sliced bread.

Lincoln would give his left nut to have her smile at him that way.

When the dude cupped her ass with his hands for all

and sundry to see, Lincoln saw red. That was not the way she should be treated in public. There were lines one did not cross. Slamming his beer bottle on the table, he strode toward the dance floor, uncaring how it looked to his friends as he marched directly toward Amber.

When he reached the oblivious couple, he grabbed her forearm. "That's enough, Amber."

"Hey, who the hell are you?" the guy snapped at him and tried to elbow him out of the way. "Find your own woman."

He ignored the dude because it took everything inside him not to clock him in the jaw for putting his hands on Amber that way. He addressed her. "You're done here, Amber. Let's go."

"Lincoln—"

"Wait, you know this guy? Screw this, I'm out. There are plenty of other chicks in this town and I don't need the complication." The man scampered away without a backward glance. In fact, he couldn't get away from them fast enough.

Good. Maybe the fucker would think twice before getting too handsy with a woman who didn't belong to him.

He shifted his hand up to Amber's bicep. Wordlessly, he steered her off the dance floor. His plan was to escort her up to her hotel room. Once she was secure for the night, he would head to one of the bars that were more low key in the resort, and find some company for the night. It was a win-win for everyone involved.

"What the hell, Lincoln!"

He grunted but didn't say a word. If he spoke up, he would make a scene. He had too much respect for her to chastise her publicly. He realized that was odd considering how much people put on social media these days. At least she didn't fight him, and kept a tight smile on her face. He knew she was going to blast him. But it seemed she was waiting until they were alone to do it.

In the elevator, he murmured, "You'll thank me in the morning for saving you from that guy. You've had a few drinks—"

"Grrrrr. I know my own mind." Her eyes flashed. Those smoke-colored orbs were full of flames.

The elevator spat them out on their floor quickly and silently. Wrenching her arm from his grasp, Amber stalked off the elevator. He admired her backside, the way her hips swayed to and fro with her angry strut, while he followed close behind. Lincoln was well aware that she was pissed.

She could be angry all she wanted, but he had saved her. Truly.

At her room, before she could protest, he took the key card from her hand and shoved her door open. He waited, needing to ensure she entered before he headed back downstairs.

Without warning, Amber fisted his shirt in her hands, straining the material, and pushed him through the door with a snarl.

"Hey! Cut it out." He glowered, his own anger rising.

She emitted an enraged growl and drove him further inside. With his hands up, he didn't resist, figuring it was easier to let her get all her anger out. That way she wouldn't do something dumb, like go find that guy again. She deserved someone who stuck once they discovered she wasn't easy pickings.

"How dare you?" she growled, getting up in his face, shoving her hands against his chest—without success—so enraged, he was surprised she didn't have smoke coming out her ears. "What gives you the goddamn right to interrupt me like that?"

"He wasn't good enough for you. You deserve better than that guy."

"Who the hell are you to determine who is and isn't good enough for me?" she snapped, shoving him again and again like she could actually move him without his consent when he was easily twice her size.

Frowning, he replied, "I'm just looking out for you."

"Well, you can stop. I don't need to be looked after like I'm too helpless to know what I want. And what I wanted was to get laid tonight, or is that too much of an issue for you?"

Fuck. "Not with that guy. You're better off without him."

She put a hand against her chest, some of the anger dissipating, only to be replaced by abject misery. "All I wanted was one night, just one night for myself, where I'm not hounded with responsibilities."

Christ, when she said it that way, he felt awful for intervening the way he did. He had let his own feelings get in the way and override his good sense. He should have left her to it. "Sorry. Didn't mean to overstep. What can I do to make it right?"

Amber pissed off and snarling at him, he could handle. But Amber looking like he'd just kicked her puppy, if she had one, wasn't something he could deal with well. It made him want to scoop her up. Soothe her. Promise her the world if she would just smile again.

"Well, you could fuck my brains out," she said with blatant honesty, and a straight face that was full of the intensity that always surrounded her.

"What?" Surely, he had heard her wrong. She had not just asked him to fuck her. Had she?

Even the idea of her asking him that had his dick twitching. God only knew, there was little he wanted more than to delve into the treasure trove of her gorgeous body.

"You heard me." Her hands went behind her back. He heard the sound of her zipper lowering.

Danger. Red alert.

Abort mission.

Escape was his only option to keep their relationship above board. Lincoln must leave before Amber pushed the envelope even further. But he couldn't move. His feet were rooted to the spot as the dress loosened and slithered down her form. The vibrant red material pooled at her feet before she stepped out of it. With lust in her eyes, she seductively approached him in nothing but a slip of lace and high heels.

Fuck me.

Entranced. Aroused. His dick strained against the confines of his jeans. Lincoln stood stock still, unable to move or to think beyond the tidal wave of need bombarding his form.

She was the most gorgeous woman he had ever seen. She had smooth, alabaster skin with high, firm breasts tipped with thick, dark rouge nipples that he hungered to taste. Her slim waist was toned with hips that flared out. His fingers itched to grip her tight, to discover how she would react to his touch, to find out if she was wet, and what she sounded like when she came.

And Sweet Jesus, he could see through the flimsy black lace to her pussy. It was denuded of hair, and made him want to drop to his knees and worship her body until she screamed his name in ecstasy. He hungered to know what her pussy tasted like, to have her come all over his tongue.

But he couldn't do any of that. She was forbidden. He might as well dig his own grave if he touched her. If he gave in to the need pounding through him.

And yet, not even gale force winds could move him. Frozen to the spot, curious at what her next maneuvers would be, he waited to see if she truly was bold enough to push the envelope further than she had.

Amber stopped inches from him, close enough that he could smell her peaches and cream scent. He kept his gaze level with hers instead of allowing it to stray to her smoking body.

"Amber," he warned in a low growl. If she touched him, he doubted he would be able to stop. He'd wanted her for too damn long. Craved a forbidden taste.

She glanced at him through her thick, inky lashes. Those smoke-colored eyes had turned molten silver with desire. She wet her bottom lip.

"One night, no strings attached, just you and me."

His gut tightened at her audacious offer. Christ, he wanted her. Wanted to give in to the startling amount of desire thundering in his veins. It was on the tip of his tongue to refuse, to tell her good night and to sleep it off.

Amber brazenly placed her hand over the bulge in his jeans, sliding her delicate fingers along the firm ridge.

He groaned low, the sound rattling around in his chest as she stroked him through his jeans.

Lincoln was a fucking goner.

The moment she touched him, there was no walking away from this, from her. Not when he craved her like he needed air, as if she was essential to his very survival.

"One night, no strings," he agreed, then yanked her into his arms and crushed her lips with his.

Amber fit against him like a second skin. Her delicate,

fine-boned hands caged the back of his neck, like she was desperate to keep his mouth on hers. He was only too happy to oblige and plunged his tongue inside. Her scent surrounded him. And her mouth... fuck, he could kiss this woman every day for the rest of his life, and it still wouldn't be enough.

But their deal was for tonight only. He intended to wring every drop of pleasure from their bodies if tonight was all they would ever have together. And if he had to ignore the possessive roar inside him, exclaiming that she belonged to him, then so be it.

Lincoln was going to hell for touching her without a thought to the consequences and surrendering to the ever-present, clawing need he had for her.

But he was going to enjoy the shit out of the carnal ride.

4

Oh my god!

He was kissing her. Lincoln tasted like beer and her darkest fantasies brought to life. His beard rubbed against her lips. Those big, strong, working man's hands caressed her body, pulling her even closer until she was plastered to him like plastic wrap. The erotic sensation of being almost nude while he was still fully clothed added to the incendiary heat.

His kiss decimated her.

Amber caged the back of his head in her hands. Her fingers threaded into his hair. It was all in an effort to keep his mouth on hers.

The energy in the air around them turned dark and greedy. Angling her head, he controlled the tenor of their kiss with rough thrusts of his tongue, deep inside the cavern of her mouth, that had her leaning into him, moaning, begging for more. He seduced as his tongue danced with hers, taking her deeper under his erotic spell with every stroke.

In all her life, she had never desired a man like she did

Lincoln. He called to her in a way that confounded her. And she was over the moon that he was finally, finally giving in.

He had the softest lips imaginable for a man so hard. And the brutally harsh way he kissed her was everything she never knew she needed. He was wrecking her, ensuring no other man would ever satisfy her, one stroke of his tongue at a time.

Her entire world altered under his heady kiss. It was as if she had been waiting for this moment her entire life. And the moment he conceded and kissed her, he knocked over the dominos fate had lined up for her.

The soft cotton of his dress shirt abraded her nipples. She pressed her torso more firmly against his incredibly firm chest.

Amber prayed that she wasn't dreaming. That he really was touching her with those big hands, with his mouth strategically kissing every single thought out of her head until her reality boiled down to him.

He exceeded her every fantasy. In turn, Amber held nothing back, giving him everything, surrendering to the rising tide of arousal while he kissed her blind.

He didn't entice with his kisses. He invaded. He conquered. He left her clinging to him, greedy for every morsel of desire. The man was still wearing far too many clothes.

Her hands slid along the firm ridges of his chest to the buttons on his shirt. She needed him naked. Longed to feel his flesh beneath her fingertips. She hastily undid the buttons, impatient and greedy.

Never lifting his mouth, Lincoln walked her backwards toward the bed.

Hallelujah!

Lincoln was all in... for tonight, at least. And she didn't intend to waste a second with him if this was all she got. She would have flirted with other men in front of him more often if she'd known this was the response she'd receive.

She moaned at the first contact of her hands on his naked chest as she shoved the halves of his shirt apart. She thought his hands, those capable strong hands were sexy. The feel of his hard chest, a body that had been honed not in a gym but through hard work, made her weak-kneed.

Lincoln tore his mouth off hers.

She whimpered at the loss.

"I want you on the bed. Leave the heels on."

The husky command shivered through her.

"I want to see you first," she panted. She had seen his upper half a time or two. It was the rest of him that she was on edge to view.

Lincoln's gaze narrowed, and his face turned downright stern. Amber didn't understand why that look got her so hot, only that it did, leaving her trembling and achy. But instead of denying her, he undid the cuffs on his shirt, shrugging the material off the rest of the way.

He was perfect, and all hers tonight.

Drawn to him, to the chance to freely explore the wealth of his hunky form, she traced his chest with her hands. He studied her through hooded eyes. But she couldn't stop herself, not when she had craved him for so long.

As she trailed her fingertips over him, the whorls of dark hair covering his pecs tickled. She traced the flat disks of his nipples and was rewarded when they pebbled at her touch. She drew her fingers down his happy trail, fingering the ridges of muscles on his abdomen. Lowering her touch to the waistband of his jeans, she teased the skin, finding his chiseled victory lines.

But she didn't dip her fingers beneath the waistband.

Instead, she circled his body, running her hands along his biceps and forearms, tracing the tribal tats along his obliques. She moved out of his line of sight, to his backside.

Amber bit her lip but even that couldn't contain her appreciative sigh.

She loved this man's back. Sexy didn't even begin to cut it. One time too many, she had watched him strip down to only his jeans and work boots during the summer as he fixed leaky cabin roofs. His muscles rippled and flexed beneath her hands as she caressed him from his broad shoulders down to his narrow waist. She fingered the small dimples low on his back. Before the night was done, she would dip her tongue in those dimples.

Circling him, her hands roved over his rock hard body, committing his form to memory. Because if this here tonight was all she would ever have with him, there was no part of him she didn't want to explore while she could.

When she'd made the full circle around him, returning to his front, she peered up at his face. His gaze had turned black with lust. And the carnal look he cast her made him seem like he was the Big Bad Wolf ready to feast on her flesh.

"On... the... bed," he chewed out, like he was having a difficult time speaking.

This time, his demand slid over any of her objections. A part of her emerged that wanted to follow his orders, that was desperate and greedy to submit. Keeping her gaze trained on him, she backed away until her legs hit the mattress.

Tossing her hair out of her way, as gracefully as she

could, she lowered herself onto the bed under his watchful gaze that missed nothing. She leaned back on her elbows and spread her thighs in invitation.

"Fuck," he growled darkly. His eyes scorched a trail over her form, drinking her in. And if she had to describe his reaction, she would say her naked body almost broke his restraint.

What did it say about her that she wanted his vaunted control to snap? That she yearned for him to unleash his darker tendencies on her?

She didn't get a chance to consider the questions buzzing around her brain.

Lincoln sank to his knees before the bed. He hauled her to the edge so that her ass balanced there precariously. Spread her thighs even wider apart to accommodate his broad shoulders. He leaned in. His face nuzzled her thighs near her apex, his beard scraping over her sensitive skin.

Amber gripped the bedding beneath her, panting, waiting for his next move.

He ripped her panties off in a single snap, tossing the flimsy material behind him, uncaring where they fell.

She gasped at the leashed violence in his actions. Her sex clenched in sweet anticipation. But she couldn't turn her gaze away, too entranced at seeing him this way.

She was left in nothing but her heels. His long fingers parted her folds. He emitted a deep, rumbling growl of pleasure when he drew his fingers through her crease. "You're so wet."

"And what are you going to do about that... Sir?"

She bit her bottom lip, worried that she'd crossed a line. But he *was* a Dominant. It was part of what made Lincoln so enticing—his command and his poise.

The moniker had the desired effect. Lincoln cast her a

sexy half grin as he teased her slit, studying her reaction. "Such a pretty pussy, and it's all for me."

She whimpered. "Yes, it is... please."

"Please, what? Tell me what you want me to do to you."

"Touch me," she begged.

"Like this?" He stroked his fingers through her slit, lightly circled her clit, and left her gasping.

"Yes. Like that. But with your mouth." It was one of the myriad number of fantasies she had about him—to have him eat her out and make her come.

He kept teasing her clit, not enough to get her off, but enough to set her body on tortuous edge.

"Please... Sir," she gasped.

It was like she had said the magic word. Because then his mouth descended to her sex. The first wicked kiss, as he tongued her slit, was like everything else Lincoln did, done with precision and determination.

Her head dropped back on a moan as he did it again, his tongue grazing her crease, from her back channel up to her clit. He experimented, like he was learning her pussy as he stroked her with his tongue, growing bolder with every pass.

"Oh god!"

Lincoln's tongue flicked and laved at her clit like it was his favorite treat. He clamped his hands on her thighs to hold her in place as he delivered his naughty kiss. This was so much more than she'd thought she would experience tonight. And she had to watch him. His dark head between her thighs. The way his tongue pierced her pussy, plunging deep inside, only to withdraw and swirl hypnotic, drugging circles around her clit.

Jesus Christ.

The man savored her pussy with a look of such pleasure on his face, it added to the eroticism, tossing gasoline on an inferno. Amber couldn't remember being with a guy who enjoyed giving her oral this much.

"Oh god, Lincoln."

He smiled. "Yeah, you're such a bad girl, aren't you? You like my mouth on your pussy, don't you?"

"God, yes."

"I fucking love the way you taste." He latched his mouth around her clit, attacking her sensitive flesh.

She whimpered and writhed beneath the delicious onslaught.

He never let up, lapping at her pussy like it was the source of his life. When her clit swelled, poking out from beneath the hood, he sucked it into his mouth like a starving man savoring steak. Her fingers gripped his head to hold him in place as she rocked her hips, needing the friction so that she would finally come while simultaneously wanting to draw it out, never wanting it to end.

Lincoln nipped her clit. Pleasure-pain razored through her and had her back arching.

Lifting his mouth off her pussy, his bearded chin coated with her cream, he snarled, "Put your hands on the bed or I will stop."

At the growled order, she complied. She was too needy and desperate for his lovemaking. If he stopped, she feared a part of her would die inside at getting so close, only to be denied.

"Please don't stop, Sir." She clutched at the bedding as he reaffixed his mouth to her pleasure bud.

Amber came up off the bed, her hips jerking when he slid a thick finger inside her sheath and curled it at just the right angle to hit the bundle of nerves in her pussy. He thrust that finger back and forth while he sucked on her nub.

"Lincoln," she moaned.

This was more than she had imagined, more than she had dreamed. All her responsibilities slid away. He made her delirious with pleasure, circling and stroking her sensitive flesh while she undulated her hips needing more, needing everything from him. She held nothing back. Her cries and moans of pleasure filled the room. She didn't care if someone heard them. Let them.

He added a second finger, stretching her, plunging those firm digits deep inside until she writhed and whimpered as pleasure built inside her in lacerating waves. He suctioned her clit in tandem with his fingers working their magic on her pussy.

Amber climaxed in a blinding explosion. Her back arched and her legs shook at the tectonic force. Surely, the world must stop turning at the pure volts of ecstasy raining through her. She wailed. "Oh god, Lincoln."

He lapped at her cream, drawing her pleasure out even longer, while she shook at the magnitude of her orgasm.

Holy cow, he had a talented mouth. If he was this skilled with oral, would she even survive the bliss when he fucked her?

5

*a*mber lifted her heavy lids as Lincoln withdrew his fingers and mouth from her pussy, then moaned deep in her throat when he put those two fingers in his mouth and sucked her juices off.

Sexiest sight ever. He groaned around those fingers, like her cunt tasted like ambrosia.

Riding her endorphin high, she watched him kick off his boots. Then he removed a condom from his wallet and tossed it on the bed beside her. When he shoved his jeans down, giving her the first glimpse of his swollen cock beneath his black boxer briefs, she rose into a sitting position on the bed.

The man was gorgeous. He had thick, muscled thighs and calves, and lean hips, but it was what was behind those black boxer briefs that had her licking her lips.

He shoved his underwear down, stepping out of both. He stood proudly in front of her. His erect shaft bobbed before her.

My god!

Could a cock be beautiful? Because his was.

"See something you like?"

Amber hadn't realized she had spoken those words aloud. "Yes."

He chuckled darkly, huskily. "Then touch me."

At his command, desire humming through every molecule in her body, she slid her hand around his cock, desperate to touch him, to feel him in her hands, to give him as much pleasure as he had given her. She gripped him at the base of his shaft.

Lincoln shuddered at her touch.

She adored that she could make such a strong man so weak with pleasure simply by touching him. His dick was broad and long. Long enough, it curved upward slightly near the head, and thick enough that her fingers didn't meet as they circled him.

She stroked him gently, exploring his cock, loving the feel of his satiny skin. It was like caressing a silken blade. The head was just as smooth, with precum seeping from the slit. This was one of the many fantasies she'd had of him—to take him into her mouth and make him come on her tongue.

Needing to taste him, she leaned forward and swiped her tongue over the head, lapping at the drop of precum. His salty musk flavor hit her tongue.

She hummed with pleasure.

She looked at him from beneath her lashes. Dark desire was splashed across his harsh features. She licked him from root to tip, enjoying his husky groan. She teased the head, tracing her tongue around his girth.

She held his gaze as she opened her mouth and took him inside.

"Jesus. That's it. Fuck, your mouth feels good."

His praise was all the urging she needed. She sucked on the crown, teasingly, loving the way he hissed with pleasure.

Amber wanted to drive him crazy, make him pant and beg for release.

She shifted her mouth, pushing farther down over his shaft, taking as much of him in as she could fit. But even as it grew uncomfortable, she breathed through her gag reflex, opening her throat and reveling in his husky groan. He was still far bigger than she could fit in her mouth but that didn't mean she didn't give it her best shot, deep throating him again and again. Using her hand in conjunction with her mouth, she moved her lips up and down his length.

"That's it." He gave her free rein as she sucked his cock —for a little while. But when she hollowed her cheeks and sucked hard on his dick, he gripped her head between his hands and began to thrust. "Fuck, that's it. So fucking good." He fucked her mouth, moving her head up and down, faster and faster as his desire rose.

She redoubled her efforts, desperate to make him as wild as he had made her moments ago. With her free hand, she caressed his balls and was rewarded with a groan. She could tell he was close as he pumped his hips, fucking her mouth. It aroused her. Her sex fluttered and clenched as she worked her lips up and down his cock.

His pace increased. It grew far less controlled. His shaft elongated, swelling with each thrust. She craved a taste of him on her tongue.

"Amber, I'm going to come. Spit or swallow?" He gritted out the warning.

Did he really think she wanted him to come anywhere but her mouth? She redoubled her efforts as she sucked him off, making that her response. Her name uttered like that was better than any aphrodisiac. He surged inside her. His shaft lengthened.

"AHHH, FUCK, I'm—" His roar echoed in the room.

Warm splashes of semen filled her waiting mouth as his climax struck. She worked her throat, ensuring that she swallowed every drop. He kept thrusting, riding the wave of ecstasy to its completion.

Lincoln lost in his own ecstasy was a sight to behold. When he stopped thrusting, she finally removed her mouth.

And the possessive look on Lincoln's face left her breathless.

Still cupping her head in his hands, he leaned down and claimed her mouth in a torrid assault. It wasn't lost on Amber that he was tasting himself on her lips, or just how fucking sexy it was.

Kicking off her heels, she rose, needing full contact with his body. She was desperate to touch and taste every part of him. Lincoln gathered her close, their twin moans at finally being skin to skin were muffled by their mouths on each other.

They fell onto the bed together. Hands stroked over flesh as they learned each other's bodies. Their mouths were fused together. She couldn't get enough of him. Couldn't touch or caress him enough. She felt his cock rise once more against her belly.

He rolled them until her back was flat on the bed and he was nestled between her thighs. Lincoln rose to his knees and grabbed the condom. He tore into the foil packet. With her bottom lip between her teeth, she watched him roll the protection over his hard length. She quivered low in her belly as he rubbed his cock, making sure it was firmly in place, his eyes on her.

He ran his crest through her folds. She whimpered, "Please."

"Someone's a little greedy for my cock."

"Yes, please."

"Tell me you want my dick in your tight little pussy." A sexy smirk slid over his lips because he knew the effect he was having on her.

"I want you to fuck my pussy with your big dick, Sir."

Lincoln's expression smoldered. He positioned his shaft at her entrance, pressing the tip against her opening.

She squirmed, her hands stroking his chest.

He leaned forward, hovering above her body, pushing her thighs even wider. But he held himself aloft, still barely penetrating her, and driving her mad with longing.

"Please. I need you," she begged, rocking her hips even as he evaded her efforts to impale herself on his cock.

"Once we do this, there's no going back."

Frustrated beyond measure, she snarled, "That's sort of the point. Now, are you going to fuck me or just tease me?"

His eyes hooded. Without warning, he slammed inside her in a single thrust. At the swift invasion, her back arched with pleasure. He pushed deeper, stretching her.

"Oh my god!"

"Fuck, you're so goddamn tight."

They held there a moment, staring in each other's eyes, Amber panting at the pleasure of having him buried deep inside her. God, he felt so damn good.

Then he withdrew until only the tip remained before repeating his brutal thrust. He did it again and again. Her mouth dropped open as he rammed her pussy.

Sliding her hands over his torso, she rocked her hips, meeting his vicious thrusts, taking him in deep.

But Lincoln had other ideas.

He snatched her hands from his body, then pinned them above her head with one hand, never breaking his stride as he thrust. The dominant move was akin to pouring lava into her system.

"Oh god."

"Yeah, you like me controlling you, making you submit, taking away your freedom as I fuck you. I can feel it in the way your cunt flutters around my cock."

"Yes." There was no denying it added an element of eroticism that had been missing in her previous sexual encounters, driving home that while she might be the boss under normal circumstances, in the bedroom, she needed to be dominated, to be controlled.

"Such a bad girl. I fucking love it. Love the fact that I get to make a mess of this pussy." He propped himself up on his other arm, and brought their torsos into alignment.

In this position, his handsome, rugged face hovered inches above hers. She could feel his warm breath. His gaze broadcast his desire. He established a torturously slow, relentless pace. Restrained by his steel grip, Amber urged him on with her hips, meeting each of his thrusts with her own.

He felt better than any of her fantasies. It was worth the wait. He had been worth the wait.

His dominance slid over her like a caress. As independent as she was, that dominance produced an atavistic response. As if her biological systems recognized he was the strongest alpha capable.

"Lincoln... please... more."

"Not yet. I want it to last."

Frustrated beyond measure, she clenched the walls of her pussy around his plunging shaft.

"Don't do that," he hissed with a low growl.

She did it again anyway. Because it felt so damn good.

"Dammit, Amber." He grunted as if he was in pain.

"This is just round one tonight. Take me, Lincoln, hard

and fast... please." She wasn't above a bit of begging. She needed to climax in the worst way.

Her response ripped through all his carefully guarded restraint. With a muttered oath, Lincoln released her hands, propped himself up on his, and fucked her. Undulating her hips, she met his forceful thrusts.

Flesh slapped against flesh. He grunted and groaned. She scored his chest with her nails. Lincoln rammed deep again and again. The pleasure built in layers, increasing in increments.

Lincoln gathered her close, burying his face against her neck.

She clung to him. Her hand smoothed along his back and dug in for purchase. She writhed as the heat expanded. Greedy for more, Lincoln jackhammered his thrusts. And, well, she had given him permission to screw her brains out.

She loved every naughty minute of his wild lovemaking.

This was what had been missing in her life. This was what she had craved in the middle of the night. This feeling of belonging, of being wanted for who she was and not who she had to appear to be.

Lincoln couldn't know that this was more than a simple one-night stand for her.

Amber had wanted him for too long, had craved to feel him surrounding her, plundering the depths of her form until they were no longer two individuals, but one being, striving to derive as much pleasure as humanly possible.

"Oh god, Lincoln," she cried as her orgasm struck with all the delicacy of an F5 tornado.

It demolished her. She clung as she shuddered in ecstasy. Lincoln followed her over. His deep rumbling groan as his body strained against hers was the sexiest damn thing she had ever heard.

They rocked their hips together, drawing the pleasure out until every drop was spent.

Amber lay there, dazed, enjoying Lincoln's heavy weight draped over her form. His lips were pressed against her neck. His beard scraped her flesh.

She smoothed her hands out, caressing the spots where she had dug her nails into his skin. She wouldn't trade this night for anything. No matter what happened, she was thrilled and sated and at peace.

Lincoln shifted, raising his head and shoulders. At that movement, she lifted her heavy lids. He was so handsome. Everything inside her shivered at the possessiveness in his gaze.

She *wanted* to belong to him. Wished that he would want to keep her past tonight, even when she knew that it was a long shot.

"As much as I would love another round, I only have the single condom with me."

A Cheshire Cat grin spread over her lips. "Not to worry, I have an entire twelve count box in my overnight bag. Consider it a challenge to see how many rounds we can squeeze in before our bodies give out on us."

His gaze hooded with desire. "Is that a fact?"

"It is." She nodded, caressing his chest, loving the fact that he was still embedded inside her. And she could feel his length hardening once more.

"Well, if all we have is tonight, we shouldn't let them go to waste. I accept your challenge."

"My thoughts exactly."

Lincoln claimed her lips in a torrid, hungry mingling. Deep down, in her heart of hearts, she hoped that after tonight, he would want more than a single night.

What would he say if he knew she wanted to keep him?

6

———

*L*incoln woke with a warm female body wrapped around his frame.

He glanced down at Amber. Her head was resting on his shoulder. Long tresses of her inky hair spilled around them. A few strands clung to his chest. He resisted picking up a lock of her hair, not wanting to wake her. Her face was serene as she slept, giving him a chance to memorize the way she looked in his arms. The high cheekbones, the thick fan of inky lashes against her cheeks, the slim nose that tilted up slightly at the end, the lush lips that had looked better than any fantasy wrapped around his dick.

She fit against his side in a way no other woman ever had.

As awareness crept in, he began to wrap his mind around the fact that last night had really happened. He and Amber had screwed each other blind. Multiple times, and in multiple ways. He knew what her pussy tasted like. Knew what it felt like to have her come on his cock. Knew the little noises she made in the heights of ecstasy. And knew that beneath her cool, composed exterior lay the heart of a submissive. All it would take was the right man, the right Dom, to bring her forth. From the small sampling he had received overnight, he wished he could be that man for her.

What had he been thinking?

He had fucked his boss. He had fucked his friend's baby sister. If Colt ever discovered his transgression, Lincoln was a dead man. There were plenty of places on ranch land to bury a body so that it would never be found again.

In truth, the moment she had stripped off her dress, his brain had shut down. A voracious, greedy need had taken hold. It had been incessant. Demanded he take what she so blithely offered. He hadn't thought about anything past feeling her slick heat around him.

His dick rose at the memory, with her peaches and cream scent all around him.

Christ, he would love nothing more than to wake her up by sliding his dick in her sweet cunt and screwing her brains out again, hearing her cry out his name as she came.

But he had agreed to her terms. One night, no strings attached.

The Dom in him seethed, demanding he stake his claim on *his* female. The bastard was acting downright possessive now that he had tasted her—and with good reason, because the moment he had buried himself in her taut heat last night, every atom in his being roared *mine*. On some level, he had known she was different, that she could upend everything he had worked so hard to build. He wasn't a man who ever wanted to give up his bachelor status, not really. And yet, Amber was the one woman on the planet who could make him change his mind. A few more nights in her arms, feeling her come undone beneath his hands, and he would sell his soul to make her his permanently. He knew that as surely as he knew his name.

Lincoln realized there was no future for a trailer park kid from the wrong side of town and a trust fund princess. Not even one as tough as Amber. And he cared about her too much to put her in the position where she would need to choose. Although, there was a dash of self-preservation tossed in there too.

Regret filled his movements as he, slowly and gently so as not to disturb her, extricated himself from her gorgeous body. She was so fucking beautiful, she made him ache. Ache to be inside her again, to hold her and love her, to hear her breathy moans as she cried his name in ecstasy.

When he finally rose from the bed, he drew the covers up over her form and watched her sleep, committing her appearance to memory because he knew he couldn't touch her again. He wasn't the right man for her.

Lincoln dressed quietly, not wanting to disturb her, and wanting to honor the deal they'd made last night.

But maybe he should wait until she woke up?

Except, if he waited until then, he didn't know if he would be strong enough to walk away. Not when everything inside him was clamoring that he stake his claim on her. That meant he would sever their agreement. And he was a man of his word. All it would take was Amber turning his way with that hungry look in her eyes and he would break completely, reneging on the deal they'd struck.

He picked up the scrap of her lace panties from the floor, stuffing the destroyed lingerie into his pocket, as a souvenir to remember this night by. Foolish, perhaps, but he had touched a slice of heaven. For a guy like him, that was as close to heaven as he would ever reach.

Quietly, so that he didn't wake her, he exited her room.

His own hotel room was only a few doors down. He entered it with no one from their party the wiser that anything had happened between him and Amber last night.

When for him, it was a memory that was etched into his brain, one that he would remember forever.

~

Amber woke in stages.

Naked. Sore. Her body well used. She had beard burn on parts of her body. Lincoln had been a revelation. Without any doubts, he had given her the hottest night of her life. Amber had come so many times, it was a wonder she was even conscious.

With her eyes still closed, she reached for him, craving another round before they had to get up and dress for their flight home. She hated the limitations of their bargain and only having a single night together. She wanted more nights with him. Deep down, she worried that no matter what, once would never be enough. She craved his dominance and his touch. Wanted to explore the submissive side of herself with him in depth.

Her hands encountered cold, empty space in the king-sized bed.

Amber's eyes snapped open at finding herself alone.

The light streaming in through the curtains was enough to see by, as she surveyed the empty bed. She rose into a sitting position, wondering if he was in the bathroom. But as she glanced around the hotel room, a sinking sensation filled her being.

His clothes and boots were gone. Lincoln was gone. He'd left like a thief in the night, ensuring their single night deal remained just that. He had even disposed of all the condom wrappers, leaving no evidence or trace of their torrid night together around.

Agony struck sure and swiftly. She was bereft, it felt like her heart had been wrenched from her chest.

She emitted a ragged sob. The pain rose from the depths of her soul. Tears splashed down her cheeks. Amber clapped a hand over her mouth to quiet her mournful cries.

She had wanted a night with him. And she had gotten what she wished for in spades. She should have been more careful of what she'd wished for, because she had gotten it all—and some she didn't want. She didn't regret last night. But he had taken her at her word that they should keep it to a single night.

He'd left her. No strings attached. No emotions. No goodbye.

At least she didn't have to do the walk of shame and hope that none of their friends saw her.

The thought made her tears fall even harder. And a painful realization struck, ripping what remained to shreds. Last night had meant nothing to Lincoln. It had been a physical release. When, for her, it had meant *everything*. It had indelibly altered her on a fundamental level. She knew now that she needed to submit in the bedroom, and that was all thanks to Lincoln.

But had last night been payback for that evening long ago?

Right after she had turned twenty-one, about a month before she and Brecken began dating, Amber had been home over Spring Break. Being a freshly minted adult able to legally drink, she had gone to Park Tavern in Winter Park for a drink and night out away from the ranch.

That had been the first time she had seen Lincoln. She had been at the bar drinking a beer, studying the appetizers on the menu, only to have him sit on the empty barstool beside her and comment, "They have some of the best nachos you'll ever eat."

He had appeared so dashing and sexy in his cowboy get up.

They ended up sharing a plate of nachos, flirting back and forth the entire time. The attraction between them was mutual even though he was eight years older. It wasn't until he walked her out to her car and kissed her that the night went awry. When he asked her where she lived, angling for an invite, and discovered she too lived on Silver Springs Ranch, he changed. All the warmth evaporated when he learned she was the daughter of the ranch owner whom he worked for. And he accused her of deceiving him.

Maybe she had by not being up front with him. But it had been nice for a change, having a man from her home town express interest in her, instead of giving her a wide berth since her dad had put the fear of god into boys to stay away from her when she was growing up. She had soaked up the attention like a person finally feeling the sunlight on their face.

Until last night, she'd thought Lincoln couldn't stand to be in her presence. It was the way he had acted ever since that night five years ago.

Only to have him prove her wrong. He had been just as greedy for her as she had been for him.

Waking up abandoned and alone after experiencing the heights of ecstasy in his arms, knowing that he had been present and right there with her the whole time, left her floundering.

Had last night been a revenge fuck? Had he only done it to get back at her for the perceived slight?

Those dark thoughts had her sobbing even harder. She

wished it didn't matter what he thought of her. She wished things were different, and that he had stayed.

No one knew how hard running the ranch had been for her. Not that she wasn't capable of the job as CEO of Silver Springs Ranch, because she totally was. It was what she had studied in college, and trained for her entire life.

But as the first woman in charge of the ranch, she had come up against some fierce, antiquated male conditioning. Not from the guys who were friends with her brother, Colt, because they all accepted her.

But there were some ranch hands—a group of the older wranglers who spent the majority of their time out in the pastures and riding herd on the cows—who had taken a stance that they were never going to accept her.

Amber worked herself to the bone day in and out just with the hope that they would one day cave. That she would no longer have to prove that she was capable and worthy of being at the helm.

If Lincoln let it slip about last night... any credence or headway she had made would be lost.

She shifted to climb out of bed, feeling ancient and utterly exhausted. Truthfully, she didn't know how much longer she could go on this way.

Whatever joy she had experienced at being made CEO had been leeched away.

The one bright spot had been her fantasies of Lincoln, of being with him. Yet even that had been a farce. If she was worthy enough, wanted enough, then he would have stayed, regardless of their agreement. And he hadn't. He couldn't even be bothered with waking her up to let her know he was leaving her room—and her bed.

Her cell phone buzzed on the nightstand with an

incoming text. Swiping at the tears, her eyes gritty from crying, she grabbed it. It was a message from Brecken.

Amber, if I wasn't clear yesterday, let me be so now. I've never stopped loving you. Have never stopped regretting the way things ended between us. And I want the chance to prove to you that we could be even better this time around.

Okay. Let's try it. She texted back before she could over-think it. She was just so tired of fighting. And Brecken wasn't wrong, they had been great together.

Yeah? Really?

Yes, really. Why don't you come spend some time at the ranch? I'm in a wedding next weekend, and you can be my plus one.

Let me work out taking some time away. I'm sure I could work remotely for a few days.

I arrive back at the ranch later today. Once you provide me the dates you can make it, I will reserve a cabin for you.

You mean I can't stay with you?

She winced, not ready to get horizontal with him that fast. And she didn't want him in close proximity because she could see herself trying to mend the hurt caused by Lincoln by having sex with Brecken. Jumping into bed with him too quickly wouldn't end well. She needed a modicum of space as they got to know each other again. *Sorry. My brother and his wife are in town, and staying at the house. Otherwise, I would make up one of the guest bedrooms for you.*

Ah, no worries. I'll get back to you on those dates.

Great. I've got to pack and get ready to fly home. Talk later?

Yes. And Amber, thank you for giving me another shot.

Warmth filled her at being wanted so much that he thanked her. It wasn't the flash bang excitement she had experienced with Lincoln. If anything, her enthusiasm was lukewarm at best. But it was better than nothing. Especially when she felt like she didn't have anyone to lean on.

No thanks necessary. I'm glad you looked me up.

It was true. If anything, she owed him thanks for drying her tears and shoring up her resolve. So what if Lincoln didn't want more than a night with her? There was a good, dependable man who did.

As for Lincoln, he could go to hell.

7

*L*ater that morning, the wedding party boarded the ranch's private Lear jet. Lincoln didn't begrudge the Andersons their wealth. After over six years of working there, he knew just how hard the family worked to run the ranch. They earned every penny they made, and then some. And they compensated their employees well. His job had afforded him a way to help his mom when she was still alive, and help his sister now while she was in college.

The group was more subdued today after their night of frivolities. Tanner and Noelle looked rather haggard, as if they'd had one too many drinks last night. The four couples seemed tired but had that *we've just spent the night sexing it up* vibe. And Amber looked like an untouchable ice princess, even in yoga pants and an oversized sweatshirt with all that glorious hair of hers up in a messy top bun.

On board, he took the seat next to Duncan and Kate. Across the aisle, wearing sunglasses even on the plane, was Amber. She avoided looking in his direction.

"You doing okay?" Bianca asked Amber.

"Just a few too many last night. I'll be fine," Amber explained with a slight smile at the bride-to-be.

Lincoln snorted. Like hell had Amber had too much to drink. She hadn't been that tipsy. If she thought to play last night off as some drunken escapade that she now regretted, so be it. But he wasn't going to tiptoe around her.

Amber whipped her face in his direction. A dark brow rose from behind the sunglasses. "Problem, Lincoln?"

So, this was how it was going to be between them now. While they hadn't been bosom buddies beforehand, now the energy she was throwing in his direction was downright glacial.

"You might want to be careful, drinking like that. Might cause you to get into situations over your head, sweetheart." His voice dripped derision as he clenched his hands on the armrests of his seat. Otherwise, he would drag her over his lap and whale on her sexy butt until she dropped the attitude.

Those lush lips of hers flattened into a frown. "Appreciate the concern but there's little I can't handle. Very little."

"You sure about that?" he seethed. But then, the two of them sniping at each other was nothing new.

"Oh, I think I know something little when I see it," Amber launched the barb. Then she turned away from him, responding to something Noelle said.

He gritted his teeth. The last thing he needed to do was make the night they'd spent together public knowledge. He might be a bastard and trailer park trash, but he would never disparage a woman that way. Regardless of whether the woman deserved it or not.

The flight from Vegas to Winter Park, Colorado, was short and sweet. They had barely taken off before the captain was announcing they were coming in for landing.

The sooner they were back, the sooner he could put some distance between himself and Amber. As much as he enjoyed antagonizing her, he also was well aware that if he stepped out of line, with the fuck off vibe she was tossing his way, he would likely be looking for new employment.

So much for no strings, no harm, no foul. He should have known better than to sleep with her last night. But he'd been thinking with his dick.

Before long, they were pulling up in front of the main hotel.

Colt and Avery stood on the steps, his arm around her waist, as their group disembarked from the caravan of vehicles. Lincoln watched Amber cut away from the group and head straight for them.

Amber shoved her sunglasses up onto her head. Colt released Avery long enough to give his sister a big hug. Grabbing his duffel from the back of Maverick's SUV, Lincoln watched as they smiled at each other before they let go, and then she was hugging Avery.

Tossing his duffel in the bed of his truck, he sauntered over to the stairs where their entire party had migrated upon seeing Colt and Avery. Although, Grace didn't stay. She said something to the couple, then hightailed it past them, likely going to pick up the baby from Mrs. Gregory.

Lincoln joined them. Colt turned his way with a wide grin.

"Fancy meeting you here. Almost didn't recognize you without a hat on," Lincoln said, taking Colt's hand in a friendly shake.

Colt chuckled. "Yeah, I've gotten used to going without one. But now that we're back for a bit, I'll have to pick it up again."

"You're staying? For how long?" That was unexpected

but pleased Lincoln to no end. He had missed having Colt around, even for something as simple as their monthly poker game. While they had added Matt and Eli, it still hadn't been the same without Colt present.

"That is yet to be determined," Colt explained, and shot a glance at his sister.

"Why don't we all give them some space? If you guys would like to come to dinner at our house tomorrow night, kids are welcome, say five o'clock," Amber offered the group.

"That sounds lovely," Grace said, rejoining them with the baby in her arms. Emmett was by their side, holding the diaper bag and car seat, looking downright domesticated.

In fact, all of Lincoln's buddies were looking that way with their women.

"We're in, as long as you don't mind the boys coming too," Noah stated.

Amber gave him a friendly smile. "They're welcome to come. I'll make sure we have food that they'll like on hand. Now, if you'll excuse me, I need to go check on how everything went while we were gone, and bribe Mrs. Gregory to help with the meal tomorrow night."

"I can help too, since I don't have to worry about the café until Monday. You might as well use me," Morgan offered rather sweetly. She was a good fit for Noah—down to earth, a good head on her shoulders, and Noah's two boys had transformed under her love and guidance, from little hellions into well-mannered kids who only occasionally got into trouble.

"You should make dinner a pot luck affair. That way you don't have to do everything," Kate added. "Because I'd be happy to make a dish or two as well to bring along. I will anyway, no matter if you want me to or not."

Duncan squeezed Kate's waist and looked at her like the sun rose and set with her.

Amber considered the group. Avery held up her hands. "Don't look at me. If you want to know about constellations and comets, I'm your girl. Unless you want some grilled cheese for dinner, I could make that in a pinch."

That got a few chuckles from the group, Lincoln included.

After studying the group, Amber nodded. "Pot luck sounds great. We can coordinate in the morning. That being said, last night was great. I'm thrilled that we all went. And now I need to get some work done."

"I think I will head in to the office with you. I'd love to take a look at things myself," Colt stated, removing his arm from around his wife.

Amber gritted her teeth and exasperation filled her eyes for a brief second before she smoothed it out with a smile that didn't reach her eyes. There was a tightness around her smile too. Lincoln doubted anyone else noticed. "All right, you can follow me in."

What the hell? Why had he never noticed the tension? How had he missed it? And what was it about? Why would she be upset? He would ask Colt. Because Amber would bite his head off in her current state.

The moment Colt and Amber headed inside, the party dispersed, everyone retreating to their own homes. The entire drive home, Lincoln replayed the past twenty-four hours in his mind—from the mind-melding intensity of his night with Amber's slim form wrapped around his own, to the way they'd left things today.

None of it sat well with him. Not when he knew deep down that one night with her would never be enough.

---

8

*C*olt followed Amber into the hotel. Employees stopped what they were doing to say hello to him. And some of the female employees flirted with him even though he was happily married. But then, he was a tall, well-built, successful man with a full head of dirty blond hair, and women had always thrown themselves at him. Besides, with him distracted, she had time to check in with Mike behind the front desk to see if there were any problems while she had been away. There hadn't been any, thank goodness.

But she still wanted to head to the office.

It was better than heading home with nothing to do but think about the implications of last night and whether she could expect some fallout.

Besides, she needed to reserve a cabin for Brecken. He had worked quickly to get time away from the office, and would be here on Wednesday. Colt followed her up to her office that had formerly been his.

"We missed you at the dual party deal last night."

"Yeah, Avery and I wished we could have made it into

town by then. But her thing yesterday evening was something she couldn't miss. We caught the early flight out of Houston and made it to the house by ten this morning."

Amber took her seat behind the desk. It was different having Colt here with her being behind the desk. It was a whole lot easier just emailing him reports than talking about it directly. Because at least with an email, she couldn't read his facial cues.

"It was fun, but I'm glad we're home. This week is going to be jam-packed with tasks because of the wedding," she said.

"Anywhere you would like me to help out, I'm at your disposal. We're staying for at least three weeks, if you don't mind. If you do, we can see if one of the cabins is available."

They were staying?

"No, I don't mind at all. As long as you two lovebirds keep it to your bedroom and I don't end up walking in on anything, we'll be good. That is not a visual I want or need." She tried to play it off like it didn't matter. She loved her brother. But having him here for the next three weeks felt like she was going to be monitored on the job she was doing. It was much easier when she didn't feel like she had him watching over her shoulder to see if she screwed up.

Reaching behind her desk, she grabbed the file folder she needed and handed it across the desk. Might as well rip the bandage off.

"That's the first quarter profit and loss numbers for this year. I didn't have time to email it to you and Dad before the party. But I think everyone will be happy with them." Or at least, they'd better be. Each quarter since she had been at the helm, profits had steadily grown.

"No worries." Colt flipped it open.

She opened up the hotel registration application on the

computer system and searched for an available cabin rental while he reviewed the numbers.

"Profits are up again."

She smiled at that. "I know. And do you see why they're up, even for winter?"

Colt studied the spreadsheets. His brows rose. And then he laughed. "All those adjustments and changes you wanted to make that I wouldn't let you, have paid off."

"I told you. I know it was an expense up front for the new computer system and converting all the cabins to solar. But when you look at what we've saved, those improvements are paying for themselves in spades."

"They really have. I wish I would have listened to you about these modifications back when I was in that seat."

The offhanded compliment warmed her and gave her confidence for the improvement she wanted to make next. "I'm glad you think that way, because I will need your help swaying Dad on my next proposal."

Colt tilted his head. "I'm listening. What do you need my backing on?"

"I want to convert the hotel to solar power."

He grimaced. "Amber, I don't know. It could harm the aesthetic appearance of the hotel. I have a feeling Dad will be more than difficult to sway on this—more like impossible."

She handed him the file with all her projections in it. "Take a look at the numbers. They're hard to ignore. And just so you and Dad understand, I want to do it in a way where the impact to the overall appearance of the hotel is minimal. I've already been talking with Lincoln about designing it in a way where it enhances the way it looks instead of detracts from it."

Colt examined the numbers for a few moments. "Wow, we would save that much? Just from switching?"

"Yeah. And from what I understand from Lincoln," she barely stumbled over his name, "because the backup generators are all solar powered, it will be easy for him to convert the whole system. I can ask him to write up a detailed summary with initial blueprint specs of what the change would look like."

"These numbers are hard to beat."

She knew she had him on her side. Knew that once Colt was swayed, their dad wouldn't be that far behind. It felt good, like she was putting her stamp on the ranch. "I know. That's why I want to push for it, with your support."

"I'll talk to Lincoln myself, get a feel for his vision. Might help me sell it to the old man with you if I hear it from the horse's mouth."

Cut herself out of the awkward middle and have her brother handle her one-night stand? Yes, please! "If you would do that, it would be a load off my shoulders. With the wedding this week and the rodeo the following, I have work coming out my eyeballs."

"I'm at your disposal. Tell me where you need me, and I can fill in."

An available cabin popped up in her search. She held up a finger and said, "Hold that thought. I need to reserve this cabin real quick."

"Who are you reserving a cabin for?"

She entered Brecken's information—what she had of it —along with her name, adding that it was all comped by her into the reservation. She booked him in through Sunday, since he had mentioned in his message that he had to be back at work in the office on Monday.

"Brecken. He's coming to the ranch this week."

"Brecken, as in your ex-boyfriend from college, Brecken?"

"Yeah, he's my plus one to the wedding." She didn't wither under Colt's stare, and was proud of herself for it. Regardless of how insecure she was feeling at the moment, she wouldn't show it.

Colt leaned back in his seat. "I'm just surprised, is all. If I remember correctly, he broke it off because you wouldn't stay with him in Boston."

"He did. But he's in Denver now, which is a much easier commute." She shrugged, trying to play it off like his breaking up with her all those years ago hadn't affected her at the time.

"So you two are getting back together?" He sounded far too skeptical.

"We're exploring that option."

"Huh. I didn't see that one coming. Always figured you'd find someone here in Winter Park."

"And who would that be, brother dear?" Lincoln's image flashed in her mind. "Some cowboy on the ranch who's an employee, or one of the many guys Dad scared away while I was growing up?"

Colt shifted uncomfortably in his seat. "Yeah, it's none of my business. I just don't want to see you hurt. I remember how upset you were when he did break it off back then."

"Avery forgave you for being a jerk and hurting her. Why can't I do the same?" Amber could be just as stubborn as her brother. It was encoded in their DNA as Andersons.

At the mention of the way he had fumbled and almost messed up his relationship with his wife, her brother winced. "Point taken. I will be nice to him. But if he hurts you again, I get to deal with him."

"Fair enough. Let's divvy up the tasks for this week and head home. I bet if you stop by the kitchens and sweet talk Mrs. Gregory, she'll make dinner for all of us and we won't need to head to the store today for supplies," she suggested, because she had not had any time to get grocery shopping done.

"Deal."

She and Colt worked their way through the full list of tasks for the upcoming week. Colt was more than willing to shoulder some of the burden, and planned to oversee many of the tasks outside of the main hotel. This would allow Amber to focus on getting the hotel prepped for the wedding, and for the influx of rodeo guests the following week. It was a win-win all around.

Plus, it helped take her mind off Lincoln, at least for a short amount of time. Because after last night, he was imprinted on her heart and soul. Damn him.

9

*I*n the days following the Vegas trip, Lincoln had thought of little else but Amber. He had begged off the Sunday night group dinner, claiming he had work piled up and that if he was going to take off for the wedding festivities later in the week, the repairs on his list couldn't wait.

Lincoln hated missing out on spending time with his friends, and Colt in particular.

He knew that he and Colt would have plenty of time to catch up this week. They were both groomsmen in the wedding, so he would be hard to miss.

But he needed the time away from seeing Amber. That woman called to him on so many levels. And yet, all he would ever be good for when it came to her was a single night, apparently.

He knew he was acting like a jilted lover.

Yet, it fucking chafed like scratchy wool underwear that all Amber wanted from him was one night. It fed into his insecurities that he was nothing more than trailer park trash, that he would never be anything but that, and while she might have descended into the gutter with him for a night, that was all it would ever be. Deep down, he knew it was for the best. He wasn't good enough for her, not by a long shot.

But that didn't make him crave her any less. If anything, now that he had tasted her enticing sweetness, it was worse. Before their night together, he'd had fantasies about her. Who wouldn't? She was fucking hot as hell with those short skirts and high heels she wore around the ranch.

Yet now he knew beyond a shadow of a doubt what it was like, feeling her move beneath him, what her skin and pussy tasted like, the sounds she made that had driven him wild, and how stunning she was when she came.

And it was worse than ever before. Because now, he knew exactly what it was that he was missing out on.

Fuck.

He promised himself he would stop thinking about her, stop replaying their night together, otherwise he was going to get himself killed. He'd almost electrocuted himself in one of the guest cabins this morning because he was thinking about her and not the electrical work he'd been performing.

Although, in his defense, she was on his mind because they had a meeting this afternoon. He was on his way in to the main hotel to discuss one of the guest cabins that had been damaged in a winter storm a few weeks ago that he had just finally been able to start repairing, only to uncover more damage than they had initially thought.

Striding into the hotel lobby, he was brought up short.

Amber was gorgeous in a black pencil skirt and blush-colored blouse. But her attire wasn't what had Lincoln rooted to the spot. She was greeting a guy who was about his height with a golden mane of expertly trimmed hair, dressed in a three-piece charcoal suit.

It wasn't unusual for Amber to greet important guests in the lobby. They had had foreign dignitaries, celebrities, and even a big time horror author had stayed in the hotel. It was the way she was greeting him that was strange.

They were kissing.

It was a full-on lip lock. When they finished kissing, the guy's hands remained on her slim waist. And Amber was laughing up at him. Lincoln had flashbacks to the night in Vegas and her on the club dance floor.

What the fuck!

Friday night, he had known she was simply scratching an itch with the help. But having it waved in front of his face that she could toss him away so easily enraged him. Yeah, he had grown up in a trailer park. And no, he wasn't the least bit respectable. But at least he was housebroken. And while he might be cavalier with tourists passing through, because there was no future, he was tied to this ranch and the life he had built, and would never intentionally be cruel.

Walking in to see this was a downright a slap in the face. Before he could think better of it, the territorial beast inside him emerged, and he prowled her way with a snarl. "Amber. We have a meeting. If you're done playing and making a fool of yourself in the lobby, I'd appreciate if we could get to it."

The two lovebirds broke apart.

Amber glanced his way. Annoyance, and something else filtered through those goddess eyes the color of a summer storm cloud, which she quickly hid before he got a full glimpse. Just what was the woman hiding?

"As you can see, I'm busy at the moment. If you want to go wait for me in my office, I'll be there as quick as can be," she replied with an imperious tone.

It made him want to take her over his knee. The woman was testing his patience and resolve to remain impartial in her presence.

The guy had his arm around her waist—the same waist he had gripped as he'd pounded inside her taut cunt while she moaned his name. Possessive fury overrode everything. How dare this guy put his hands on what belonged to Lincoln?

"I have a lot on my plate today with the wedding this week. You've got five minutes, or the meeting will need to be rescheduled and the maintenance won't get gone before the wedding," he seethed, clenching his hands into fists. It was either that or he would throttle her.

The guy held his hand out for him to shake. Lincoln couldn't deny that they looked good together. He was tall and golden, while she had her dark raven tresses spilling around her shoulders. They looked like a power couple that one would see on the cover of a magazine.

Begrudgingly, he took the offered hand and shook it.

"It's my fault. I arrived later than expected. Brecken Harrison. I'm Amber's boyfriend," the man said with a gregarious, charming smile.

Lincoln kept himself from sneering at the man. Boyfriend? When had Amber started dating someone? Had she already been seeing him Friday night, and cheated on the guy with him?

Anger roiled and raged, filling every corner of his being. Lincoln had the urge to pummel something, anything, to unleash his wrath. But what he really wanted to do was give Amber the spanking of her life.

"Ex-boyfriend," Amber admonished him with a smile playing around her lush lips. The same lips that had sucked him off with voracious glee the other night. That memory had been fueling Lincoln's fantasies the last few days. He had stroked one out in the shower this morning, thinking of it—and her.

Brecken sent her a sly grin chock full of inuendo. "Not for long, if I have anything to say about it."

Amber playfully slapped him on the chest, and rolled her eyes.

What the hell! She was acting like nothing had happened between them Friday night. And yes, he realized they had the whole no strings attached, no harm, no foul deal. But it was like she had completely blotted out their night together.

When for him, it was all he thought about, day in and out. He went to bed at night with the memory of that night in his mind. He thought about all the ways he had taken her. And god help him, he yearned to do it again.

But Amber acting as if it had been nothing, when he knew damn well she had been present and right there with him, enraged him. Fury engulfed him. He snarled, "Forget it. I see that you're busy. If shit doesn't get fixed before the wedding, it's on you, not me."

Without another word, Lincoln swiveled on his heel and strode off. It was either that or he would go caveman on Amber. Toss her over his shoulder, and carry her to the office or anywhere private and get to the bottom of her blatant disregard.

The problem remained that he didn't know exactly what it was he *did* want from Amber. He knew the best thing for him to do was forget it, and her.

But that was like asking him to forget the sun.

Friday night, he had fought his desire for her, and succeeded—until she put her hand on his pants and gripped his dick. Really, there was only so much a guy could handle.

He had attempted to be a gentleman even after she dropped her clothes. But the hand on his dick had shoved him past the point of reason, and every argument for turning her down fled in a heartbeat.

Mainly because he'd wanted her for years. Ever since that fateful night years ago at Park Tavern, the night they met.

He'd kissed her that evening with every intention of trying to convince her to go home with him. And then he had discovered she was Colt's sister. It was right after he had been offered the position as Head of Maintenance for the ranch. He needed the income too badly to mess around with the boss's sister.

Which had him putting up walls—accusing her of hiding who she was as a defense, to make her want to walk away from him, instead of gazing at him like he was some goddamn superhero.

Lincoln headed back to work, starting with one of the cabins that only needed a few repairs. This was one of the high mountain chalet cabins. This high up and far away from the bulk of civilization, the cabin was completely off grid. It was fully solar powered. And the water came from a nearby well. There was a septic tank that they had to drain and clean each year.

But they had another month before they brought in the local contractors to handle that task.

Outside, there were a few boards on the porch that were rotted. He replaced those first.

Inside, the kitchen faucet had a slow leak on it, but the leak was tied to the garbage disposal. He replaced the disposal system, and changed the washer in the sink that was out of whack. Before he left the cabin, he double checked the electrical system and solar output.

Over the past year, they had been slowly but surely switching each cabin over to solar power. While it was pricey to do up front, in the long run, it saved the ranch oodles of cash. And it kept the cabins from losing power too often during storms. It made it easier for the ranch to offer year-round getaway cabins when they always had power.

That was pretty much how the rest of his day went. How all his days tended to go. He went from guest cabin to guest cabin, repairing what needed it. Granted, he didn't head to the cabin on the ridge with all the work that needed to be done, because he had not been able to speak to Amber.

He was given full range and authority to repair and replace what was needed. However, over the years, they had established a method where for anything above a certain dollar amount, Lincoln would report it—first to Colt and now to Amber—before fixing the issue.

It didn't mean that it wouldn't get fixed, but at times, they had prioritized what absolutely couldn't wait to be repaired and what could wait.

By six that night, he was finished for the day and he headed home. He had his own two-bedroom cabin set back away from the main hub of the ranch, amidst a bevy of trees. He liked the quiet stillness of his place. And while it technically belonged to the ranch, as did every blade of grass and tree around his place, it was home.

He had made it his through grit and hard work.

Inside, he tossed his keys in the bowl by the front door and stripped his boots off. He grabbed a beer on his way to the shower. He wasn't a huge drinker, as there had been far too many residents of the trailer park he had grown up in who had turned to drugs and alcohol as a way to endure their crappy living situation.

But today called for a drink or two.

It wasn't every day that the woman he had literally just spent the night with, tearing up the sheets until the early morning hours, appeared with a man at her side.

After his shower, he fixed himself some dinner. It was nothing fancy, he just heated up some leftover meatloaf that he made a sandwich out of, and tossed some chips on his plate. He put a basketball game on while he ate, and washed dishes.

When he grabbed a second beer out of the fridge, a knock sounded on his front door. Who the hell could that be?

It was just past eight in the evening. Late around here for a visitor. He just hoped there wasn't an emergency maintenance issue. He'd deal with it if it came to that.

Lincoln shoved the door open and felt like he had been struck by lightning.

Amber.

Lust sizzled along his spine at finding her standing on his front stoop, looking beautiful and uncertain. The normal business attire she wore had been traded in for yoga pants and an oversized sweatshirt that made her appear earthy and real.

"Hi, sorry to bother you at home, but I wanted to explain—"

He didn't want an explanation. He wanted *her*.

To hell with their one-night agreement.

---

10

*L*incoln yanked her inside without a word, slamming the door shut. Then he pressed her against the closed door, crowding her with his body. Before she could utter a protest, he crushed her mouth, taking what he had wanted every day since they left Vegas.

The Dom in him demanded he show her that he was her master, the only man who would ever be able to fully satisfy her, not that city slicker in a suit.

Amber froze against his erotic assault.

For a moment.

She moaned in the back of her throat. Her body turned fluid as she slid her hands into his hair to hold his mouth in place. Her response was the only green light he needed.

He slid his hands down her sides, past her perfect tits and the indent of her waist, over the flare of her hips to her thighs. He lifted her right leg up around his waist. It was the only prompt he needed to give her. She brought the left up on her own.

He ground his pelvis against hers. Even with the

clothing barrier in place, he felt the heat pulsing off her sex. His dick strained against his sweats, greedy to feel her cunt.

They needed a bed. Now.

Otherwise, he would fuck her up against the door. And while that idea had merit, he wanted her in his bed more. He had fantasized about taking her in his bed, about seeing her on her back with her hair spread out over his bedding. Never breaking his hold on her, his mouth ravenous as he kissed her, he carried her through the living room with his destination in mind. His bare feet padded quietly over the hardwood.

Lincoln didn't linger on the journey, he strode straight to his room, and the bed. The king bed with the pine headboard and footboard might not be fancy but it was comfortable and clean.

And by the time he was done with her, it would no longer be clean.

He lowered her gorgeous body onto his bed. Then regretfully released her. He reached overhead and yanked his tee shirt off over his shoulders.

Amber stared at him, her breath huffing in and out. The pulse in her neck beat wildly, and her pupils were dilated.

"If you don't want this, say so now. But if you do, strip. You're wearing too many damn clothes, and I want you naked."

Victory flooded him as she rose off the bed just enough to remove the sweatshirt. She tossed it behind her, but he didn't pay any attention to its trajectory. Beneath that sweatshirt she wore a satin bra with daisies on it. Her nipples were stiff hard points poking against the material, making his mouth water.

He shucked his sweats and boxers in a single move. Stepping out of them, he reached into his nightstand and drew out a foil packet. Her breasts spilled out as she removed her bra.

On a rough groan, he leaned over her on the bed, swooped down, and latched his mouth around a dusky areola. Her hands threaded into his hair as she arched her back. Her gasp of pleasure had his dick jolting.

She had the most glorious tits—full, firm. He kneaded the other as he laved and nipped at the pert bud. They fit perfectly in the palms of his hand as if they had been molded just for him.

Lincoln took his time with her breasts. As much as he craved to feel her cunt wrapped around his cock once again, he loved the way she tasted. Loved the little garbled moans and cries she emitted when he bit down on a swollen point. There were so many things he wanted to do with her tits. He wanted to see how they would look with clamps on them. He wanted to fuck them. Glide his dick between the globes and then come all over her chest and face.

"Lincoln."

The sound of his name uttered in that throaty breathless manner had his inner caveman roaring with the need to claim her, mark her, make her his in every way imaginable. She had fueled so many fantasies over the years. And the reality of her was even better than he had dreamed.

His mouth moved down her belly. He hooked his hands in the waistband of her pants and drew them down. He yanked them off her lithe legs, then ran his hands up her calves and thighs to her apex covered by the same daisy yellow satin.

She lifted her hips up slightly, helping him as he drew her panties off.

He stared at her for a minute, lying in his bed, with her inky hair spilling over the blanket. Her nipples were angry red from his ministrations. Her thighs were spread, giving him a premiere view of her dew slicked pussy. She was wet for him.

Fuck.

It looked like she belonged there. In his bed. And not simply for one night.

Before he could delve too much into his psyche over that little tidbit, he commanded, "On your hands and knees, with that sweet ass of yours turned toward me."

Desire shrouded her as she complied. She rolled over and rose sinuously. Her toned body had been honed not from good genes but because she worked out religiously. He knew because he'd visited her house multiple times, only to locate her in the home gym, sweating it out.

When she presented her ass to him, he about fell on her like a raving beast. She had the most perfectly shaped, rounded ass. He drew his hands down her sinuous back and cupped her bottom. He massaged the globes, parting them wide.

Unable to wait any longer, he leaned in and tongued her slit, from her clit all the way to her naughty back channel. At her gasp of pleasure, he applied himself to the task. With his tongue, he laved her pussy, lapping at her cream, letting her musky flavor roll over his senses.

Flicking and circling her clit, he rubbed at the nub until it swelled for him. Then he suctioned the firm bud into his mouth.

"Oh god. Please." Amber rocked her hips, pushing her cunt against his face.

Clamping his hands on her thighs, he growled as he imprisoned her. Plunging his tongue into her pussy, he began to fuck her with it, loving the little sounds of ecstasy she emitted.

He brought his fingers into play, swirling two digits around her clit.

Curious at her response, Lincoln dragged his tongue along her crease, then inserted those two fingers in her pussy. Pulling her ass cheeks farther apart, he swiped his tongue over her anus.

She moaned, rocking her hips against his fingers and tongue.

When she didn't protest the illicit caress, he did it a second time. And her throaty groan was all he needed to continue.

Lincoln rimmed her with his tongue as his fingers pumped in her slick heat. She canted her hips, thrusting back. Growling at her response, he took it up a notch—he firmed his tongue and pressed against her back door entrance, sliding his tongue in and out, slowly at first.

Amber lowered her face to his bed and gripped the covers. Her muffled moans spurred his actions. He wanted her ass like he wanted air to breathe. Not knowing whether this was going to be the last time with her, he went for gold.

She thrust her hips back, undulating against his tongue and fingers. Her cries and gasps filled the room. He felt precum seep from his cock, desperate to slide into her wet heat.

Amber came, her pussy clutching at his fingers, her ass spasming around his tongue.

He pumped his fingers until her spasms relented. When he withdrew them, she held herself there, still trembling with aftershocks.

Unable to withstand it any longer, he sheathed himself in protection, rolling the latex over his shaft. Lincoln climbed up into bed and repositioned her slightly to give himself room. He nudged her thighs wider apart. Gripping his dick, he rubbed the head through her crease.

"Oh please," she begged, wriggling her hips.

Amber pleading with him, desperate for his cock, was the sexiest damn thing in the world. Positioning his crest at her entrance, he clasped her hips and rolled his pelvis, thrusting deep inside until he bottomed out.

Oh fuck.

Amber's cunt gripped him tight. He groaned as she squeezed him. It felt like coming home after being denied entrance. Need rose in battering waves. Unable to hold still, he withdrew until only the tip remained and slammed home, again and again.

"God, you feel so fucking good. I could fuck this sweet cunt all night long."

She whimpered.

Clamping his hands on her hips as he drove home, bottoming out in her taut heat, he asked, "Do you want that? Want me to fuck your pussy all night long?"

"Yes. Give it to me."

"Such a bad girl, aren't you?"

"Yes. Only for you."

"That's right. You're *my* bad girl."

He grunted as he established a steady pace. He wanted this to last as long as possible. Watching his dick disappear inside her pink pussy was akin to a holy experience. She canted her hips, meeting his thrusts as the tide of pleasure swept her up into its grasp.

Had there ever been a more perfect woman made?

Being with her like this made all the other women he had been with fade. He didn't think he would ever get enough of her. She arched her back like a cat, tossing her waterfall of hair. He wished she had worn it up in a ponytail. That way, he could wind the length of her hair around his hand.

He wanted to own her. Wanted to mark her, have her wear the proof of his ownership and keep all other men from coming near her. Including that city slicker in the suit. At the dark thought, he smacked her bottom for the offense.

The crack of his palm echoed in the room. Amber stopped at the rough swat. For a split second, he worried he had gone too far.

But then she issued a deep, throaty moan. "Oh god, yes."

Entranced by her response, he smacked her rump again. Hard this time. Hard enough he could admire the red outline of his handprint on her milky flesh.

"Oh god, more, please."

Someone liked a bit of pain with their pleasure, making her damn near perfect. He peppered her behind as he thrust. Amber transformed into a wildcat, writhing and canting her hips as she moaned.

The spanking changed their lovemaking, taking it darker, greedier as he fucked her roughly—so rough, he was certain he would leave bruises on her hips. That thought snapped his remaining hold on his indomitable control in two.

He boosted his pace, pumping his dick brutally again and again while she clawed at the sheets.

Christ, this woman in her pleasure was a goddamn goddess. In all his years, he had never beheld such a glorious sight.

Lincoln leaned his chest against her back and slid a possessive hand around her throat as he pounded her cunt. She might never be his in truth, but he understood her needs better than any other man ever would because they matched his own. He nipped her shoulder as he thrust, marking her while he savaged her pussy.

"Lincoln," she whimpered.

"That's right. You like the way I fuck you, don't you?"

"Yes."

"And you liked my tongue in your ass, didn't you?"

"Yes." She sobbed.

"Ever have a man fuck your ass?" He had to know. He wanted her ass like he wanted air to breathe.

"No." She shook her head and moaned.

"Well, you're about to," he growled, removing his cock from her tight pussy.

The need to claim her ass gripped him, because he knew no other man would ever take her there. It would be the one place that he would claim that would always belong to him.

He reached into the nightstand and withdrew a small tube of lube. He rubbed some on her back entrance and more over his index finger. "Deep breaths for me."

Then he gently pressed his finger against her anus, inserting merely the tip and thrusting it in and out. With his free hand, he rubbed her swollen clit. And his finger slid in deeper and deeper with each thrust. When Amber began thrusting her hips back, he added a second finger, beginning the whole stretching process over again.

When he had three fingers gliding unimpeded in her ass, he pulled them out, slicked more lube over his shaft, then positioned the head against her entrance. He held her hips steady as he pressed forward, going slow, letting her body adjust to his intrusion.

He kept rubbing her clit as he gently thrust, progressing deeper with each pass. Her moans of pleasure spurred him on until he was fully embedded in her ass.

Mine.

Being the first man to take her ass unleashed something primal in him. When she began to writhe and rock her hips, he withdrew until only the head remained, and thrust deep.

"Oh god," she cried.

"Yeah, you like me fucking your ass. Don't you?"

"Yes. Please... harder."

Baby.

She was his, even if she never acknowledged it. Lincoln gripped her hips and pumped his shaft. Her ass was so tight, fuck, it was amazing. He had thought seeing his cock glide deep into her pussy was great, but seeing his dick slide deep into her ass was spectacular. He wished for a moment that he was taking her bareback. That there wasn't the thin latex membrane separating them.

"More," she pleaded on a deep groan.

With that plea, Lincoln cut loose. The shackles fell off. He fucked her ass like his life depended on it. The sounds she made drove him wild. He gripped her hips tight as he fucked her, ramming his dick over and over again in her ass. He reached around her hip and rubbed her clit, knowing he wasn't going to last long, not with how good she felt clamped around him.

He leaned over her back once again, peppering her channel with deep, rough thrusts. Amber's legs gave out with the intensity of her pleasure. He followed her down. His body surrounded hers as he fucked her ass. Her moans of ecstasy competed with the slap of flesh.

He pinched her clit as he thrust, and felt her explode. Her ass gripped him, spasming tight.

"Lincoln," she sobbed as she came, quaking beneath him.

It was all he needed to send him hurtling over the ledge into ecstasy. "Oh fuck, I'm—"

He roared. His cum splashed inside the condom as he plunged in her ass again and again. The tidal wave of ecstasy rocked him to his core. He couldn't ever remember coming this hard. He thrust until his balls were drained of cum and he began to soften.

Lincoln slumped against her briefly to catch his breath. But he didn't want to squish her because she really was a small thing. That thought—the desire to care for her as if she were in fact his submissive, and see to her comfort—had him rolling off.

He lay on his back with his arm tossed above his head, staring at the ceiling and gulping in oxygen.

He had fucked his boss. Again.

They were developing a pattern. "You had something you wanted to see me about," he said, and shot her a glance.

She was face down on his bed. Her hair was a mess. Her body was limp, and glistened with a slight sheen of sweat. And he had never seen a lovelier sight. If they were different people, he would pull her close and hold her while they talked. But they weren't, and he worried if he tried the other approach, he would be rejected.

She shifted onto her side, facing him with a sheepish expression on her face. "Yeah. I wanted to explain... about Brecken."

"You mean the guy you're cheating on with me." It still rankled him that he had been used that way, regardless of whether he had let his emotions, his need for her, override his good common sense.

"We aren't dating. He's my ex from college, and is interested in rekindling things between us. That's all. I wasn't expecting him to kiss me like that, and I can see how it would be interpreted as such."

"And yet, you're here in my bed." He drew a finger down her arm, marveling at the softness of her skin.

She blushed. After everything they had done, the fact that she could still blush charmed him.

"Not intentionally, but yes, I'm in your bed. And no, I don't know what I'm going to do about Brecken—or you and this, for that matter."

He could already feel his ardor rising. "Well, you could stay... for the next round."

Amber visibly shivered. "I could, couldn't I?"

"I can see I'm going to be a bad influence on you."

But she surprised him. She straddled his hips, took his hands in hers, and pinned them above his head. "Maybe I'm the one who's the bad influence on you. Ever think of that, tough guy?"

"I don't know. After tonight, I know where you live now. That you're a bad girl who likes to be naughty and depraved, who likes her sex rough and kinky, and needs to submit." He ground against her slit.

"And if I do?"

"Then you've come to the right place, because I understand what you need." The woman was playing with fire. But when it came to her and this, he was willing to risk the burns. His cock sprang back to life as she leaned down. He ran his hands over her slim back.

"If you plan on corrupting me some more, I'm game. Fire away, bad girl. Show me what you've got," he teased her darkly.

But then he gripped her head between his palms and kissed her, surrendering to the madness, to the wicked pleasure that only she could give.

11

*W*armth surrounded Amber. She blinked as the room swam into focus.

Hazy, predawn shadows filled the room. But it wasn't her salmon-colored walls surrounding her. Nor was she alone. Lincoln's rugged aroma reminded her of peat smoke and sandalwood. Her head was cradled against his chest. Her arm was tossed over his torso. And one of her legs was tangled up with his, while his arm was wrapped around her body with his hand resting upon her hip bone.

She'd slept with Lincoln again. But she used the term *sleep* loosely. They had screwed one another senseless. Twice. Her rear was sore from having his dick in her ass. Amber had always wondered about anal sex and whether it was something she would like. She had fantasized about it but had never brought it up with any of her bed partners. But Lincoln seemed to know intuitively what turned her on.

He hadn't been wrong last night. She adored rough sex and kink and having him dominate her. It was freeing not having to worry about being in charge. And for all his gruffness and their contentious past, she trusted him. He would never truly hurt her physically.

But last night complicated an already minefield-laden situation.

Sleeping with Lincoln once could be explained away as a fun drunken night in Vegas. To do it twice, well, that was sheer idiocy on her part. Lincoln wasn't a relationship kind of guy. Complicating last night's dalliance was her status as his boss. Legally, she was putting the ranch in a rather precarious position.

Meaning that she was being reckless with the Anderson legacy she had been entrusted to preserve and protect.

Except, she had never wanted anyone the way she craved Lincoln. It went beyond mere lust and desire. He overwhelmed her. She thirsted for his dominance. While at the same time, she feared what continuing their clandestine nights would do to her heart.

In the predawn gray light, she studied his profile. His dark chestnut hair was in total disarray from sleep, and likely from her fingers gripping on tight. His broad forehead was interrupted by thick slashes of brows. Dark fans of lashes lay like black crescent moons against his face. With his eyes closed, she could study him without the intensity of his gaze upon her.

He kept his dark chestnut beard trimmed, and she could feel the beard burn on her neck and thighs. She shivered at the delicious memory.

She had never planned on staying the night. But then, she had never planned on sleeping with him again either. When she thought about everything they'd done last night, she felt a deep residual ache in her girly bits.

Physically, they were fantastic together. He understood her needs, taking her into darker realms that she might not have ventured into without him there to guide her.

It also made him dangerous. Not physically. No, he was hazardous to her peace of mind, to her hard-fought independence, and to her heart. The crush she'd had on him was deeper than a mere crush. Leagues deeper.

It was why she had to leave. Now. Before he woke.

Leaving before he roused wasn't payback for the morning after in Vegas, either. She had to get home before she was missed. Even though it pained her to walk away.

She wanted to cuddle more with him. Yearned to wake him up by taking him in her mouth. But that was venturing into territory that could damn her, and unmake everything she had worked toward.

Gingerly, she slipped from his bed—or at least, she was giving it a good college try when a hand clamped on her forearm and the other circled her waist before she could sneak out of bed.

"Going somewhere?" His sleep-filled husky timbre shivered along her spine as he reeled her back against his criminally rock hard form until they were spooning.

Did he realize how potent he was? That she had very few guardrails in place, and his touch was demolishing even those?

"Yes. Home." She tried to wriggle out of his hold, really, she did. Against her rear, she felt the firm evidence of his desire rise. He intentionally pressed his cock against her bare bottom. She bit her lower lip to contain her mewl, and prayed that she would find the strength to leave.

"You could stay." His hand around her waist drifted south to her mons. He nipped at her earlobe.

Lincoln was temptation personified.

"No, I can't. I never should have allowed this to happen

in the first place." She bit back the moan as his fingers parted her folds and delved between, rubbing slow, hypnotic circles around her clit.

Oh god, oh god, oh god.

He knew just the right amount of pressure to exert with his fingers to put her body on edge without offering any release. He dangled that carrot just far enough away that she would have to reach for it, agree to his illicit offer.

"Why, because of your boyfriend?" he challenged, never stopping the movement of his fingers, circling and teasing her pussy.

She was seconds away from caving, and dug into her last reserve of strength. "Like I said yesterday, he's my ex-boyfriend. But more importantly, you're my employee. It was wrong that I allowed last night to happen."

He nipped her earlobe again, his fingers rubbing her clit, making her delirious with pleasure. "You like being wrong with me. Even now, your pussy begs for my touch. Weeps to feel my cock."

God help her, she did. So damn much. She had little defense against the mind-numbing pleasure he offered.

"That's not the point," she protested, not even sure what the point was any longer. She rocked her hips against his fingers and cock.

She couldn't allow this to happen again. But god, his touch incinerated all her good intentions.

"You're not going to be honest and tell him about the two of us, are you?"

She closed her eyes. No. Brecken did not need to know that on the same day he came to the ranch, she spent the night fucking another man. "There's no point. It doesn't matter."

Lincoln stiffened behind her. "You mean I don't matter. What we did, didn't matter to you."

She glanced over her shoulder at him. "I didn't say that. You did."

Because it did matter; *he* mattered to her. But she couldn't voice her emotions after being let down the other night.

Lincoln rolled her body under his so fast, she barely had time to gasp. He fit his big body between her thighs so that his hips intimately pressed against her sex, with the firm ridge of his cock against her slit. He held her hands prisoner at her sides, fury emblazoned on his face. He ground his pelvis against her crotch, studying her response. "You wanted me last night, wanted me inside that tight little cunt of yours, making you come screaming my name. Don't try to deny it. Even now, your body wants me, wants what I can do to it."

"Yes. I did. And I do, even when I shouldn't, I want you," she admitted. She was paving her own road to hell as she hooked her legs behind his back, bringing him even closer.

His gaze positively simmered. If she had to go out on a limb, she would say he was fucking thrilled by her response.

"Then stay. And give me a chance to convince you to choose me instead," he murmured, kissing along her jaw, with his beard scraping deliciously along the delicate skin of her neck. "Then we can be wrong again together every night."

"Wait, what?" Did he really just say that?

"Instead of Bilken." He dragged his teeth over that one spot on her neck that had her eyes crossing at the pleasure.

"Brecken." She gasped.

"Whatever. I think you should choose me instead."

"But I thought we were doing a no strings attached, just for the night deal."

He finally lifted his head and stared down at her in a way that made her heart tremble. "And obviously we haven't kept it to just one night, nullifying the terms of the agreement. All I'm asking is that you consider me. Because we seem to keep doing this. I want to keep doing this with you."

"But you left. In Vegas, you left—"

"Only because I was trying to abide by the terms you set forth. When I would have much rather stayed, and done more of this."

Lincoln's lips sought hers. He claimed her mouth in a drugging kiss that obliterated any remaining objections. There was no turning from this, from him. Until Lincoln kissed her, she had never fully understood what the term ravish meant. She did now, because that was exactly the way he kissed her. She clung to him, begging him for more as she kissed him back. His mouth evoked a primal response in her body. She surrendered to it, and him, caving to his wicked kiss and her own desires. Need blasted her system.

"I'll consider you," she whispered on a ragged moan as he nibbled along her jaw.

"I knew you'd see it my way," he murmured against her throat.

God, he was right, she enjoyed being wrong with him. But was it really wrong when it felt so right?

He headed directly for the gold too. His fingers sought her pussy as he sucked a pebbled nipple into his mouth. He plunged two fingers inside. Her hips jerked at the sudden intrusion.

"Lincoln," she gasped, rocking her hips as he thrust his

fingers. He hit that bundle of nerves that left her clinging and writhing.

"You're so fucking wet," he growled, pumping his fingers in and out.

"All for you." She moaned, so close to coming already, she no longer cared whether this was right or wrong. All she cared about was feeling him inside her again.

"Yeah, that's right. Because you like being a bad girl with me, don't you?"

"God, yes."

"Then tell me, bad girl, what do you want me to do with this pretty pussy."

"Fuck me," she begged, mindless from the slow finger-fucking driving her wild.

"With what? My fingers?" He thrust them deep.

She shook her head from side to side. "No. Please."

"Hmm, with my mouth then?"

"No. I need... oh god."

"Tell me, bad girl. Say what you want."

"Your cock, in me, fucking my pussy," she moaned.

"See, now was that so hard?" he crooned, pumping his fingers faster.

"Lincoln, please... Sir."

Her words spurred him into action. Lincoln removed his fingers from her pussy. She watched as he licked them clean. Then he reached into the nightstand drawer and grabbed a condom. Shifting, he rose onto his knees, pushing her thighs even wider apart, and protected them both. Lincoln caressed his shaft, ensuring that the condom was firmly on.

He rubbed his shaft through her slit, teasing her clit with the head.

"Please."

His eyes hooded. "You want this cock, bad girl?"

Amber was past the point of no return. There was no retreat, no denial, no escaping the pulsating need for him that eclipsed all else. "I want you to fuck me with your big cock, hard and fast, and make me come, screaming."

Lincoln's gaze blazed with lust. "Then have me."

He positioned the head of his shaft at her entrance, gripped her thighs, and thrust, filling her, stretching her with his girth. The first stroke took her breath away, it felt so good. The second had her back arching at the pleasure swamping her system.

Lincoln settled his big body against hers, aligning their torsos. He took her mouth in a hungry exchange as he established a blistering pace. This wasn't the long, drawn out coupling of the previous night.

It was a race to the finish line.

He pounded inside her. She undulated, meeting his rough thrusts. Amber clung to him as he rammed deep again and again. Moans tumbled out of her mouth. She dug her nails into his back. Sweat coated their skin.

How would she ever do without this again?

"Oh god, Lincoln!" she wailed as the climax struck. She bucked against him. Her legs shook and toes curled as ecstasy ripped through her. She held on tight as she quaked around his plunging member.

"Amber, fuck, I'm coming," he bellowed as he followed her over, straining, pumping his cock as he came, stroking deep until every ounce of pleasure had been extracted.

They lay together, limbs wrapped around each other, holding on as they gasped for breath. Sex with Lincoln defied all expectations. It redefined the term *pleasure*. Sex with him set a new bar that she was deeply afraid no other man would ever be able to rise to the challenge and meet.

He was ruining her, one delicious orgasm at a time.

When Lincoln shifted, rising above her, she finally lifted her lids, knowing that she had feelings for him on top of their insane chemistry. How could she not? They had been in each other's lives for years, working in close proximity. But what she found in his dark gaze rocked her to her core.

Emotions blazed within those dark espresso depths, with a healthy dose of surprise as he stared at her—like he couldn't believe what he was feeling but it was there just the same, naked and on display.

The idea that he was just as stunned and moved by their connection as she was left her marveling over it. What did it mean? Could there be more between them? Was there a chance they might have a future?

The possibility spun her for a loop. Emotions battered her in rapid succession. Excitement. Fear. Joy. Desire. Hope.

"So you'll think about it, about me? Consider dating me instead?" he asked.

Like there was any doubt. She hadn't been able to erase him from her mind, and had tried. But there was guilt present as well. "I will... but I'm also considering Brecken."

Lincoln's face hardened. He withdrew, rolling off her, severing the intimate connection. His response made her regret her words, even though they were the truth. She couldn't send Brecken packing, not when she'd promised to give him a chance to win her back.

On his back, staring at the ceiling, he said, "If that's what you want, I won't stop you. But consider this while you ponder who you want to be with. I'm the one you spent the night with on his first night here on the ranch, not him.

You might want to ask yourself why that is before you come to any conclusions."

He was right. And she hated that he appeared hurt that she wasn't making her decision today. "I know. And I'm sorry. I really thought we were done after Vegas, with the way you left that morning. And I get why you did. But until last night, I was under the impression that we had our night and you didn't want more from me than that. If I had known..."

Lincoln glanced her way, his face a stern, unreadable mask. "Would it have made a difference?"

Honestly? Yes, it would have, but she couldn't admit that, not when they were discussing hypotheticals. Solemnly, she replied, "I don't know. Maybe."

It was as close to the truth as she was willing to venture. And she had lingered with him this morning long enough. Amber rose from bed and hunted down her clothing, scattered about the room in their haste last night. She dressed as she found each piece, her bra first and panties second, while he lay in bed and silently watched. His eyes caressed her body.

"Stop that." She pointed at him after putting her sweatshirt back on, and then donned a shoe.

"Stop what?" A sexy smirk appeared on his face, because the man knew precisely what he was doing.

"I don't have time for another round this morning. I've got to get home and make it look like I was there all night."

"Ashamed that you spent the night fucking the help?"

She scowled. "No. But some of the cowboys on this ranch already have a hard time with me running things around here. If they discovered I was sleeping with you, it would denigrate any amount of respect I've earned over the past eighteen months. Not because of you, but because I have girl parts."

"It can't be that bad."

She shot him a stare. "You're right. It's been worse than that. And it's not like Colt or my father didn't have issues with ranch hands from time to time, but they never had to keep proving they were worthy of running things around here. They were just accepted. But when it comes to me, nothing I do seems to matter."

She shook her head as Lincoln rose from the bed.

"Who's giving you such a hard time? I want names." He glowered with such menace, she shivered. Like he planned to go knock some heads together.

It was super sweet that he wanted to defend her. It thrilled a dark corner of her heart, but she couldn't let him do that. Dressed, she patted his bare chest. "I appreciate the sentiment, but I can't do that. I need this place to continue to run seamlessly, as much as it ever does around here. And if you went around, threatening to beat up any cowboy who gave me a hard time for being a female, it would only make things worse, not better. Please forget it."

She shouldn't have even shared that much with him.

"I'll figure out who, and take care of it."

Searching his face, she pleaded. "Please drop it, Lincoln. If you go to bat for me, they will know something's up. And they're like vultures, jumping on any perceived weaknesses. If you want me to consider you then that's what I need you to do."

He searched her face, like he was attempting to see past her mask to the very heart of her. But then he finally nodded in agreement. "I'm not happy about it, but I won't make your job any harder than it already is. I also have an ulterior motive, though. I want you in my bed on a more permanent basis."

She quivered low in her belly at his words as relief flooded her. "Thank you. I've got to go."

Lincoln tugged her against his hard body, cupped her nape, and kissed her. After all the hungry exchanges, this deep and tender mingling devastated her. It knocked her off her axis. Had her sighing into him until she was clinging to him. Only then did he release her, with a satisfied gleam in his eyes.

Dizzy with all her conflicting emotions, she pressed her fingers to her mouth. She could still feel his lips on hers. "What was that for?"

Lincoln appeared pleased at her response. "Just pleading my case so you'll think of me when you're with Bradley."

"Brecken."

He shrugged nonchalantly. "It doesn't matter. Will I see you tonight?"

"Um, I'm not sure." He had thrown her completely off her game and spun her for a loop with the whole tossing his hat into the ring spiel.

"Don't make me wait too long."

It was rather difficult to concentrate and form words when he stood before her in nothing but his birthday suit, completely unfazed by his nakedness.

"Um, I won't. But now I've really got to go or I'm going to be late to the office. You don't need to see me out. I know the way." She hightailed it out of his house and into her vehicle.

What the hell had she been thinking last night?

Sleeping with Lincoln in Vegas was one thing. Doing it again on the ranch, where anyone could have driven by his cabin and seen her SUV parked in his driveway, was another story entirely. She hadn't lied about the ranch hands. If they discovered she was sleeping with a subordinate, she would never live it down.

They would treat her like she was just another piece of ass. Some pretty fluff for a guy's arm and bed, but not capable of running a ranch.

It was an antiquated attitude, for sure. But the thing was, here in the remote regions of the Rockies, change came slowly—so slow, she had witnessed snails move at a faster pace than some of the attitudes and forward progress did here. It didn't matter that it was the twenty-first century because many of them hadn't progressed into the twentieth century with their mindsets.

And what she hadn't mentioned to Lincoln was that she didn't know if she wanted to stay. That she was exhausted from the constant, daily uphill battle for acceptance. Amber didn't care if they liked her, it was whether they accepted she was in charge that mattered.

Then he had to go and change the script on her with his whole choose him deal.

She made it home and did her best to shove those thoughts away. The two-story mountain chalet-style home she had grown up in had always been a refuge. She loved this house with its wood and stone exterior—even if she didn't particularly love her job at the moment, there were a metric tons of good memories here.

Now for the hard part: sneaking inside before Colt and Avery got up and caught her.

Carefully, and as quietly as possible, she unlocked the door. She opened it, tiptoeing inside like a ghost. After relatching the lock, she headed for the back staircase by the kitchen. It would be the best way to avoid running into them. Besides, the stairs were closer to her bedroom on the second floor. All she had to do was make it to those stairs, and she should be home free.

She silently crept down the hall. She spied the stairs and picked up her stride.

"I know the walk of shame when I see it. Spend the night with Brecken?" Avery asked from her perch at the kitchen table.

Amber winced at being caught and shot her sister-in-law a small smile, wondering how the hell she was going to play this off. She couldn't think of any excuse. She shook her head. "No. Lincoln. And please don't say anything to Colt. He wouldn't understand. Or to Brecken until I've figured out how to broach the topic."

Avery lifted a brow. "You've got it, although I expect the full story some other time. And just so you know, Colt's in the shower right now. If you hurry up to your room, he won't catch you in the clothes you left the house in last night."

Grateful, Amber headed over and hugged her sister-in-law. "Thank you, on all fronts." Then she raced up the stairs to her bedroom. It wasn't until she stood under the hot spray of her shower that the night and the situation finally caught up with her.

She had two men who wanted to date her. In her whole life, that had never happened. And she didn't know if she felt comfortable with the idea, let alone the practice. Nor did she have any idea whom she should choose. Then again, when she let Brecken know that he wasn't the only one in her life, he could tell her to go to hell. Especially given the fact that she'd said she wasn't seeing anyone.

But what if he was okay with it? Did that mean she would be dating them both?

12

*B*y the time Amber emerged from the shower, she felt somewhat human and ready to tackle the day ahead. She would be much better off as soon as she had some coffee. Though for once, the lack wasn't as bad as normal. In fact, she couldn't stop smiling even with the problems she faced having two men in her life. And her good mood could be laid solely at Lincoln's large feet.

Then again, fabulous, earth-shattering sex could make a person see the world through rose-colored glasses.

As she dressed for the day, she mentally went through the list of tasks she needed to complete before heading to the final bridesmaid dress fittings with a local seamstress today.

At the buzz of her phone, she glanced at the incoming text message. Instantly a wave of guilt flooded her. Brecken. What had she done? He'd never speak to her after this. And frankly, she wouldn't blame him. God, what a mess!

Dinner tonight?

Dammit. She was going to have to tell him about

Lincoln. With their history, he deserved honesty. But not over text. Over dinner, and face to face.

Sure. I have the final dress fitting for my bridesmaid dress this afternoon but should be done by five-ish.

That works for me. Let's plan for six. I can pick you up.

Out of guilt, she conceded. *Sure, that sounds wonderful. See you then.*

I can't wait.

She wished that Lincoln had told her all this stuff sooner. Then she wouldn't be in this mess. Although, it wasn't all his fault. Being emotionally distraught, she had pulled the trigger with Brecken quickly. And that was solely on her head. If she would have given herself some time and space, then maybe...

She sighed. She could play the maybe game until kingdom come. It wouldn't change the situation she found herself in.

Ready for the day in her business attire, Amber headed down to the kitchen with her phone and purse in hand. Colt and Avery were at the kitchen table, finishing breakfast together. They were such a beautiful couple. Her brother positively doted on his wife.

"Morning." Colt nodded congenially.

Memories of all the years and meals they had had together at that very table surfaced. "Hey, any coffee left?"

"Made a full pot, there's plenty."

"Thank goodness." She tossed her purse on the kitchen table and made a beeline for the coffeepot.

"There's some muffins and fruit if you're hungry," Avery piped in.

Amber spied them on the counter. Colt must have sweet-talked Mrs. Gregory into making them. They were her cinnamon streusel muffins, and absolutely divine.

Although Morgan and Kate had these iced lemon muffins at the café that were in a heated competition as Amber's favorite.

"I don't know that I have the time." She checked her watch and winced. If she ate, she would be cutting it close to her meeting time with marketing for the new summer campaign.

But she rarely got a chance to see her brother and his wife. If there was one thing she had learned over the years, it was that family came first, above all else. The rest could wait. If she was a few minutes late, then she was late. "Thanks. I'm starving this morning."

"I can't imagine why," Avery murmured with a secretive smile.

Amber sighed as she added a muffin and fresh berries to a plate. Avery was going to tease her about this morning forever. Amber grabbed the plate along with her mug of coffee, and headed to the table.

"I'm glad we're able to catch you before work and all the festivities this week get underway." Colt leaned back in his seat with an empty plate before him.

"Me too. I've missed you guys around here. How's Tank doing?" Tank was her brother's horse, and just the sweetest stallion.

"Good." He shot a glance loaded with meaning at Avery as they had a wordless conversation in front of Amber.

Something was up with them. "Okay, you two, spit it out. What's going on here?"

"Well, we were wondering if you minded if we stayed on longer than the three weeks I mentioned the other day."

"A lot longer than three weeks," Avery chimed in, laying her hand on Colt's forearm in support and solidarity.

"Sure. This is your home too. Why do you think you

need to ask that?" Amber appreciated that they were asking, but it was still just as much Colt's home as it was hers. And yes, if he stayed longer, it would cause some complications with the staff, but she would weather that like she always did.

"I think you're misunderstanding me. Avery and I were considering making a permanent move back to the ranch for the next few years," Colt explained, watching her reaction.

Years? Amber could see with perfect clarity all the hard-fought battles she had won on the ranch being for nothing. She did her best to school her features. "But I thought you wanted to see the world and all that jazz."

"I did. We did—"

"What your brother is trying to say and failing is that we're starting a family, and have decided we want our child to have a stable foundation," Avery said with her hand over Colt's.

"You're pregnant?" Amber glanced from Avery to her brother and back again.

"Yeah. Three months along. My due date is in September."

"Oh, I'm so happy for you both." She put a hand on her chest and felt her eyes fill with happy tears. They were starting the next generation of Andersons.

Colt glanced at Avery and lifted her hand up to his mouth, brushing a kiss over her knuckles in a super sweet gesture.

"Oh my goodness, that means I'm going to be an aunt." Amber couldn't believe her brother was going to be a dad.

"It does. And we're not here to cramp your style. We can find a place in Winter Park, or maybe one of the larger unused guest cabins—" Colt began.

"Nonsense, you guys will live here. It's your home too.

This house is the perfect place for a family," Amber stated, waving him off. This house had been home to three generations of Andersons. Their child would be the fourth in this house, as it should be.

"Are you sure you won't mind?" Colt asked sounding unconvinced.

"If I did, I would tell you. When have I ever minced words with you?"

Colt barked out a laugh. "Never, in my recollection. But thanks. We appreciate it. And if there's a position you need filled on the ranch, I figure I can help out."

"You don't want your old job back?" She figured it was what he would want. What their father would want, especially, regardless of the job she had done.

"Hon, it's your job now. I knew what I was giving up when I left with Avery. I would never take it away from you just because we've decided to move back to the ranch. I figure I can fill in and help out in the stables. There's always work to be done in that arena. I'm going to start with the stalls here, and get everything fresh for Tank and Daisy."

"Daisy? You got another horse?"

"Daisy was a gift to me from your brother on our one-year anniversary." Avery stated with a small smile at Colt.

"She was." Colt winked at Avery. "I'll have to fly down and drive the trailer up with the horses, and oversee the movers, but will do that after the wedding. I've got people looking after them while we're here."

"Well, that's just great." Amber glanced at the time on her phone. "And I would love to stay and chat, but I have a full morning before the dress fitting shindig this afternoon."

After putting her empty plate and mug in the dishwasher, she went back over to her brother and gave him a big hug.

"Congratulations. I'm so happy for you both." She hugged Avery too.

She kept the smile on her face until she was in her vehicle. Her brother was coming back. She should be relieved. She should give him a boatload a duties to take some of the burden off her shoulders.

She loved her brother. And was thrilled that they were having a baby.

But how was she going to manage the ranch now with him always underfoot? There was a part of her that just wanted to hand him back all his responsibilities and leave the ranch.

To do what? She hadn't the foggiest clue.

Besides, if she left so soon after his return, Colt would think it was something he had done. Which could cause a rift, and was the last thing she wanted to do.

Amber was stuck between a rock and a hard place with no idea how to move forward. All she knew was she couldn't continue this way indefinitely.

One way or the other, she needed to figure out what exactly it was that she did want, both with the job and the men in her life, before it all came tumbling down about her ears.

13

*P*enelope's Dress Shop was located in the older section of downtown Winter Park, a few blocks over from the main road, which wasn't all that far away from the newer section. It was a quaint little shop where they served tea, coffee and, for bridal parties, champagne.

Penelope had been a year behind Amber in school. They hadn't been in the same circles back then. But Amber liked her. The spunky brunette had a good head on her shoulders, and her dresses were gorgeous. She had all the normal designers but also did her own line. Bianca had chosen one of Penelope's creations for her wedding dress, and it was a real humdinger.

Amber was late for the fitting. Granted, she had been running late all day, so what was one more tardy? She strode inside, the bell above the glass door chiming as she entered.

Toward the back in the seating area was Bianca, looking lovely in ivory slacks and a pink blouse, along with the rest of the bridal party.

"You made it." Bianca smiled the moment she spied Amber.

"I did. Sorry. It's been one of those days," Amber said, giving her a hug.

Up on a small, raised dais stood Morgan in her silver, chiffon bridesmaid dress with cap sleeves and a beaded bust. The v-shaped neckline was lovely, and the bead work on the bust and sleeves was exquisite. She had her dark hair in a thick braid that fell over one shoulder.

"You look lovely, Morgan," Amber said.

"And it still fits. Mostly. I was a little worried about the fit what with my growing belly. I've put on five pounds in the last two weeks," Morgan replied proudly.

"I'm going to let it out for you. Just an inch to give you and baby some breathing room. Last thing you want to do on the day of the wedding is pass out because you can't breathe," Penelope commented, on her knees beside the circular dais, checking Morgan's dress length and pinning a few spots.

"That's true," Morgan agreed with a small chuckle.

"You'll be glad you did. I remember trying to make myself fit into my pants when I needed to go up a size because of Jamie. I almost passed out at the office with a waiting room full of patients." Grace shook her head at the memory.

"Ah, then I have something to look forward to," Avery stated with a grin.

Heads turned in her direction. Kate's mouth was open wide.

"Are you pregnant?" Bianca exclaimed.

Avery nodded. "Yep, Colt and I are expecting. We're due in September."

Kate, Bianca, Morgan, Noelle, and Grace all went nuts

over the news. They took turns hugging Avery. Noelle was there for support even though she wasn't one of the bridesmaids.

"You don't seem surprised," Penelope noted as she rose from her position on the floor.

"They told me already. The perks of being the sister and future aunt," Amber explained, taking a sip of champagne.

"Why don't we get you taken care of next? The dressing room is in through there." Penelope handed her the dress and nodded toward the fitting room at the back of the store.

"I'm on it." It would give her a few minutes alone when she felt like she had been under siege today. As she slid the dress on and zipped it up, Amber took a little time to center herself. Her brother had spun her world on its axis this morning with his news—not the baby, but moving back and making the ranch their permanent address.

Adding to the confusion and turmoil in her life were Lincoln and Brecken and the choice before her. She hated that she had no idea what she wanted on either front. Amber prided herself on being decisive and a go getter. She wasn't a fan of chaos.

Right now, she felt like she was on one of those multi access trainers that astronauts used to use in preparation for going to outer space, and she was spinning out of control.

But she wasn't going to be able to decide her fate in the dress shop fitting room so she headed back out to the little group and climbed up on the dais. The fitting area had a bunch of mirrors along one side of the wall, giving her a full length look at herself in the gown. It really was a gorgeous dress, and the fit was superb.

"So, a little birdie told me that someone has a date to the wedding," Grace stated with an arched brow.

"She does. A man by the name of Brecken, if I recall her text from the other day, about adding him." Bianca smirked.

"I met him the other day when he came to the café. He's rather dreamy with his sun-kissed golden hair and lovely blue eyes. Plus, he's a good tipper too," Morgan added.

"This is the part where you spill all the deets." Kate gestured.

"About both of them." Avery chuckled.

The girls all gasped. Dammit. Amber hadn't wanted to say anything about Lincoln to anyone. At least, not until she was able to break the news to Brecken. Granted, she knew they wouldn't say anything or gossip about it. But still.

"Two men?" Bianca exclaimed, her mouth wide open.

"What is Avery talking about?" Grace asked with a confused frown.

"Oh ho, now this is getting good. Spill, missy," Morgan stated, peering up at her with wide eyed excitement.

Amber shot her sister-in-law an unamused stare. "Thanks for that."

Avery shrugged. "Your brother isn't nearby to hear it all now. I covered for you this morning. It's only fair that we get to hear all the juicy goodness. And, since we're all together, you can get it out of the way in one swoop."

"Yeah, like, who is the other man?" Grace stated.

Amber glanced around the room at her friends and smiled, knowing she was about to drop a whopper of a bomb on them. "Lincoln."

"What!" Morgan shrieked.

"No!" Grace laughed.

"Avery, what did you see?" Noelle asked, shooting Amber a loaded look that they were going to talk later. Amber understood it because she had kept her best friend out of the loop on this one. And now she felt horrible about that.

"All I know is that Amber was doing the walk of shame this morning after a night with Lincoln." Avery chuckled.

"It wasn't the first time, either," Amber said, and then realized she had said that out loud.

"When?" Bianca gasped.

"How?" Morgan demanded.

"You're almost six months pregnant, do you really need an instruction manual?" Avery questioned her, laughing over it.

"Of course she doesn't. But there's a solemn oath with female friends when it comes to things like this: that we are required to tell our best girlfriends everything. Remember, ladies, chicks before dicks," Noelle stated with a straight face.

"Oh, I like her," Penelope said with a laugh.

"Yep, she's a riot. If you will all quiet down long enough, I will tell you everything. As it is, I can't get a word in edgewise." Amber stared them down.

"We'll be good, just please, please, please tell us and leave nothing out," Morgan begged, with nods from the rest of the lot.

"Okay, so when we went to Vegas..." Amber filled them in on everything, from the call from Brecken Friday morning before they left for the airport, to her and Lincoln hooking up, to him leaving her before she woke up.

"Girl. Oh my god!" Noelle exclaimed.

"Right. This is so juicy. Two men duking it out to be with you." Morgan put a hand over her heart.

"I don't envy you one bit," Bianca said, "Okay, maybe a little. Depends how this Brecken fellow is in the sack."

"The bigger question is, are you leaning toward one

over another already?" Grace asked, always the level-headed, practical one out of the bunch. It was one of the reasons they had clicked so well when Grace first moved here.

"I don't know," Amber said. *With any of it.* It seemed like her entire life had been completely upended. She was lucky she knew her head from her ass because it was one of the only things she was certain about. She had been going down one path for so long, tossing in all these alternatives left her spiraling. She felt like she was on that amusement park ride—the one where you stood in a circular room with your back against the wall and then it began to spin, the floor dropped away, and you were completely powerless as it spun you round and round until you were ready to puke.

"Well, we're here if you need to talk it out," Avery offered.

"And whichever one you don't want, you could send them my way," Penelope added from her position by the dais.

That got laughs out of everyone. But now for the bigger conundrum: dating both men so that she could choose one. That was if Brecken didn't tell her to go to hell.

Was it wrong of her to hope that Brecken would get upset and take the decision out of her hands?

14

---

*B*recken Harrison III came from a distinguished family out of New York. His father's company, Harrison Investments, had offices in New York, Boston, and London, with an expansion into Denver.

Amber had just finished putting the final touches on her face, adding a frosty pink lipstick to her lips, when the door-bell rang. It was time. She steeled herself for the upcoming conversation they needed to have. She didn't want to hurt Brecken, but she also believed in honesty in relationships. If they couldn't resolve this issue, then they would never make it through life's inevitable hurdles together. But she also understood that this situation was bizarre.

Grabbing her purse, she heard Colt's heavy bootsteps on the hardwood floor downstairs, and then the sound of male voices in the foyer, which moved into the kitchen. She headed down the back stairs.

Amber traipsed down the stairs with her coat draped over her forearm and found her brother leaning back against the kitchen island with his arms crossed in front of his chest. For all appearances, he seemed relaxed, but Amber knew better. Colt was one of the most perceptive people. And he was studying Brecken closely for flaws when he commented, "It was nice of you to come to the wedding."

"It was last minute, but you know your sister," Brecken remarked just as she made her presence known.

"I do at that. Amber, your date is here." Colt had a shit-eating grin on his face and a raised eyebrow which he promptly lowered before Brecken caught his teasing look intended for her. Jesus, her brother was acting like she had never been on a date before.

"Thanks, brother dear. Shall we go?"

"You look fantastic." Brecken held his arm out for her to take, all smooth and debonair. But then, he had always been this way. It was part of his charm. He was very old school in a lot of ways when it came to dating.

"Thank you. So do you." He did. Brecken had that golden boy, all American sheen to his appearance, from his golden head of hair, to his bright blue eyes that twinkled when he smiled with his perfect white teeth. Tall and muscular, much like a swimmer, he filled out the mint-green dress shirt and dark charcoal slacks extremely well. She accepted his hand, glad to see that she had not gone over-board with her dress. It was a sleek little black number that hugged her curves. The pencil skirt fell just below her knees. Even though it was April, there was a crisp chill in the evenings. Before they left, she donned her gray twill pea coat with Brecken's assistance.

Colt looked like he was about to bust a gut laughing. "Don't be out too late. If you are and need me to, I can handle things in the morning for you. Just text me and let me know."

"It will be fine. Tomorrow, we're getting everything ready in the ballroom for the wedding on Saturday. But other than that, the schedule is fairly light," she stated through gritted teeth while trying to maintain a pleasing smile on her face for Brecken so he wouldn't think anything was amiss. Colt was already pushing her out the door. It angered her, and she wanted to let him have it because she was just so tired of it all. All this back and forth was making her feel bipolar.

"Let me know if you do. You kids have fun." Colt nodded. "I've got to get dinner started for the missus. Avery's having a lie down right now."

"You could always ask Mrs. Gregory to help."

"Nah, I won't bother her. Avery will be fine. She just tends to get morning sickness in the evening. Soup and crackers are what work best for her. I think I'm skilled enough in the kitchen to heat up some chicken soup."

"We'll get out of your hair. I made us some reservations at the steak place in town. Hope that's all right," Brecken explained, towing Amber down the hall.

"No. I don't mind. Steak sounds wonderful."

He escorted her out the door and to his car. The luxury black Audi sedan was out of place here in the mountains and not practical, but then, he was only passing through.

"What was that all about? I couldn't help but notice some tension between you and your brother."

She smiled as he drove off the ranch and headed toward town. "Picked up on that, huh? It's nothing. Well, not nothing, but he and Avery have decided—because they are starting a family—to return to the ranch."

"Ah. Puts a crimp in things around the ranch for you."

"It does. I love my brother dearly. But being a woman running a ranch, there's been a lot of uphill battles with some of the older cowboys who don't take too kindly to a woman being in charge."

"It's the twenty-first century." Brecken glanced at her with shock on his face.

"To them it's not. They have one way of doing things, their way, and if you buck the system, they tend to be rather ornery cusses. But what can I do?"

"You think your brother moving back will undermine your status?"

"Yes. I think it's rather inevitable." She would bet there was already talk in the bunkhouse and on the range over Colt's return, and that would only increase once they realized he was back full time.

"You'll figure it out. I have faith in you." Brecken escorted her into Tucker's Steakhouse.

This restaurant, while nice for Winter Park, probably wasn't even close to the places he normally dined at on a regular basis. But they did have amazing steaks here, even if it was a bit touristy.

She'd always liked it here, with the dark wood floors and crisp ivory linen tablecloths. All the waiters wore black slacks and dress shirts with ties. The aroma of sizzling steaks filled the air.

Once they were seated, Amber asked, "So, I've got to know why you're still single. Has there been no one since we broke up?"

"I dated around, quite a bit, actually. One relationship even got rather serious, but in the end, we wanted different things. You've been the only woman I've ever loved."

"I see." She tried to focus on the menu and not his words. They didn't fill her with excitement, only confusion. She had loved him, but that was in the past. Could she fall for him again? Perhaps. If Lincoln wasn't in the picture, she would reply with a resounding yes. Except, Lincoln *was* in the picture. And that made this complicated.

"And what about you?"

This was the part she had been dreading. If he got upset, she would call Noelle and see about getting a ride home. "I need to be honest. When we were talking last week, I wasn't seeing anyone—or really, he wasn't seeing me. But that's changed. Since then, he asked for a chance to date me. And now I'm left with trying to decide between the two of you. I'm so sorry. I truly didn't see this coming, from either of you. I understand if the whole situation is too weird for you and you just want to remain friends. I will even go Dutch on dinner—"

Brecken leveled her with his calm blue gaze as he placed his hand over hers. "I'm glad you told me, but I haven't changed my mind. Who is it? If you don't mind my asking."

She let out a somewhat relieved breath. He was always so polite, but that was part of his upbringing and charm. It tended to put people at ease. "His name is Lincoln. He's the head of maintenance for the ranch. We've known each other for many years."

But have only recently started banging each other's brains out.

"Oh, that rather angry guy from the other day? The one you had an appointment with?" Brecken appeared genuinely shocked.

Amber got it, really, she did. Lincoln was the polar opposite of Brecken. While Brecken was smooth and debonair and refined, like a finely aged scotch, Lincoln was rough and tumble, gritty, and hard enough to chew nails. He was a shot of fireball whiskey that burned all the way down. Her attraction to him didn't make sense, other than he was the kind of man she had grown up around. "I forgot how good your memory is. But yes, that was Lincoln. And to finish answering your prior question, he's been the only one since you and I broke up. I mean, I've had a few dates here and there, but it's hard when you're the boss."

The waiter chose that moment to appear. The guy looked barely old enough to shave, but he was nice enough, and took their order like a seasoned pro.

Once the waiter was out of earshot, Brecken finally replied, "I get it. There are lines that shouldn't be crossed. But he's the only one since me? Really?"

"Yep." Brecken looked far too pleased by that statement. It just made Amber feel inept—that the whole time she had been back home since college, she had been virtually dateless.

"The men in this town must be fools."

Their waiter brought their wine, and she waited for him to leave before responding. "It's not all their fault, I can assure you. I tend to be quite the workaholic."

"You always were that, even in college. It's why you outpaced me in most of our classes together." Brecken took her hand in his. She was proud of herself for not yanking it back.

It wasn't that she didn't want him to touch her. There should be something soothing and familiar about it. But it had been three long years since they'd split. As much as he might not want to admit it, they were different people, and it would take time to relearn intimacy between them. She steered the subject away from her dateless existence on the ranch. "So, tell me about this new division you're heading up for the firm."

"It's a really exciting time for the market with all the crypto currencies, and we're wanting to make trading more accessible to normal people—show them how to invest, and what type of stocks and bonds to look to invest in. My division is the IT mobile application. We're in the process of making it even easier for people to manage their investments with a few clicks on our app."

"Sounds exciting." She had never really been all that intrigued by the stock market. Oh, she had her own investments, but she used the market to play the long game. It wasn't something she obsessed over.

"It is." His enthusiasm for his work was something she had always liked about him.

"And how are your parents?" she asked after the waiter set their meals down.

"Dad is still working sixty hours a week. We can't get the man to slow down. And Mom is now acting president over that children's cancer charity. It's a cause she really believes in, and she takes a lot of pride in the work they've accomplished."

"Sounds like they're still living the dream. And what about you and your move to Denver? When did you transfer here?"

"Three months ago, right after the first of the year."

"And you waited all this time to contact me?" She mocked being offended by the news.

Brecken grew serious. "I didn't know how an overture from me would be received after the way I had left things. Not to mention, I was still trying to figure out the best way to approach you. I don't think you realize just how formidable you are."

Amber snorted. "I'm not that scary, am I?"

"No, not at all. It's just, I worried, quite a lot actually, about whether you would even take my call after the way I ended things," he admitted solemnly.

This was something she could lay to rest for good. "Look, you were right. We both had to go our separate ways back then. I had to sink all my time and energy into the ranch. And Colorado to Boston? We never would have seen one another with our combined work schedules. We could have tried, but I think the end result would have been the same. Breaking up really was the best thing for us at that juncture in our lives."

"I know you're right, but I still hate it just the same. And I am thrilled that you consented to see me and have dinner with me tonight." He gave the waiter his card with the check, not even looking at the total.

While Amber had money, what her family had in their accounts made them look like paupers in comparison to Brecken and his family. They were billionaires. Just Brecken's trust fund alone was in the billions of dollars. That didn't include his stock options and the real estate he owned. They were filthy rich.

"No matter what, it's been great seeing you." She meant it. Here was someone who never for a single second made her feel unworthy, not even with his much larger bank accounts.

"So you've made your choice then?" Brecken's face fell.

"No. I just... my life feels like it's been turned upside down with my brother coming back to the ranch, and you and Lincoln. I don't know which way I'm supposed to go. I'm not used to indecision in my life so it's driving me a little crazy. I would totally understand if it's too much for you. If our roles were reversed, I don't know that I would stick with you under the same circumstances. And I wouldn't blame you if it was too much."

He took her hand and squeezed. "I'm not going anywhere, unless you tell me to. I want this—you and me back together again, Amber. If that means I have to fight for you, then I'm game."

"All right. But you'll let me know if you change your mind." She yawned, even though she tried to hide it, because the day was catching up with her.

"Why don't I get you home? You've had a long day. And I'm sure the next few days are going to be busy for you with the wedding."

"They really are, and I appreciate it." Still, work wasn't the full reason why she was so exhausted. Much of it had to do with Lincoln and spending the night in his arms last night. Even the memory of it was enough to heat her blood and liquify her insides.

Brecken drove her home, holding her hand in his, the whole way back. "Remember that one time when we made out in the stacks and almost got caught?"

"What do you mean, almost? We did get caught. Your hand was down my pants, and my top was on the floor."

He barked a laugh, his voice rich and cultured even in joy. "That's right. We did actually get caught. I forgot about that part."

"That's because you weren't the one showing everyone your chest. I'm surprised we didn't get suspended for that, or even worse, expelled."

"It wasn't the first time or the last that students got busy in the stacks."

"It was the last time for me, if you remember." She recalled the abject mortification, and how they had laughed all the way back to his dorm room, where they had finished what they had begun in the stacks.

"No, exhibitionism wasn't for you."

No, she wasn't into exhibitionism at all. However, she did happen to adore a little bit of domination.

Which brought Lincoln's sexy image to mind.

He'd asked her to come over tonight. But she had turned

him down in a text message this morning because of her date with Brecken.

Guilt flooded her. Dammit. She shouldn't be thinking about Lincoln while on her date with Brecken. It wasn't fair to Brecken at all.

When they arrived back at her house, Brecken did the gallant gentlemanly thing and walked her up the stairs to the door. In the dim front porch light, he really was handsome. Amber didn't fight him when he pulled her into his arms and kissed her. She laid her palms against his chest at his tender, exploratory kiss. His lips were soft. Her head swam. He tasted like the wine they'd had at dinner. The kiss was nice, comfortable even, and familiar.

His hands smoothed along her back, heading south and cupping her rear to deepen the exchange. Warning signals blared. She was not ready for intimacy with him yet, not beyond a few kisses. It was bad enough she'd slept with Lincoln last night, and again this morning.

If there was one thing she was not built for, it was bouncing from one man's bed to another's. She pushed her palms against his chest and disengaged the kiss.

Brecken smiled with smoldering intensity. "Just like old times. Are you sure I can't convince you to come back to my cabin tonight?"

She hated to crush the hope in his eyes. But she had to set some boundaries. "It's a nice offer. But I need to go slow with this. Very slow. I hope you'll be patient with me."

"I understand." He dropped his hands from her sides, quickly hiding his disappointment with calm understanding.

"Thanks for dinner. I had a lovely time." She kissed his cheek. He really was a good man. He was the type of man she should choose.

"Then I will say goodnight."

With guilt riding her, she offered, "We've got the rehearsal dinner Friday night, if you're interested in going with me."

Brecken smiled like she had just offered him the Holy Grail. "Just tell me the time and place, and I'm yours."

His happiness at the invite didn't waylay her guilt in the slightest. But perhaps it was a start. Brecken was everything she should want. They had been great together once, and could be again if she could just make a damn decision. But he didn't need to know the internal struggle she faced. "It's at five thirty in the hotel ballroom, followed by dinner in the private room in the restaurant. It's casual, slacks and dress shirts."

"I'll be there. Let me know if you need any help setting up. I'm here and available, so you might as well use me."

"Thanks, Brecken. Goodnight." She headed inside with his goodnight following her in. He really was one of the good ones.

She'd thought the night out with him would make things clearer. If anything, it had only confused the situation even more. She had feelings for Brecken. Of course, she did. He had been such a huge part of her life. Going out with him tonight was like putting on her favorite pair of well-worn jeans. It was comfortable and familiar.

But then there was Lincoln.

He touched her, and she couldn't see anyone but him. Was it just lust with him, or was there more?

She didn't know. And that was the problem.

15

*T*he phone ringing woke Lincoln from a dead sleep.

Praying it wasn't a maintenance emergency and that he could at least get a cup of coffee before work, he fumbled for the phone and hit the answer button. "Hello."

"Linc, I'm so glad I caught you. Thanks for sending that check. The registrar's office was beginning to hound me for the payment." His sister's voice drifted through the line.

"No problem, Nicole. I'm sorry it took me so long to get it into the mail. It's been crazy around here lately." Lincoln flipped on the bedside lamp and yawned. It was close enough to the time he had to be up for work, anyway.

"Are you sure that it wouldn't be easier if I just took out a loan? I know Mama's medical care took a large chunk of your savings."

Rubbing a hand over his face, wiping the sleep from his eyes, he shuffled out of his bedroom, heading for the kitchen and his coffeemaker. "No. I told you that I would handle it. Nicole, you're the first member of our family to go to college. I don't care what I have to do, but I will make sure you don't have to worry about tuition so you can focus on other things, like becoming the best damn pediatrician in the country."

"I don't know about in the country, though I appreciate your faith in me. But I hate that you've taken on the financial burden of my tuition. There's been so much that has fallen on you, between Mom and me. It's not right."

They had had this argument multiple times. But there was no way he was going to let her suffer and stress out over money when he had the ability to help out. "Nicole, I have a great job where I don't have to pay for my house. I don't need much in the way of money other than groceries and utilities. I don't want you to worry about it."

"I know, but—"

"Listen. Once you've graduated and finished your residency and are a bigwig doctor, you can fly me out to wherever you end up and take me to dinner." Like hell was he going to let his sister suffer financially when he knew damn well she was working her ass off.

"Deal."

"How are classes going?" The scent of coffee brewing filled the kitchen as he pulled a clean mug out of the dishwasher.

"Good. I can't wait for this semester to be over. I think I'm going to sleep for a solid week." Nicole laughed.

"You'll make it. I have faith in you."

"You're the best big brother ever. Sorry for waking you up. I gotta run into class. Love you."

"Right back at you. Later."

If there was one good thing he had done in his life since he started working at Silver Springs, it was taking care of his family. Before getting the job on the ranch, he had sent home money for his mom when he could.

Cleaning houses hadn't left his mother with any spare income.

But then he'd started here, and his housing was part of his salary—first in the bunkhouse and then, once he was here long enough and became a permanent employee, he'd earned the right to one of the empty employee cabins.

The furniture and everything inside belonged to him. The electric was solar powered, which helped keep the cost of utilities way down. Having the cost of living and this place as part of his salary had enabled him to send his mom a check each month to help her out—ease the burden for her, financially at least. And in the last few years, he had also been helping his sister pay for medical school—what wasn't covered with her grants and fellowships.

Then their mom had gotten sick with bare bones health insurance, which barely paid for any of her medical care. The cost of the lifesaving treatments was astronomical. Lincoln had helped however he could each month. Not that any of it mattered, she'd died last summer, with the cancer winning in the end.

He put his empty cereal bowl in the dishwasher and filled his coffee mug back to the brim, figuring he would take it into the shower with him to finish caffeinating himself for the long day ahead. He was in charge of helping set up the ballroom for the wedding rehearsal tomorrow, and wedding on Saturday.

While he was on his trek to the bathroom there came a knock at the front door. Who the hell could it be at this hour? The sun was barely above the horizon.

Setting his mug on the coffee table, he back tracked to the front door, and yanked it open.

Amber.

"Is everything all right?" he asked as she marched inside.

Stripping off her sapphire-blue blazer, she tossed it onto the nearby living room chair. But she didn't stop at the coat. She stepped out of her heels, and unzipped her black pencil skirt. "Everything's just fine."

Fuck, she was gorgeous. And he couldn't stop the lust flooding his system over her little striptease. When she started unbuttoning her blouse, he grabbed her hands. "Amber."

She looked him in the eyes. Finally. There was a wildness to her that he had only seen when he was buried deep inside her. Her eyes were frantic and pleading.

"Tell me what's going on."

"I thought that would be pretty obvious. I need you. Right now." The moment her blouse was off and tossed over her blazer, she launched herself at him.

Lincoln stumbled as his arms were suddenly full of wanton woman.

Her mouth fused to his, and he staggered under the full brunt of her desire. Jesus, she tasted like hopes and dreams he had long since buried. Her lithe body clung to him. And her hands were everywhere, caressing his chest and back, playing with the dimples on his lower back, only to rise up and slide into his hair to grip him tight.

He groaned. All thoughts of a shower and work and anything but the woman in his arms fled. Arousal pounded through his veins. He was instantly hard and needy.

Christ, he might die from this woman.

And then his only thought was getting inside her as she scored his chest with her nails before she reached one hand down beneath the waistband of his boxers and gripped his dick. He groaned into her mouth as she stroked him.

Fuck.

His dick was hard enough, he could pound nails with the damn thing. And her hot little hand fondling him had pleasure sizzling along his spine to pool in his groin.

If he wasn't careful and didn't take control quickly, he was going to come before he ever made it inside her hot little cunt.

With their mouths fused, they headed in the direction of his bedroom. They made it as far as the hall. He pressed her up against the wall, desperate to feel her. Using the wall to keep her lithe form propped up, he delved his hand beneath her panties and found her dripping.

"Jesus. You're so fucking wet."

"I know. I need you. Right now. No more foreplay. Dick. In me. Now." She shoved his boxers down far enough to free his erection.

He yanked her panties to the side. Panting, he hesitated. "I need a condom, babe. Hold on."

"No. I'm on the pill and clean. Just fuck me already."

Lust barreled through him as the thought of taking her without anything between them. He wasn't going to ask her to reconsider. He was a greedy, selfish bastard, and the thought of fucking her bareback had his cock jolting in excitement. With her assistance, he lifted her legs up around his waist.

"Look at me," he demanded as he notched the head at her entrance. She was so fucking drenched.

Amber lifted her gaze. The moment their eyes connected, he thrust, needing to see her expression the moment he filled her bareback. And he couldn't stop his deep groan at the fucking spectacular feeling of her pussy clamping down tight, or the glazed pleasure that spread over her face as he bottomed out inside her.

Fuck.

It felt like he had plugged his dick into a hot velvet vise grip. And the Dom in him growled *mine.* Possessiveness infused him. The muscles in her pussy squeezed him.

"Don't do that. I won't last." He grunted at the way it caused his entire body to tighten and draw in as it prepared to climax.

"I can't stop. You feel too good without a condom."

Assuming control, he clasped her hips tight and leisurely stroked inside her. "You forget who's in charge here, and it's not you. You'll get to come when I say you can, and not a moment beforehand."

She whimpered, her eyelids heavy with lust.

He couldn't stop the smirk from spreading. "Yeah, your greedy little cunt loves my cock, doesn't it?"

"Yes. Please."

On a rough groan, he crushed her mouth, flexing his pelvis. Desire ratcheted up to new heights that went far beyond his ability to control. Like a dam overflowing, need overwhelmed his self-control. He pistoned hard and fast inside her. Amber was right there with him, undulating her hips, holding on tight as they barreled toward ecstasy at lightning fast speeds.

The fact that Amber trusted him enough to accept him into her body without protection shifted something inside him. It went beyond the territorial possessiveness that seeing her with her ex-boyfriend had brought up. Because everything inside him proclaimed this woman belonged to him.

It was ridiculous. He'd grown up in a double-wide trailer in New Jersey. She'd grown up the spoiled princess of the ranch owner.

They didn't make sense. From the outside looking in,

they wouldn't. But he could no longer deny the things she made him feel.

The etchings of his climax rippled along his spine, pooling in his balls. His cock elongated as he thrust, nearing the point of no return. But he needed to ensure her pleasure first. He reached between them and rubbed her clit.

She tore her mouth from his. "Oh god, Lincoln."

"That's it. Come for me."

Clasping him tight, she wailed. Her pussy spasmed around his pistoning shaft. The squeezing flutters clamped down on his dick. It was all that was needed to send him leaping over the edge, following her into bliss.

He groaned against her neck as he came. The orgasm was so powerful, his knees shook and his legs turned to jelly as he spilled rope upon rope of semen inside her quaking channel. As they stood there, panting, their hearts racing from their mad dash sprint, a thought struck Lincoln that left him trembling. It was an image of her belly swollen and heavy with his child. He'd never wanted children, never even put it on his radar. Over the years, he'd even avoided dating women who had kids.

His dad had been a son of a bitch who walked out on his family shortly after Nicole was born. Lincoln knew what it was like to grow up without a father around. And he worried that he would follow in the old man's footsteps—have a family who depended on him, needed him, and just walk away when it got to be too much.

But he saw the image with perfect clarity. And there was a part of him that wanted it fiercely. It fucking terrified him how much he wanted with this woman.

He would never be good enough for her. But he was a selfish bastard. As much as he knew he should let her go, let her be with someone better suited, like that city slicker of an ex, he just couldn't do it. Not now that he knew the noises she made when she came, and the way she felt clasped around his cock.

Lincoln lifted his head from the crux of her neck, watching as her eyes fluttered open. "Not that I mind at all, but that was rather unexpected."

A pretty blush spread over her cheeks. It charmed him that she could blush after they had fucked each other blind. "I know. Sorry. Didn't mean to…"

"Use me like your own personal fuck toy? Do I look like I mind?"

"No."

He rubbed his thumb over her cheek. "You can use me like this whenever you want to, Amber."

She gifted him with a small smile and wiggled against him, signaling that she wanted him to put her down. "I should probably get dressed and head into the office."

But he liked holding her, liked being this close and intimate with her. He watched her erect walls between them now that their ardor had cooled. "I'll put you down on one condition."

"What's that?" she asked suspiciously.

"Go out with me tonight." He hadn't been lying. He wanted a shot at dating her. It might be wrong and rather reckless, given that they worked together. But hadn't they already crossed so many lines that there really was no coming back from it?

"What?" She frowned.

"Ashamed to go out on a date with the help?"

"No. I'm just surprised, is all. I didn't think this was anything more than… this." She gestured at the two of them naked and still intertwined.

"Amber, I wasn't lying the other day. I want to date you

and explore what else there might be between us." Lincoln finally withdrew and lowered her onto her feet.

Amber stared at him, searching his face like she didn't entirely believe him, before she finally nodded. "All right. I'll be ready by six."

"It's a date."

"Okay, I'm game."

"Good." He put his boxers back on, while she went into the bathroom to wash up and dress. He would have to say something to Colt today—give him a heads up that he was taking his sister out.

When she walked out of the bathroom, looking like she hadn't just climaxed screaming his name moments before, Lincoln said, "I'm telling Colt."

"What?"

"About us, Amber. This way, there are no surprises. He's one of my best friends, and it's wrong of me to keep this from him."

She sputtered, her objections written all over her lovely face. "But—"

"No arguments on this point. This isn't to hurt you or put you in a tight spot on the ranch. If we keep this from him and he finds out from someone else, he will consider it a betrayal. You know that about your brother."

Amber sighed as she donned her jacket. "Fine. You can tell him."

"Glad you agree." He reeled her in for a kiss. He kept it brief. Any longer, and they would end up right back in bed.

But when he released her, she had a dazed expression on her face. Pleasure seeped over him at keeping her off kilter, at the way she had melted into him. And at the knowledge that if he pushed the envelope, he could haul her into his bedroom and take her again, with her eager participation.

"I've got to go."

"I'll see you tonight." He walked her to his door, watched her climb into her vehicle and pull out of his driveway.

Lincoln rubbed his chest at the monumental shift in their relationship. It was no longer going to be in the shadows, but out in the open.

He just hoped that Colt would take the news of him dating his sister well.

That afternoon, Lincoln located Colt in the stables behind his house. "This place is looking good."

Colt shot him a grin after he finished hammering the board on the stall. "Yeah, there's not too much wear and tear on it. Amber made sure to keep it maintained while I was gone. Just want to make sure it's ready for Tank and Daisy when they arrive."

"You're moving Tank back to the ranch?" Lincoln helped him lift the next board he was replacing, and held it as Colt nailed it in.

"I guess the news hasn't broken yet. Was planning to announce it soon after we got past the wedding this weekend. Avery and I are moving back to the ranch."

"Are you, really? That's great news." But it made him wonder how Amber was taking it. "What does Amber think?"

"Oh, she's fine with it."

"She's fine with you taking over again?" Lincoln doubted that. And, if that wasn't the case, he would be miffed at his buddy for doing that to her. Amber had done a great job with the ranch in Colt's absence.

Colt shook his head with a slight laugh. "No. I might not be the brightest bulb in the socket, but even I know better than to do that. No, Amber will remain in the CEO position, and I will help out and fill in where needed."

Lincoln would just bet she loved that idea. No wonder she had been so prickly lately. "What brought this move on, if you don't mind me asking?"

"Avery's pregnant. And after a lot of discussion, we both decided that we wanted a firm foundation and place to raise our kid. The ranch seemed like the best place."

Lincoln slapped him on the back. "I hadn't heard the news. Congrats, dude. How far along is she?"

"Three months; she's due in late September."

"I'm happy for you. Truly. It will be nice to have you back."

"Thanks. Is there something you wanted?" Colt asked. The guy had always been rather perceptive.

Lincoln eyed the hammer Colt held in his hand, and decided to risk it. Colt wouldn't bash his brains in for dating his sister. At least, he didn't think that he would. Feeling rather sheepish, he rubbed a hand through his hair. "Yeah, the thing is, I'm dating your sister. Before things progress too far, I wanted to give you a heads up."

Shock filtered over Colt's face, followed by confusion. "I see. But I thought she was dating that Brecken fellow."

"Yeah, she's sort of dating both of us until she figures out which one she wants to be with." It still chafed that she could be with Lincoln and lose control the way she did, but still be considering the other guy.

At his response, Colt burst out laughing. The dude

laughed so hard, he slapped his chest with the hand not holding the hammer.

"What's so funny?"

"I appreciate you telling me. Amber's a grown woman, and I have no control over who she dates, nor do I want that. And I don't have to tell you not to hurt her. You two will find your way, or you won't. But I'm laughing because I recognize the signs, and the look on your face."

"What are you talking about?"

"Don't bullshit me. You care about her. You might not have figured out just how much yet, but I see the signs."

He did care about her. There was no doubt about that fact. "Yeah. Your point?"

Colt clasped his shoulder. "I can't think of a better man for my sister. And I wish you luck."

"That's it? No threats?"

"I'm sure you'll both fumble and make mistakes. I know I did with Avery, quite a bit at the beginning. You'll muddle through and figure it out. But you're also both adults, and I know that even if it's not a relationship that goes the distance, you won't be cruel should you part ways. That's all anyone can ask for when it comes to dating."

Relief flooded Lincoln. "Thanks, dude. I appreciate it. Want some help with the rest of the boards?"

"You have the time?"

"Yeah, I've got the time."

The other work on his agenda could be pushed to tomorrow morning. None of it was urgent. Besides, his friends were his family. And family took the time for family.

16

"You and Lincoln? Really?" her brother asked when she entered the room, putting her jacket on.

Amber eyed Colt. It seemed that Lincoln had talked to him today. It was fine. She didn't care for secrets anyway. "Yeah. I know he's an employee, which makes it tricky. I'm being careful in that regard. But he and I have been circling each other for quite a while."

Colt was leaning back against the kitchen counter as he considered her. "I get that. Although, you're kind of missing my point. You're dating Brecken and Lincoln, at the same time?"

"Seems like. Why do you ask?"

"I'm just worried, is all. I don't want it to blow up in your face."

She didn't either, but until she had a clearer idea of who she really wanted, that was the way it was going to be. Well, as long as Brecken and Lincoln were cool with it. "I appreciate the concern but I'm not in pigtails any more, haven't been for a while. And the thing is, I don't know who

I really want to be with. That's what I'm trying to figure out."

"I just don't want to see you hurt."

"That's the last thing I want too. How did you know Avery was it for you?"

Colt raised a brow. "Other than you calling me out on my shit for being an idiot, you mean?"

"Yeah. That was fun—for me, anyway. But how did you know?" That was the part of the equation she was struggling with the most. It was like both men represented two different paths for her life, only she didn't know which was the right one for her, not when they both had appeal.

"With Avery, it was easy. We gelled almost instantly. And even though we challenged each other's beliefs about what was possible, and disagreed from time to time, when I looked to the future, she was in it. I couldn't imagine my life without her."

"If that's the case, then Brecken would be the winner. We have a past and history together." She shrugged, rather disappointed by that thought.

"Then why don't you seem happy about it?"

"I don't know." Except, part of her did. Lincoln had been in her life for a while too.

"And Lincoln?"

"Nothing with your pal Lincoln is easy," she said, although that wasn't quite true. Now that they had cut through the red tape keeping them apart, the physical aspect was easy. And they seemed to be working on the rest.

"Perhaps easy isn't the right word then. We were in sync with each other, everything flowed naturally. There was a level of comfort there right from the start. Does that make it clearer?"

"To know what to look for, yes. Do I have any clue? No.

Not a chance. I think I need to get through the wedding this weekend, and then take a moment to think."

The doorbell rang.

Amber went over and gave Colt a hug. "Thanks. Now, don't wait up."

Colt hugged her and grimaced. "I don't want to know."

She left Colt in the kitchen, grabbed her purse, and headed out.

At the door, Lincoln's gaze slid over her body like a hungry caress. "You look good enough to eat. Ready?"

"Yes." He had ditched the cowboy hat tonight in favor of jeans and a dress shirt with his boots. Lincoln escorted her with his palm on her lower back to his truck. On the way into town, he asked, "How's Bayer?"

"For the last time, it's Brecken. He's fine."

"So you haven't told him to get lost yet?" he teased, but there was a note of seriousness in his voice.

"No. Are we going to spend the entire evening talking about Brecken? Because if so, you might as well turn the truck around and take me home." If this was going to be a date for them, it should be about the two of them getting to know each other in this capacity.

"It's not that I want to talk about him. I've never been in a situation like this, and can't say that I like it."

"And you think I have?"

"I don't know. I'm coming to realize that I don't know you as well as I thought I did. I can honestly say I don't recall you going on any dates—at least not to my knowledge —since you've been back." He shot her a glance across the cab of his truck.

"That's because I haven't. At least, not since I took over as CEO."

"Why not? You're a beautiful woman."

The off-handed compliment had warmth spreading through her chest. "Because it's been hard enough getting people to accept me as the CEO. If I was dating, it could cause issues. Not to mention, it doesn't help that I tend to work eighty hours a week even with all the employees we have."

"And how long did you and Brecken date for?"

"You really want to do this now?" she asked.

"If not now, when?" He pulled into a parking space outside of Margarita Cantina.

"We're having Mexican?"

"Is that a problem?"

"No. I could use a margarita. But to answer your question, we dated for almost three years."

He escorted her inside the brightly lit establishment. They were seated quickly, given it was a week night. On the weekends, this place had wait times that could stretch up to an hour or longer. But it was worth it for their top shelf margaritas and the best queso dip. Amber and Noelle had whiled away a few nights here.

They put their order in with the waiter before starting the conversation back up.

"That's quite a long time. And why did you break up?"

"Because my life was already planned out for me." She couldn't stop the sigh.

"Is working at the ranch not what you want?"

"I've not given other avenues much thought because there was no point. The ranch is where my life is. I'm not unhappy."

"But are you happy?"

That was a loaded question. More than she wanted to fully delve into tonight. "I'm trying to be. What about you and your dating past? Any exes I should know about?"

"I've dated here and there, but nothing serious." Lincoln shrugged.

"Have you ever had a serious relationship?"

"Not really. There have been women I've dated for a few months now and again... until things fizzled out and came to their natural conclusion."

"But what about having a family and kids, that type of thing?"

"I don't want to have kids," he stated seriously.

"You don't?" Well, that was something not in his favor. Because it certainly was something she wanted for her life. Not right this second, but eventually.

The waiter dropped off their drinks and chips and queso, promising to have their dinner out shortly.

After taking a drink of his beer, Lincoln finally replied. "No. I'd be too worried that the apple didn't fall from the tree."

"What do you mean?"

"My dad lit out when I was eight, leaving my mom and the rest of us in the lurch. My sister was barely a year old at the time, and doesn't even remember him. And I would never want to have a kid I might leave. I know what it's like growing up without a father around."

Oh, that was so sad. She knew he'd had it rough growing up, but had no idea just how bad it had been. "And you think you would leave them? If you had kids?"

A plethora of emotions passed over his face before it settled on resignation. "I'm not like you in that respect, Amber. My childhood was not easy or pleasant. I grew up in a trailer park. My mom cleaned houses. I helped raise my sister. I became a bit of a delinquent in my teenage years. Enough that my mom kicked me out at seventeen."

Shock had her gasping. "She did what? But you were still a child."

Lincoln leveled her with his serious expression. "By the time I was seventeen, I was already an adult. I had already seen more than most seventeen-year-olds ever did. Whatever childhood notions I had, those were burned out, and buried long before then."

It made her feel awful for him. She wanted to hug him and soothe away all his hurts. Kiss all his scars until they no longer ached. "But where did you go? How did you live?"

"I slept on couches at friends' houses for a while. Slept on a few park benches. And that's where I ran into an army vet. He was handing out meals at a homeless shelter, invited me to come get something to eat. I peppered him with questions. My eighteenth birthday was a few days away. And I was set to graduate from high school in another two months. The next day, he took me down to the army recruitment office, where I enlisted. Did a stint for four years."

She had known he'd served in the army for four years. It had been on his job application. She had made it a point to go through every employee's file when she was promoted to CEO, to have a clear understanding of who her people were. But she hadn't known the rest, or the circumstances around his upbringing.

"Did you and your mom ever make amends?"

"Yeah. Before I went to basic training, I went to her trailer and told her what I was doing, and that I would be sending part of my pay back to help with Nicole, my sister."

"And you think you wouldn't make a good father, or would follow in your dad's footsteps and abandon your family? Don't you get that what you did to help your mom and sister, that's exactly the kind of thing a good father does?"

He seemed to digest her words. "I appreciate your faith in me. But I'm not willing to risk it. I won't even date a woman who has kids."

"I see." That was... disappointing.

"Do you want kids?"

"Yes. Not right this second, mind you, but eventually, with the right guy. Or, if there ends up being no guy, I'll adopt or something."

"If you're done, I have another place on our agenda for tonight."

"Sadly, yes. I love the enchiladas here, but they always fill me up quickly."

She hadn't thought they would have much to talk about, but she had been wrong. Once they actually let their guard down around each other, things flowed between them. It shouldn't be a surprise, not with the way they were in bed—or out of it, as the case might be.

Lincoln walked her back to his truck. They were only in it for a few moments before he pulled into a familiar parking lot.

"This is where we're going?"

"It's a good spot."

"But with our history with this place?" she questioned him, studying the entrance to Park Tavern with its heavy wooden front doors and the neon sign over the entrance. It was where they had first met. And flirted. And kissed.

"It's just a bar. They have live music tonight. And I thought you might like to dance."

Her heart fluttered in her chest when she realized the thought that had gone into this date. He wasn't just winging it and hoping for the best.

Giving him the benefit of the doubt, she let him lead her

inside. They found two open spots at a bar table, and ordered some beers.

"I'm surprised you would want to come here with me," she said.

"Really?"

"Yes. Are you forgetting our history with this place?" she asked, because she hadn't. She'd never be able to forget that first kiss, or what followed afterward.

"I was an ass that night."

She laughed in surprise at his response. "You were. I was shocked too. Didn't realize my last name would cause such a stir."

Lincoln was toying with a lock of her hair, rubbing the strands between his fingers. "It shouldn't have. I liked you, and then when I discovered you were part of the family that owned the ranch, it left me worried about my job, and not you. It wasn't the right way to handle the situation. But I needed that job, and was still new enough to be worried about potentially losing it. I figured if anyone found out I had been hitting on you—"

"You did a lot more than hit on me."

"It's not like you didn't flirt back."

"I did." She remembered thinking that he was the most gorgeous man she had ever met. How he had stirred up feelings inside her that night that she had never felt before. And that, while she hadn't been a virgin, with the age difference, it had been her first time flirting with a man.

"And when I saw you at the ranch, you ignored me like we had never met," he stated solemnly.

"I didn't realize it mattered to you. And it was a knee-jerk reaction to having someone I played tonsil hockey with, call me a liar. I was hurt and angry."

He put his hand over hers on the table and squeezed. "I'm sorry. I could have handled it better."

"We both could have. You made me cry, and I retaliated."

"You? Really?"

She hadn't meant to tell him that. But it was the unvarnished truth. Tonight seemed to be the night for them. "Yes. Since we're clearing the air here."

"I'm sorry for it just the same. I can't take it back, but I can try to make up for it."

Intrigued, she lifted a brow. "How?"

He held out a hand for her to take. "Dance with me."

He was asking her to join the people already on the dance floor. The move would put the two of them front and center for anyone to see. Tongues would start wagging. But Amber had been pushed to the point where she no longer cared what anyone thought.

Her choice made, she slid her hand in his waiting one. "Show me what you've got, cowboy."

At his deep chuckle, she quivered. Lincoln led her out onto the dance floor. She didn't expect to have fun. Yet when he pulled her in close and danced her around the wooden floor, she found herself laughing up at him.

The rest of the people in the bar faded. He was all she could see. And he was different than she had imagined he would be. Now that they had finally cleared the air, they could be two people who were interested in one another. All the artifice slid away.

Her heart quivered.

She didn't know how she felt about his whole no kids stance when she had always seen herself with a few. But it was a worry for another day.

When the music changed to a slow country ballad, he

pulled her even closer. They were lined up, torso against torso. His hands on her lower back. Her arms wrapped around his neck.

"You're good at this."

"Be more specific." He cocked a dark brow.

"Dating."

He leaned in and, with his mouth by her ear, said, "There are lots of things I'm good at, and I can prove it."

Before she could respond, he cupped her nape and kissed her. Right there in the middle of the dance floor for everyone to see.

Except the moment his lips touched hers, the rest of the bar and dance floor disappeared. They could have been on Mars for all she knew or cared. Lincoln dominated with his kiss. Molded her being. Demanded a response.

It devastated her. Rocked her foundation to its core.

She returned his kiss with all the pent-up desire from the day. This was what had been missing with Brecken's kiss last night. It had been nice—pleasant, even.

But Lincoln consumed her with his kiss. He demanded her complete surrender. He made her feel feminine and delicate and protected. He made her *feel*. Emotions she usually kept bottled inside flowed freely, as if he held the key to unlock everything she kept hidden.

And instead of being freaked out by the sudden epiphany, she was relieved. In his arms, she was her most essential self. With his lips, he stirred every part of her being—her body, soul, and yes, even her heart, trembled to life.

When he finally broke the kiss and lifted his mouth, she opened her eyes and almost swallowed her tongue at the desire flaring in his eyes. The hungry look activated a primal response inside her.

She ached to feel him inside her. Leaning in close, so that no one else would hear, she whispered, "Take me to bed."

His hand tightened on her waist at her demand. Then he ushered her off the dance floor, retrieved their jackets and headed out.

She quivered at the need humming through her when she climbed into his truck. When he joined her in the cab, she said, "Lincoln."

His face was partially hidden in the shadows of night as he started the truck, and replied, "Yeah?"

"Hurry. I really need you."

"Fuck. Hold on." He put the truck in drive and pulled out, determination written across his face.

And yet, even with need pulsing through her veins, she was no closer to making up her mind. All she did know was that she wanted Lincoln in a way she had never wanted anyone before.

17

They barely made it inside his front door before he was on her, shoving her up against the door. His mouth ravaged hers. He kissed her like a man coming back from war, worshiping her mouth, leaving her gasping and clinging to him. Keeping his lips on hers, he scooped her up in his arms, and carried her the rest of the way to the bedroom. It was the first time she had ever had a man carry her this way—like she was a bride on her wedding night being carried across the threshold.

His thick, muscular arm beneath her knees made her feel cherished. As if she mattered to him.

He lowered her feet to the floor beside his bed and finally lifted his mouth. "Tonight, I'm going to restrain you. And you're going to need a safeword for what I have planned. I know we haven't ventured too far into BDSM but tonight, we're going to."

"How about Harvard?"

A crooked smile appeared on his face at her use of her alma mater. "Harvard it is. Turn for me. Let's get you out of this dress."

She obeyed his husky command without fail. No matter what, here in the bedroom, they gelled. They might not always get along elsewhere but here, they did.

He lowered the zipper on her dress. She nibbled on her bottom lip. Wouldn't he be surprised?

"Oh fuck! It's a damn good thing I didn't know what you were wearing under that dress."

"I'm glad you like it. I wore it for you."

He stepped back, his gaze sliding hungrily over her body. "Turn, let me see all of it."

She stepped out of her dress and faced him in the itty-bitty thong with the sheer black lace and mesh corset. Amber knew she looked good in the lingerie. But Lincoln's reaction was better than she had imagined. She could see the outline of his erection pressing against his jeans.

Lincoln wiped a hand over his face. "Lie back on the bed and touch yourself."

The command whipped through her. Backing up to the mattress, she reclined on it, propping herself up on one elbow as she spread her thighs. She pulled the flimsy material of her panties to one side, exposing her sex to his gaze. Then she drew her fingers through her slit to give him a good show. He wanted to restrain her, which was fine by her. She wanted to see how far she could push him before he lost control.

Lincoln's expression darkened. Lust slid over his visage.

At first, her actions had started for show to drive him crazy with desire but they switched as her ardor rose. She rubbed her clit in continuous circles. Her eyes hooded with pleasure. She rocked her hips as she dipped her fingers in her pussy. But they weren't enough—she needed him.

"Lincoln," she whimpered, uncaring that she was begging.

Lincoln stripped until he stood nude before her. His ruddy cock jutted out from his pelvis, and had her licking her lips with the desire to taste him.

"Look at you, bad girl. Making me want you. Touching yourself that way." He prowled closer.

He grabbed her hand, pulling it away from her sex. He lifted it up to his lips and sucked her fingers into his mouth. His tongue fluttered around her digits, lapping at her cream. And then he pulled her to her feet and drew her over to the full-length mirror in the corner.

He positioned her body in front of his. They looked good together. Like they fit. And then he wrapped a hand around her throat. She didn't understand why but the possessive gesture turned her on. His other hand delved between her thighs. Pushing the flimsy material out of the way, he stroked her sex.

She started to close her eyes as the pleasure grew too intense.

"No. Keep them open. I want you to watch what I do to you." His dark command slid over her like a caress.

She moaned.

His eyes were hooded with lust. Their gazes were connected as he fingered her pussy. It was highly erotic, watching his fingers stroke her folds. She was hypnotized by the sight. It had never been like this with anyone. She had never felt need arise this way with anyone.

"Play with your tits for me."

The order slithered through her. With her gaze trained on their erotic silhouettes in the mirror, she laid her hands on her belly and slowly slid them up over her torso. The silky mesh and lace added to the eroticism.

When she reached her boobs, she circled her nipples with her fingers. The mesh of the corset top was see-through. Her nipples hardened as she teased the sensitive flesh, never taking her eyes off Lincoln in the mirror.

He bent her forward, his hand still wrapped around her neck. "Spread your thighs for me."

She widened her stance, then moaned low as he rubbed the head of his shaft through her slit. He notched his cock at her entrance and then slowly entered her—so slowly, she could watch every inch disappear inside her in the mirror.

"Oh god."

"Fuck, I love the way your pussy feels, how it squeezes my dick like a hot velvet clamp." He set a leisurely pace, flexing his hips as he stroked deep.

She watched his cock spear her depths. And this angle of penetration had him hitting that bundle of nerves inside her pussy. Her mouth fell open on a harsh moan.

Her thighs and calves burned from standing in this position. But she didn't care. All she cared about was that he did not stop screwing her. She bit her lip, moaning. Sex with Lincoln was the most incredible experience. He overpowered her. Swept her up in the tide of his dominance and lovemaking.

But Lincoln withdrew his shaft. She whimpered at the loss.

"Remove the panties and heels, and then I want you on my lap." He sat on the padded leather bench at the foot of his bed, still facing the mirror.

She nearly ripped her panties in her haste. Need pounded in her body. She ached for him to fill her again. Still in the corset, she padded over to him. His thick cock jutted up from his pelvis. Before she could reach for it, and him, he swiveled her body around.

"You're going to act like a cowgirl tonight, and ride my

cock." He helped her onto his lap, positioning her legs on either side of his thick thighs so that she was straddling him.

She lifted her hips up. He fit his crown against her entrance. She glanced in the mirror at the sight, and her pussy clenched. Ever so slowly, she sank down over his wide shaft, taking his full length inside.

Palming her ass in his hands, Lincoln growled. "Oh god, you feel so fucking good. Ride me. Show me what a good cowgirl you can be."

Placing her hands on his knees, she rocked her hips. Amber set a steady, driving pace. Keeping her eyes on the mirror, she marveled at how good they looked together this way. It was like watching a porno but with the two of them as the stars of the show.

She rode him, undulating her hips, enjoying his grunts and groans as she took him inside.

He gave her the lead, for a time. Until it grew to be too much. He rose with his cock still embedded. Positioning her on her knees on the bench, bent over the back end of the bed, he gripped her hips in his hands, and unleashed himself.

It was like his control snapped in two. He fucked her. Hard. Ruthlessly. She moaned and writhed. Dark, greedy pleasure swirled around them. He reared back and peppered her behind with solid whacks as he plowed inside her.

The pleasure-pain mingled, driving her closer and closer to that glorious peak.

At the next firm smack, she imploded.

"Lincoln." She keened as she came, clamping down on his thrusting shaft. Her body quaked from the unimaginable ecstasy.

"Fuck, babe," Lincoln growled, straining. Hot splashes

of semen filled her pussy as he thrust. "That's it, milk my cock. Take all of it."

It set off a secondary round of tremors. They moved together until the final burst of pleasure subsided.

Still embedded in her pussy, he drew her up, turned her face, and took her mouth in a drugging kiss. She could kiss this man for the rest of her life, and it still wouldn't be enough.

He finally lifted his lips, and said, "Stay tonight."

"I don't know, we have a long day tomorrow. I—"

"Stay. I'll get you home first thing in the morning. I'm not done with you tonight. I still have every intention of tying you to my bed and making you scream."

"Oh well, when you put it that way..."

He gave her a sexy smirk. "Thought you'd see it my way. Now, let's get you into my bed."

"Ready for round two already?"

"With you, I'm always ready," he admitted, and kissed her again.

She turned into him, wrapped her arms around his neck, and sighed when he lifted her into his arms. He deposited her in the middle of the bed, and followed her down.

It was a long time before they came up for air. But she didn't regret her decision to stay the night. She was becoming attached to Lincoln in a way that terrified her. Because she realized, as he slipped inside her once more, that she had fallen for him. That was the reason she had been so fixated on him all these years.

She was in love with Lincoln Sinclair, and had no idea what to do about it. Because she didn't trust that he could love her in return.

18

*T*he night of Bianca and Maverick's wedding rehearsal dinner dawned. Over the last two days, Amber had overseen the set up in the ballroom for the wedding and reception. And she had thought about little else but the situation with Lincoln and Brecken.

She was in love with Lincoln. But she didn't know if he would ever feel the same. She worried that the only reason he was even dating her was because she presented a challenge, what with Brecken coming back into her life so shortly after their hookup in Vegas.

Maybe she should have waited to contact Brecken. She had been emotionally wrecked at finding Lincoln gone after their first night together.

Did that make Brecken a bandage? She hated to think a part of her was using him, especially since she had a lot of guilt over her handling of the situation. She had promised to give Brecken a chance.

But was she truly giving him a chance? She hadn't slept with him. As much as she knew she should, to give him equal footing, she wasn't a woman who could bounce from one man's bed to another.

Brecken escorted her to the rehearsal dinner.

"You look rather dashing tonight," she told him.

And he did, in his charcoal suit with a light blue pinstripe dress shirt and black tie. Then again, Brecken had always been fashionable. It was one of the areas where they had always gotten along.

"I'm not the only one. I've barely been able to speak because you look so hot tonight in that dress." His cerulean gaze simmered and traveled over the forest green dress she had on.

"We've always been the best dressed in the room," she said.

"You're right about that. Shall we?" He held out his elbow like he always used to do.

Amber threaded her hand through his arm. "Lead the way, good sir."

"Remember that time we crashed the pharmaceutical conference banquet?"

"How could I forget? We made up aliases, and everyone thought we worked there. Well, until we ran into the HR department, who knew for a fact we didn't work for their company." She chuckled at the memory.

"Yeah. I've never seen a woman run so fast in high heels before," Brecken teased her good naturedly.

"Hey, if I recall, you were running right beside me, and almost outpaced me."

"I was just watching over you. Didn't want to leave you behind."

"Uh-huh. Likely story."

Inside the ballroom, the chairs and ivory bunting were arranged. The flowers would be delivered in the morning.

Amber had a team of employees who would help get everything set up while she and the bridal party used one of the suites to get dressed.

At least they weren't the last to arrive. Emmett and Grace strolled in a few minutes later.

"Sorry we're late. Jamie was being fussy, and I wanted him to calm down before handing him off to the sitter," Grace explained, looking rather frazzled.

"Now that everyone is here, we can begin," the wedding minister stated.

Brecken released Amber and took a seat in one of the chairs near the front of the aisle. They began pairing the bridesmaids with the groomsmen.

"Fancy meeting you here," Lincoln murmured at her side. Because of course she was going to have to walk down the aisle with Lincoln.

Bianca winked at her. Oh Jesus, she had set them up together. Amber could see the wheels turning in her friend's mind. As much as she appreciated the gesture, with Brecken here watching, it only made her feel awkward. This was why she had never dated more than one guy at a time.

"I'm surprised you own a suit," she told him.

"I actually have a few."

"Well, you clean up real nice."

"Yeah, but you like it when I'm dirty," he murmured so that only she would hear.

God, did she ever. It didn't matter that Brecken and her brother were present. Lincoln had awoken something elemental inside her that only he seemed capable of igniting.

He left her side and followed the rest of the groomsmen to the front of the aisle, where they lined up in order behind

Maverick. The wedding planner made each of the brides-maids and the bride practice walking down the aisle and lining up.

The minister went through the details of the ceremony so that everyone understood the part they would play, and the timing of everything.

Then they had to walk back down the aisle in pairs. Grace was the Maid of Honor, and Noah was the Best Man. They were followed by Colt and Avery, then Duncan and Kate, then Emmett and Morgan. Amber and Lincoln brought up the caboose.

"You look incredible tonight," he whispered out the corner of his mouth.

"So do you."

"How are things going with Bobby?" He nodded toward Brecken in his seat.

Amber rolled her eyes. "It's going well. He's a good man."

"And he hasn't given up yet."

"Neither have you. If I didn't know better, I would say you were jealous."

"And if I am? What are you going to do about it?"

She glanced at him then. The stark truth was visible in his gaze.

"You really are." She wouldn't have believed it if she hadn't seen it with her own eyes. Warmth speared her chest. It had to mean something.

"It's killing me knowing that you'll go home with him tonight instead of me," Lincoln admitted.

Brecken stood at the end of the aisle, waiting for her. Amber felt torn in half. One part of her wanted to head off with Lincoln. And the other wanted to head for Brecken and the warmth and comfort he offered.

Before she could reply, Brecken was there. "You did beautifully. Let's go get a drink."

She glanced at Lincoln, at the stern expression on his face. Was this hurting him? He couldn't actually care about her, could he?

She knew he enjoyed screwing her brains out. But she'd never imagined that she could matter to him.

Lincoln let her go, let Brecken take her hand and part them.

Brecken escorted her from the ballroom into the restaurant's private room. Mrs. Gregory was the purveyor of the feast this evening, while Bianca had brought in a world-famous chef to cater the reception.

Even Mrs. Gregory, who was as hard a sell as any, had been bowled over by Chef Leon and his delectable food. Amber had spied those two in the kitchens this morning, trading taste tests of their signature dishes. In the private room, they had put all the tables together to make one long table.

Tanner, Matt, and Eli joined them as the ushers. Noelle was here tonight too.

Amber and Noelle needed to have a girls' night soon. She knew that Noelle was busy with her school work, with her second grade class. But they'd not had time in ages for it to be just the two of them. Noelle had been Amber's roommate through undergrad. She had gone on to teach at the college level, until the campus mass shooting a year ago.

Noelle was doing well tonight, but Amber would keep an eye on her. Since the shooting, Noelle had panic attacks in social situations. It was why she had convinced her friend to move to Winter Park once there was an opening at the local elementary.

Brecken was his charming self throughout dinner. They

were seated near Colt, Avery, Duncan, and Kate, while Lincoln was seated at the opposite end of the table.

Amber found herself glancing his way throughout the evening, only to find his stoic gaze on her. And every time she did, she felt a twinge of lust. But there was more than that, so much more, because her heart was engaged. She wanted to eliminate the scowl from his face as he glared at Brecken.

But then she would participate in the conversation with Brecken and their group at the end, and it felt right too. She and Brecken got along like peanut butter and jelly.

Ugh!

Why was this so difficult? Brecken's hand rested on her thigh—a definite sign of possession. She didn't mind his touch. But she couldn't deny she yearned for Lincoln.

She had to stop this. She was with Brecken tonight. And she was doing him a disservice by paying attention to Lincoln. Throughout the rest of the dinner, she ignored Lincoln as best she could. It was harder to do than one might think, because Lincoln saturated the space with his energy, making him difficult to overlook.

But she did her best focusing on Brecken. She smiled, and talked with Colt and Avery.

Amber breathed a sigh of relief when the rehearsal dinner ended. The bride was spending the night in the suite they were using tomorrow to get ready. She spied Lincoln striding out of the room without a backward glance.

She needed to figure her stuff out, and soon, otherwise she would just continue hurting people. She was either hurting Brecken or Lincoln, and both were such good men. They didn't deserve to be treated this way.

Brecken held Amber's hand on the drive home. She stared silently out the window, lost in thought. But the silence wasn't awkward, it was comfortable. Like her favorite blanket she liked to curl up with on the couch at night while watching television.

At the house, Brecken escorted her up the front porch stairs to the door. Before she could stop him, he pulled her in and kissed her. She liked Brecken's kisses. They reminded her of lazy Sunday mornings in bed doing the New York Times crossword puzzle together. And if that extra greedy flare of need wasn't present, she was okay with that.

Brecken took her assent at his kiss to try and deepen the connection, to take it further. He skimmed his hands down her back and tugged her in close, letting her feel his desire for her. But she wasn't ready to get horizontal with him. As much as it pained her to do it, she placed a palm against his chest and removed her mouth from his, stopping his advance. "I'm sorry but I'm not ready. I know it's not what you want to hear, but—"

He caressed her back. "Hey, there's no rush. But I need you to understand that I'm all in. And I know you well enough to know that you're not happy here. You can pretend with other people but not with me. I think, from past experience, that we could be very happy together."

He had always had that ability with her. It was what had made them so good together. He was everything she should want: handsome, kind, successful, a good kisser, and wealthy. Yet even as she thought that, Lincoln's image from the other night, standing before her in nothing but what was god given, bloomed in her mind.

Dammit! She squelched the thought and corresponding ache in her girly bits. Just because she loved Lincoln didn't mean that love would ever be returned. Doubts swirled in her mind.

This was the guy for her, right here and now. Brecken wanted her. He was proud to have her on his arm. Treated her with kindness and respect.

She kissed him again, pouring herself into the kiss, ignoring the unrequited truth that it paled in comparison to kissing Lincoln. That was all lust and pheromones anyway. When the ardor cooled, she doubted there would be anything left.

"Thank you for understanding," she said.

"I meant what I said. I'm in this. In fact, I want to give you something. You don't have to answer me right away. Just think about it." He pulled a small, pale blue Tiffany box from his coat pocket. "Open it."

She took it with shaky fingers, flipped the lid, and almost dropped it.

"It's four carats, princess cut. If you say yes but don't like the ring, we can find a new one." Brecken looked at her with such admiration and hope in his eyes. She wanted to tell him that she wasn't worth all this fuss. That he shouldn't want to propose to her when she was dating two men, and sleeping with one of them.

"I'm not sure. This is really fast." She tried to hand him the box back.

He stopped her, put his hands around hers with the box, and stared with such earnest intensity, she wanted to cry. "Keep the ring, and think about what I'm asking. I'm talking marriage, kids, the whole nine yards. You don't have to answer me right away—in fact, I don't want you to. But you should also know that with my move to Denver, if you say yes, you will still be close to the ranch. Close enough that we could hire a manager to oversee the daily operations while you live in Denver. This way, you would be close enough that you could be here inside of two hours or so, traffic permitting. And then you could do what you want every day instead of working yourself into the ground for someone else's dream that's not making you happy."

The truth of his words struck a chord inside her. She *had* been working on someone else's dream, relentlessly. Working herself into the ground, and for what? To have assholes give her a hard time for being female, for making her work twice as hard as a man and still not think she was worthy to lead them?

"I'll think about it." The offer he was making wasn't too good to be true because she knew him. She knew that he was being as serious as a heart attack. If she said yes to his proposal, she would never have to worry about another damn thing. Oh, there would be prenups of course, given they both had money and investments and such. But she would want for nothing.

A little voice whispered, *that's not entirely accurate. What about passion and desire and love?*

But Lincoln didn't love her. And having it go unrequited would slowly drive her crazy.

Brecken brushed his lips over her cheek. "You know we're good together. My parents adore you. And I believe I can make you extremely happy. Think about me, and what I'm asking."

"I will. I promise. I should get inside. Tomorrow is going to be a long day, what with the wedding."

"I'll see you there, and make sure no one steals your seat."

Amber hugged him. She loved him. It wasn't the flashy kind of love, or sexy, but it was calm and deep and comfortable. Releasing him, she murmured, "Goodnight."

"Sweet dreams. See you tomorrow."

Amber stood by the front door as he climbed into the

Audi and pulled away. She was more confused than ever before. She knew she should accept Brecken's proposal. Hell, three years ago, she would have been over the moon if he had proposed instead of breaking up with her.

So why couldn't she pull the trigger and say yes?

19

*L*incoln stood at the front as the musical procession began to play. He wasn't someone who had ever really thought about weddings all that much. But with all his buddies getting hitched over the last couple of years, he was starting to understand the routine. And while he didn't love dressing up in a tux, he had to admit they had done a great job transforming the ballroom.

And then he saw her. Amber.

All his attention and focus shifted instantly to her. She glided gracefully in her silver bridesmaid dress on her trek down the aisle toward him. She was stunning. But it was more than that. There was a huge smile on her face. He could tell it was three parts happiness, one part booze.

When their gazes connected, his entire being flared to life. It felt like she was smiling just for him. And that she was walking down the aisle toward him.

The woman took his breath away.

He couldn't take his eyes off her. Not even when she made it to the front of the aisle and took her place. Instead of watching the rest of the procession, he watched her.

Christ, she made him ache.

She made him question his long held beliefs, like whether he wanted to have kids or not. A month ago, he would have definitively said no. But with Amber, he wavered on his stance. She made him want to be a better man. Even when he knew deep down with a certainty that he could live a hundred years and still never be good enough for her, she made him want to try.

He was trailer trash who had managed to land on his feet in a cushy environment.

She was a trust fund princess with the world at her fingertips.

They didn't make sense, not even to him. Only, he knew without a doubt that she made him feel a surfeit of emotions. He wanted her to belong to him. He wanted to lay claim to her body and soul.

Hell, he was even having thoughts of marrying her, legally binding her to him. And the notion didn't terrify him. If anything, it felt right, as absurd as it might seem.

Bianca was beautiful as she joined Maverick with happy tears in her eyes. Throughout the ceremony, Lincoln's gaze strayed again and again to Amber. He imagined how he would feel if it was the two of them speaking vows and promising forever.

At one point, when Bianca and Maverick were exchanging rings, Amber caught him staring, and blushed. A secretive smile played around her lips.

Christ, he wanted to erase the distance, no matter who was watching or where they were, and kiss her.

He'd missed her last night. Missed having her warm little body curled against him. He wasn't a man who got attached to women. He could change them as often as he changed his underwear.

But with Amber, everything was different.

She was special. He kept himself from rubbing at the ache in his chest.

"I'd like to introduce to you for the first time, Mr. and Mrs. Maverick Greyson," The minister proclaimed.

Everyone in the ballroom broke into applause. Then Maverick and Bianca headed down the aisle as music played. When it was Lincoln and Amber's turn to walk down the aisle, it felt momentous. Like a domino had been kicked over, starting a chain of events that couldn't be stopped.

"You look stunning," he whispered out of the side of his mouth as they walked together.

"You don't look so bad yourself. Love the secret agent look."

They made it to the end of the aisle and Brecken, damn the man, was there to whisk her away from his side. Although it was temporary. Because then they had to pose for what felt like a million pictures before they were finally able to take their seats.

But Lincoln wasn't sitting near Amber for the reception. She was at another table with Brecken, laughing at his jokes and carrying on.

As the night progressed, his jealousy grew. She was his, or she should be. It would be far easier if Brecken was an asshole to hate. But the guy was an affable, down to earth sort whom everyone loved.

Was he standing in the way of Amber having the best match? Brecken could provide her with so much more than he ever could. And not just financially either. The guy was connected. Lincoln had done his research after he'd appeared at the ranch. Brecken's parents dined with presidents. Not just of other companies, but of the country.

There was no earthly way he could compete with that. A body plopped down in the seat beside him.

"Stop brooding," Colt said, handing him a bottle of beer.

"I'm not."

Colt snorted. "You are. I've known you a long damn time. You like nothing more than a good, long brooding session."

He ground his teeth. "Your point?"

"If you're really hung up on Amber, you're going to have to go big or go home."

"Who says I'm really hung up?"

Colt cast him a withering glare. "Dude, seriously? Come on. Don't bullshit me. You're the one who came to me to tell me you were dating my sister. You, not Amber. And the fact is, I know the look. It's the same one I had on my face with Avery."

"I'm not good enough for her."

"Says who? Because once I got over my initial shock—I have seen you two together, seen the way my sister looks at you and the way you look at her, and think you are good for each other."

"She's dating Brecken and me at the same time. Who do you think will win? He can give her far more than I ever will." It was Lincoln's greatest fear being shoved in his face. That he could run as far and as fast as he could from his past, but he would never truly be able to scrape the gutter off himself.

"You sure about that? Brecken's a good guy. I like him. I remember when he and Amber dated while she was in college. But I also remember the way he broke her heart when he called it off. Amber didn't emerge from her bedroom for a week solid, other than to eat. And I worry that he considers Amber disposable, given the history."

Lincoln vaguely remembered hearing about that incident. Mainly because Colt had been worried about her at the time. For that, he wanted to wring the guy's neck. He didn't like the thought of Amber hurting.

"Perhaps. But it's up to Amber who she chooses." And for the life of him, he couldn't imagine her choosing him. Even though Brecken broke her heart years ago, they still seemed to fit rather seamlessly together.

"Sometimes, my friend, you need to push the envelope a bit to make sure they know how you feel, and what it is you want with them. Ever think that Amber hasn't made a decision because she doesn't know how you feel?"

No. It had never even crossed his mind. Which just went to show how twisted up inside he was over Amber—that he didn't consider the obvious. He had to tell her what he wanted, and he would.

As soon as he figured out exactly what it was he did want with her.

"I'll consider it."

"Good. Now, I'm going to go dance with my wife." Colt slapped him on the back as he rose from the chair.

Tell Amber how he felt. That was easier said than done. Especially when he didn't have it all figured out himself. But he watched for an opening. The moment Brecken stepped out of the ballroom, Lincoln beelined toward his quarry.

He leaned down and murmured in her ear, "Come with me."

"Where?"

"Just trust me." He held his hand out and held his breath.

When she placed her hand in his, victory shot through him. He drew her to her feet. Then, like a thief in the night, he led her out of the ballroom through one of the rear exits. It led to a hall with smaller executive conference rooms. He ducked into one, flipping on lights as they entered and closing the door behind them, locking the rest of the world out.

Before she could ask him the questions he spied in her gaze, he cupped her face in his hands and kissed her, drawing her in until their bodies were aligned.

He was greedy, devouring her mouth, walking her backward until they reached the conference table. Her hands raced over his chest.

Colt was right. He needed to put himself out there. He lifted her up onto the table and finally tore his mouth off hers. "Come out with me later tonight."

"I can't." She shook her head. "Brecken is heading back to Denver tomorrow."

He growled. "Tell me you don't want me. Tell me that you're choosing him, and I will back off."

Even as everything inside him rebelled at the idea. He lifted the skirt of her dress up. His hands sought her pretty cunt, needing to touch her, show her what she meant to him, because the words were stuck in this throat.

She shook her head. "I'm undecided."

She wet her lips as he shoved the dress up to her waist, exposing her lower body. She was wearing the tiniest pair of bikini panties he had ever seen. He palmed her.

"Fuck, you're so wet." He stroked her pussy through the material. She didn't stop him when he shifted it aside and teased her slit.

He pressed a finger inside, thrusting it deep. She moaned, loudly.

"Hush, unless you want them to hear you come." Capturing her mouth, he greedily drank down her moans as he fingered her, adding a second finger, stretching her, making her writhe against his pumping digits.

She clutched at his chest. Her moans grew louder. She tore her mouth from his. "Fuck me," she begged.

Lust stole his breath. But he wasn't going to stop, not when he dearly wanted the same. Removing his fingers, he licked her cream off before removing the cummerbund around his waist. He made short work of his zipper, shoving his pants and boxers down.

She gripped him. Guided him to her opening. He groaned at the need mirrored in her gaze. She was as hot for him as he was for her.

Together, they positioned his dick at her entrance. He stared into her eyes as he thrust, gliding in deep. Amber wrapped her legs around his back. Their mouths met in a tangle of lips and tongues as he thrust.

Fuck, she felt like heaven. Like he would die if he didn't have her.

This was no meandering pace. It was a torrid rush to the finish line. He fucking loved the way her pussy gripped him tight. And the little moans she made were heady. He claimed her mouth as her cries of ecstasy crescendoed.

He snaked a hand between them, rubbing her clit as he pounded her tight channel. He wanted everything with this woman, regardless of whether he was good enough for her or not. There was no denying the way she made him feel. Like he had been gifted the keys to heaven.

Amber fit him like no other. He had tried to stay away. He'd spent years erecting distance between them, ever since that first kiss all those years ago, before he knew she was an

Anderson. How stupid had he been to deny her because of her last name?

Maybe if he had worked through all his hang-ups, they wouldn't be in this situation they were in. She would belong to him already, body and soul.

With his climax burning a path up from the base of his spine, he pinched her clit. She wailed into his mouth as he thrust, feeling her spasms clamp down on his dick. It was the catalyst. And suddenly he was coming, his orgasm rocketing through him as he thrust wildly, pouring ropes of semen inside her quaking sheath.

Lincoln thrust until the final tremor had been spent.

He finally lifted his mouth from hers. He brushed a knuckle over her alabaster cheek. She was precious to him. He wanted to protect her, wanted to take care of her, wanted to claim every part of her being.

She lifted her lids, and then sucked in a breath. "I need to get back. I've been gone for too long."

"Back to him, when I'm still buried inside you?" he snapped.

She winced. "I'm sorry. I don't know what to do or who I should be with. I feel so guilty. I'm hurting you both."

"Stop thinking so much about what you *should* do and start looking at how you feel, at what you feel."

"What are you saying?" she whispered.

Cradling her face in his hands, he said, "I care about you. Deeply. I know it might not be the answer you want. I have feelings for you. Ones that I want the chance to explore, and see just how deep they run."

Her eyes widened. "Oh."

"If all this is for you is getting your rocks off, I understand. Tell me I'm wrong. Tell me there's not something here, and I will walk away."

"There's something here."

Thank fucking god!

He kissed her then, and felt her words wriggle down and crack open his chest to slip beneath the surface. Those words arrowed straight into his heart.

When he lifted his mouth, he said, "Let me help you clean up. Then we can get out of here."

He tucked himself back in his trousers, then grabbed some tissues and helped her clean up. While he was affixing the cummerbund back around his waist, she said, "I have to go back to the wedding. Brecken will be wondering what happened to me."

"You're still going back to him tonight?"

"Please don't make this harder than it is. I came with him tonight."

"And you just came with me a few moments ago. Did you mean what you said, or was that all bullshit?"

"I meant it. But that doesn't mean I've decided anything."

Fury engulfed him. He nodded. "Fine. Come find me when you do figure it out."

He stormed out of the conference room with her calling his name. But he didn't stop. If he turned around and went back to her, he would take her over his knee and give her a damn spanking.

It didn't matter whether she cared about him or not if she was still going to run from his arms to another man's. Because he was getting tired of only getting the leftover scraps.

20

By Wednesday, Amber still had no clue what to do about the men in her life.

Brecken was back in Denver for work, but he texted her multiple times each day. He planned to be back Friday evening to stay the weekend again.

And she hadn't seen Lincoln or heard from him at all since the angry words between them Saturday night.

She hated it. Hated that she couldn't seem to decide which man she wanted to be with. Especially when her head and heart were not in agreement. They had both taken up staunch positions on a battlefield, neither willing to move from their stance.

This left her even more miserable than before. Maybe if she knew Lincoln was serious and trusted it, she could move forward.

It was just, he'd left her the morning after Vegas. She understood his reasons why. But the thing was, there was a part of her that was waiting for him to leave her again. For her to wake up and find him gone, relegating their entire affair to just a memory.

She drove past all the preparations for this weekend. Brecken would be staying at the house, in one of the guest bedrooms, because they didn't have a single open cabin or room. This weekend, they were hosting a rodeo at the ranch.

It was why Maverick and Bianca weren't leaving on their honeymoon yet—so Maverick could be here to help oversee the festivities, with all the people expected to attend. And Colt was here to help out as well. He had slid seamlessly back into ranch life. Avery was already beginning to nest at the house, even though she was only three months along in her pregnancy.

Amber didn't doubt that by the time the baby arrived, the whole house would be baby proof.

And she was beginning to think that she was going to need her own place. It wasn't that living with Colt and Avery was difficult. But she also hated intruding on them and feeling like the third wheel. The other night, they had been in the kitchen, making out when she arrived home. While it was sweet how in love they were, she also would bet if she had walked in the door even five minutes later, she would have found them in a compromising position.

The very last thing she wanted was to accidentally walk in on Colt and Avery doing the wild thing in the kitchen.

Maybe she should find a place in town. Granted, it would make the drive to the ranch tough when the weather went south, and in some cases, she would have to work remotely. Or maybe if there was an open cabin, she could set herself up there. Although, there was enough room on the property for her to build her own place, the idea of which did have a lot of merit.

Especially since she couldn't take Maverick's cabin. When his and Bianca's house was finished in a few weeks,

Eli was slated to move in there. He had earned it as a valuable member of the team.

And it wasn't like she could go live in the bunk house. Maybe one of the guest cabins that was a bit out of the way... or Lincoln's place, if she decided he was the one she couldn't live without.

Then again, if she chose Brecken, she wouldn't be living on the ranch. She would end up living with him in Denver.

She had far too many choices, and not a single one clicked for her.

Amber pulled up and parked beside Lincoln's truck. On her trek to the cabin door, she spied trees on the verge of budding. Wildflowers were starting to poke their heads up out of the ground.

She was more than ready for spring. It had been a long, hard winter. Granted, just because the calendar might say it was spring that didn't mean a damn thing to Mother Nature up here in the Rockies. While the weather for the next week called for balmy temperatures in the sixties each day, that could change in a heartbeat, and they could end up with a blizzard and a few feet of snow.

Classic rock music blared from inside the cabin, with a deep baritone bellowing something about a house of the rising sun in New Orleans. The music was too loud for anyone to hear her knock, so she strode right inside. It was a guest cabin, anyway, and she knew there was only one person working here today.

Lincoln.

Just being in his presence, her entire being came to life.

Surveying the interior, she noted it looked like he had already replaced the floorboards and was working on the wall now. She stood back, admiring his form in jeans with a toolbelt slung around his lean hips. He had the sleeves of his long-sleeved gray Henley pushed up to his elbows, displaying his powerful forearms. His cowboy hat was resting on the kitchen counter. He wore protective goggles.

Desire pooled in her belly.

He was utterly sexy. So handsome, he made her ache. She rubbed at the pang in her chest. Loving him was never going to be easy, because he wasn't an easy man.

He turned and halted, his eyes wide at spying her here. He shut off the music. "Amber. What can I do for you?"

She strutted his way, putting a little extra sway into her hips. He narrowed his gaze, his jaw clenched, but she spied the lust. He couldn't hide it even if he tried now that she knew what to look for with him.

She swaggered up to him, hooked a hand around his neck, went up onto her tiptoes, and kissed him.

She poured everything the man made her feel into her kiss—all the fear, longing, and love, but it was the last one that concerned her the most. Because with a few words, he could crush her heart into dust.

Her free hand drifted down his torso and cupped him through his jeans, leaving no room for misinterpretation as to her intent. She wanted him in ways she didn't even understand. It went beyond love and lust.

He was elemental to her being. She craved him, and the way he made her feel. She very much feared she was addicted to his lovemaking.

He groaned, gripping her tight. He removed his protective eye coverings, only to angle her head the way he wanted, assuming command. She went all buttery inside. She fumbled with his belt. Clawed at the zipper of his jeans, desperate to feel him.

Lincoln lifted his mouth and growled as she fisted her hand around his cock.

"You're going to be the death of me, woman."

"Not possible. Take me."

"So demanding."

"Your point?"

"Just wanted it noted that it's not all one-sided here," he murmured.

"It's never been one-sided. On the couch." She jerked her chin. It was covered in plastic to protect it from dust, and wasn't near where he had been using the electric saw or sanding or nailing anything.

She led him over and shoved him onto the seat, which gave her the opportunity to straddle him. Drawing her skirt up, she shifted her panties to the side, never taking her eyes off him. He didn't touch her, waiting for her to make a move. Taking his cock in hand, she fit the crown at her entrance.

She sank down over his length, taking him in, deeper and deeper until he bottomed out inside her. He was so large, he stretched her almost painfully. His gaze turned black with desire.

She held on to his shoulders and began to undulate, never taking her eyes off him. Even as she rode his cock, she wondered about the need she had for him. It wasn't normal. Then again, nothing about this situation was normal.

He gave her the lead for a short time before he finally gripped her hips and began to thrust.

Lincoln was rock hard, and knew just the spots to hit to drive her wild. "You like my cock, don't you?"

"Yes." She rolled her hips, taking his shaft deep as he thrust up.

"You look gorgeous riding me. Your pretty, pink pussy grips me so tight. This pussy is mine, don't you think?"

She was so far gone, the words spilled out on a sob. "Yes. It's yours."

"That's what I thought. Mine, do you hear me? All mine." He gripped her tight and pummeled his shaft inside her.

Mindless with need, she cried, "Yes, yes, yes!"

His mouth crashed down on hers, swallowing her cries. She undulated and writhed, slamming her hips down again and again as he filled her deeply. She was half mad with lust. Again and again, she canted her hips, the smacks of flesh filling the cabin.

Her climax struck swiftly, her back arching as she keened unintelligible words. Lincoln's heavy groan sounded unbelievably sexy as he followed her over into bliss, filling her pussy with his cum, igniting a secondary round of ecstasy.

"You finally told the suit to get lost?" he murmured into her neck.

"Brecken? No, I didn't."

His hands on her stilled and he lifted his face. "So, you just had an itch you needed scratched, and figured I would do?"

"No. I had some work to discuss with you, but I looked at you and couldn't help myself. I can't seem to control myself around you, or say no. I think I'm addicted to you actually, and I—"

Lincoln kissed her, stopping her diatribe mid-sentence. He kissed her until she went pliant again before he broke the kiss.

"It's a step in the right direction at least." He rubbed his hands over her back. "Now, what did you want to discuss with me?"

He didn't move to shift her off his lap or remove his

shaft from her sheath. He just held her, rubbing those big working man's hands up and down her back.

"The rodeo this weekend. I'd like you to be in charge of overseeing the set up and tear down. Make sure they don't damage anything of ours, and if they do, note it so I can present it to the company as a reason to keep the deposit in addition to the fee."

"I can do that. It won't interfere with the events I'm participating in on Saturday."

"You're participating?"

"Of course. Going to come watch me ride in the barrel riding competition?"

The thought of watching him on horseback had desire curling in her belly. "I could be persuaded."

"Well, then. I should get started on that immediately. Don't you think?"

"I think that would be best."

His sexy smirk set her entire being aflame. Amber was being reckless. Anyone could walk in on them here. But she didn't care. She didn't care that she was up to her eyeballs in tasks she needed to complete today. She didn't care that she still had to make a choice between the two men in her life.

All she cared about in this moment was that Lincoln kept touching her. His mouth captured hers in a drugging kiss. Amber gave herself over to his mastery, to the ever-present inferno his touch ignited.

And then all her thoughts scattered to the wind as he pulled her into the firestorm of his lovemaking. It was a long time before either of them came up for air.

21

The morning of the rodeo dawned sunny and warm, like Mother Nature was blessing them with a beautiful day before a storm system moved into the area later on in the week that promised to snarl life on the ranch.

Around the outskirts of the hotel, they had event stations and arenas set up. There was the rodeo corral they'd constructed with the rodeo's help yesterday, surrounded by fan stands. That area was for the professional bull riders and bronco riding. Lincoln would be stepping up for some of the riding, himself. He wasn't breaking a bronco, it was an obstacle course with barrels, which was timed. He wasn't savvy enough on horseback to do more, even with the time he had spent training with Maverick and Noah.

His thoughts veered, as they always did lately, to Amber.

He'd not seen her last night because Brecken was back at the ranch and staying at her house. The idea left him clenching his fists with the need to defend his territory.

Amber could lie to herself all she wanted but she and Lincoln were made for each other. He didn't understand her reluctance to make a decision. The way she acted made him feel like her dirty little secret even with their date the other night. That she came to him for sex, and little else.

It didn't matter that it was really great sex. Who was he kidding? Sex with Amber was on another level entirely from any woman he had been with, and without a doubt the best he had ever had. The other day, she had confessed she was addicted to him. He had kept quiet on that account, instead of babbling that he was just as addicted to her. It smacked of vulnerability. Something he wasn't willing to showcase when he didn't know if she would pick him.

And it irked him that Brecken was getting an all-access pass this weekend to her gorgeous body. Especially when he didn't know if she would even come see him because Brecken was in town.

Lincoln stood in line, waiting to check in for the three events he was participating in. He glanced up from his phone.

Shit. Speak of the devil and he appears.

Brecken approached the line he was in, until he was standing behind Lincoln.

Lincoln nodded, assessing him. Gone was the usual suit attire. Brecken wore jeans and hiking boots. And he still managed to look like a city slicker.

"Morning. If you're looking for the spectator line, it's beyond the fence on the other side." Lincoln jerked his chin in the general direction.

"I'm participating but thanks for the advice," Brecken stated, his smile tight.

Well, that changed things considerably. "And what events are you doing?"

"The axe throwing and target shooting."

"I'm doing those, as well as the barrel riding." Lincoln studied him in a different light since he was going to be an opponent in two of his competitions.

Brecken tossed out a gauntlet challenge. "Care to make a little wager on those events?"

Lincoln calculated what he was willing to risk, sizing the man up, the wheels turning. "Sure. How about the winner gets to take Amber to the rodeo show this evening?"

Brecken's eyes narrowed as he assessed Lincoln, before nodding in agreement. "You're on. And I'll even add the barrel riding to round it out. That way, its whoever wins the best two out of three events to make it a fair fight."

"Works for me." The guy surprised him. It took guts to agree to compete in a sport that you hadn't trained in. Lincoln shook his hand in agreement.

"Look, I know its awkward since we're both competing for the same woman. But you need to know I'm here to win her back, and I make a habit out of winning. I never should have let her go in the first place," Brecken stated as they made their way up the line.

"Why did you?" Lincoln asked, because he didn't understand. Not when everything inside him demanded he claim her for all time. That she belonged to him.

"Because I was stupid. A woman like Amber comes along once in a lifetime. And I'm willing to fight for her." Brecken sounded deadly serious.

"I am, too. And I'm aiming to win," Lincoln said, even though he knew that Brecken was the better choice, that he could give her more than Lincoln would ever be capable of providing. None of that mattered when he held her. His world winnowed down to her, and her alone. Made him feel like she was the reason he existed.

"Well, we know where we stand." Brecken nodded.

"No hard feelings, one way or the other. I can tell you care about her. We both do."

"Yeah, I might actually like you if you weren't trying to steal the woman I love." Brecken smirked.

"Likewise. Best of luck to you." Lincoln nodded and filled out all the entrance forms.

First up for Lincoln was the axe throwing event. It was something he and the guys practiced throughout the year. It wasn't as easy as it looked.

In the stall next to his, Brecken was competing. At least it would make it easy for them to determine the winner. And Lincoln's focus shifted from trying to beat everyone, to simply beating Brecken.

They each had a series of targets. Each one was rated for hitting the mark, and then dropping in points the further out the strike went. In Lincoln's peripheral vision, he noticed Amber looking like a million bucks in her cowgirl get up. She had foregone the heels in exchange for cowboy boots and jeans. And those jeans looked like they had been painted on.

He felt her gaze on him as he hit the marks.

He had to doubly focus on his task. Whenever she was around, he tended to pay more attention to her than anything else.

Throw after throw, he racked up points, hitting the target again and again. He edged out the competition. This was one of his sports, and he was good at it. It came as no surprise when he was declared the winner of the event.

He nodded at Brecken, who acknowledged his win with a jerk of his chin.

Next up for Lincoln was the target shooting. This event was located much farther from the hotel, in another field.

Lincoln made the hike over, grabbing a bottle of water on the way. He'd wait to have a beer until he had won, both the competitions and the bet. He was looking forward to escorting Amber to the rodeo tonight.

"It seems we're matched in all the events," Brecken stated, walking up beside him.

"Seems like it."

They checked in for the target shooting event. Lincoln nodded at Duncan, who was overseeing this event. The former Navy Seal was the best shooter Lincoln had ever encountered. Duncan liked running the event to, as he said, *keep idiots from doing something stupid with a firearm.*

Lincoln was highly skilled with a rifle. Not as good as Duncan, because there were few who were, but he'd also had Duncan train him.

As he was getting himself set up, Duncan stopped by his station. "You've got a look in your eye. You sure you're up for this?"

"Yep. I only need to beat Brecken." He jerked his chin in the guy's direction.

Duncan's brows rose at his response. "And what's the prize?"

"Winner gets to take Amber to the main rodeo event tonight."

Duncan whistled. "Well now, that's quite the bet. Better you than me."

"You've already got your woman. If it was Kate for whom you were competing, wouldn't you do it?"

"There's not much I wouldn't do for that woman," Duncan replied, his eyes warm as he spoke of his fiancée.

"I feel the same way about Amber," Lincoln admitted out loud.

Duncan considered him for a moment. "Is that a fact?

Took you long enough. Remember what I taught you, and you should be fine."

The shooting match began with the targets placed twenty-five yards away. And then with each round, the targets were moved back five yards farther. Lincoln kept hitting the bull's eye with every progression.

But so did Brecken.

Lincoln started sweating when the targets reached fifty yards, then sixty. The other players had already fallen by the wayside. He and Brecken were neck and neck. Tied for first place. When the targets were moved to seventy-five yards, three quarters the length of a football field, Lincoln missed the bull's eye.

Grimacing, he watched Brecken sight and shoot... and break the damn tie by hitting the bull's eye.

Son of a bitch!

Brecken shot him a satisfied smirk.

He nodded in acknowledgement of the win, and that this bet wasn't over. Lincoln couldn't believe he had lost the marksmanship competition. "That was a damn fine shot."

Brecken smiled proudly. "It was, wasn't it?"

"Where'd you learn to shoot like that?"

"I grew up skeet shooting." Brecken shrugged. "You're not half bad yourself. Where did you learn?"

Lincoln nodded toward his buddy. "The guy overseeing the event over there, Duncan, was a Navy Seal. He taught me everything he knows."

"No shit. No wonder you gave me a run for my money."

"And now we're tied, one to one."

"I'll see you at the corral in an hour." Brecken walked away.

On his trek back toward the horse corral, Lincoln stopped and grabbed a snack, needing to focus. This was a timed event. He knew the horse he was riding, Apollo, so he had that advantage. He had practiced courses like what had been set up with Noah and Maverick in their spare time. He might not have grown up on a ranch, but he had taken to living on one better than a fly being introduced to shit.

Noah was there, helping coordinate the horses with the riders. Noah slapped him on the shoulder. "You ready for this?"

"As I will ever be."

"Just focus on letting Apollo have his head, he knows what to do."

"I will." Lincoln didn't have to win the entire event, he just needed to beat Brecken. He spotted Amber in the stands, and tipped his hat.

The horse he was riding today was Apollo, a fifteen-hand black stallion with a decent demeanor, who liked winning.

"What do you say, boy? Think we can beat him?" He rubbed the stallion's inky nose.

Apollo snorted and shook his head. They waited their turn. When Lincoln's number was called, he mounted Apollo. They trotted toward the corral. Inside the fencing, they had an obstacle course. It was meant to test the dexterity of not just the horse but the rider as well. And it was timed.

Whoever had the fastest time through the obstacle course without any errors, won. It was as simple and as difficult as that. Apollo leaped forward with a nudge of Lincoln's knees at the sound of the buzzer.

Lincoln focused on moving him around the barrels. They moved as one. Apollo's hooves pounded against the ground. He smiled at the way they moved through the barrels, at the time on the scoreboard. In, out, and around

the course three times, he spied the finish line, urging
Apollo toward the marker. Apollo sensed they were headed
toward the finish and lengthened his stride, hoofbeats
pounding over the ground.

Lincoln finally glanced at the score after they crossed
the finish line. They had made it in fifty-nine seconds. And
they were the riding duo to beat. Satisfaction flowed
through him as he dismounted and gave Apollo a treat. One
of Noah's employees took Apollo back to his stall, promising
to give the stallion extra hay for a job well done. Lincoln
would stop by after the competition to help with him.

There were three other riders after him in this competition—two where he didn't care whether they beat him or
not. And Brecken. If this were a superhero movie, he would
be considered Lincoln's archnemesis.

The first rider completed the course in one minute,
twelve seconds. The second rider finished in one minute,
twenty-two seconds, so both were out of contention to take
top honors.

And then it was Brecken's turn.

Lincoln watched Brecken and one of the ranch horses,
Axel, trot out into the arena and take their position. When
the buzzer sounded, he held his breath. Keeping an eye on
the time, he watched horse and rider weave in and out of
the barrels, and the concentration of the two. They were
flawless together. It looked like they had been riding
together for years instead of it being the first time.

Brecken and Axel reached the home stretch with fifty
seconds on the board.

On edge, Lincoln kept glancing between the rider and
the time. The final galloping stretch seemed to slow to a
crawl but actually went by in a flash. They roared across the

finish line to the thunderous approval of the crowd. The time stopped on the scoreboard.

Fifty-seven-point-five seconds.

Brecken had won.

Lincoln rocked back on his heels.

He'd lost the bet, and the competition. To say that he was stunned would be putting it mildly. Brecken was all grins as he dismounted Axel.

"Congratulations, on this and the bet." Lincoln nodded, still having a hard time wrapping his head around the fact that he'd lost.

"Thank you."

"Have a great night." Lincoln didn't want to act like a sore loser. But losing Amber to this guy, even if it was just for the night, rankled.

He could only hope that it wasn't a portend of things to come. Because he had no idea what he was going to do if he lost Amber completely.

22

*A*mber sighed as she entered the house with Brecken in tow.

"I'm glad I came this weekend, to see the ranch in full swing. I understand why you love it so much," Brecken stated with his arm around her waist.

"Yeah. It has its good points." It also had its bad, just like anything else.

"Amber, my dear, you should come to bed with me. Make the day even better." He nuzzled her neck.

She rolled her eyes. "You're drunk. You should go to bed and sleep it off."

"What does a guy need to do to win you?" Brecken asked. He had been thrilled about winning the bet with Lincoln.

She still couldn't believe that Brecken had beaten Lincoln. And then had clued her in to their little wager on who got to take her to the rodeo tonight.

Men and their competitions.

"Brecken, we've talked about this. When I'm ready to

take that next step, I will let you know." She wasn't there yet. She kept stalling on taking the next step with him.

She helped him up the stairs to the guest room.

"You know what I think?" he stated as she ushered him into the guest room.

"No. What do you think?"

"That I screwed everything up between us. Losing you was the biggest mistake of my life. And now you don't trust that I really want you to be mine. Forever," he said, sounding rather defeated. It made her guilt that much worse, even when she knew that a good part of his present melancholy was because he'd had a few too many.

"Come on. Why don't we get you into bed?" She maneuvered him onto the mattress. Helped him get his boots off.

"Hmm. That's good. You're right. Tonight, I wouldn't even be able to get it up. Tomorrow will be better. We should have sex then."

She didn't say that tomorrow he would have one hell of a hangover. She tossed a blanket over him. Before she left the room, she grabbed the trashcan out of the bathroom and set it next to his bed. At his light snore, she felt like he was hunkered down for the night.

Rather tired herself, she headed to her room. The rodeo was one of their best events each year. They hosted two annually—once in the spring, and again in August. Other than a few drunk and disorderly individuals the sheriff helped them with, the event had gone off without many glitches.

In her room, she removed her boots and sighed. She liked her heels over boots any day, and was contemplating a long hot bath before calling it a night when her phone buzzed with an incoming text.

Lincoln. *Go to the window.*

What? Even via text, he was tossing out orders.

Don't argue, just do it.

And I'm looking for what? She strode over to her window and glanced down.

Leaning against his truck, looking hotter than sin, stood Lincoln. His face was upturned toward her room window. She shoved the window open.

"Are you out of your damn mind?"

"Don't think too hard about it. Just come out with me."

"You're crazy. You know that? Where are we going?"

"You'll just have to trust me," he stated with his hands on his hips.

She debated whether she should go. How would it look to Brecken if she poured him into bed and left to go out with another man? Even though he knew about Lincoln, it still would put her in a precarious position.

"I can always come up there if you're not going to come out."

Panic decided her next steps.

"I'll be down in just a minute." The last thing she could do was have Lincoln come up and stay in her bedroom tonight. She could already see the fireworks in the morning, with a hungover Brecken and her brother finding Lincoln here.

But as she descended the stairs, she wondered why it was that she couldn't seem to say no to Lincoln when she had no problem saying no to Brecken. It had to be because her connection with Lincoln went beyond love.

Outside, he held the passenger door of his truck open for her. Once she was situated, he joined her in the cab and then started driving.

"Where are we going?" she asked when she realized they were heading away from his cabin.

"You'll see."

"Sorry about today."

He laughed. "Yeah, surprised the hell out of me as well that he beat me."

"Now, about that bet. Whose idea was that?"

"Does it matter?"

"No, but I'm curious. Indulge me."

"It was mine. It rankled me that just because he's in town, he automatically takes precedence over me and whether I get to see you."

"You seem to be seeing me just fine now." Her voice dripped sarcasm in an effort to hide the guilt that was near to drowning her.

It couldn't go on like this. One way or another, she was going to have to make a decision, and soon. Only, it felt like the most important decision of her life. What if she made the wrong choice? She doubted that, if she chose one over the other and then decided she had made the wrong choice, the other would think kindly of her.

"I can hear that mind of yours working away. What's going on in that big brain of yours, hmm?"

"I'm worried that I'll make the wrong choice," she admitted.

"Is that what's stopping you from making one?" he asked, pulling off the main road. He drove another fourth of a mile before stopping.

They were at one of the overlook points on the ranch. It was deserted this time of night. But the stars were out in all their glory.

She hesitated before answering. "Partly."

"What does your gut say?"

"It's not talking to me at the moment. When I know, you'll know," she lied, hating that she wasn't being honest with him. But what could she say? That she was in love with him but worried that this was nothing more than a passing fancy with him? That her head told her Brecken was the right choice while her heart told another tale?

~

"Come on," Lincoln said.

"Where are we going? Isn't it dangerous to go hiking at night?"

He cast her a sly grin. "We're not going hiking. I have something better in mind."

She quirked a brow. But her curiosity got the better of her just like he knew it would. He strode to the tailgate and pulled it down. Hauling himself up, he unrolled the combined sleeping bags on top of the padding he had laid down before heading to her house. It was little more than the thick foam workout mats he had retrofit for the bed of his truck.

It was an idea he'd had this past week.

He even had a few pillows laid out where the bed of the truck met the back of the cab.

"What's this?" She studied everything he had in the truck bed.

"I figured we could have a stargazing date. Tonight's the best night for it for the next little bit."

Amber stared at him. Her entire being softened under the moonlight. "It looks wonderful."

He held out a hand. "Let me help you up."

She really was a tiny thing with a big commanding presence. As he lifted her up onto the bed of his truck, he was struck again by her delicate frame. Especially when Amber was anything but delicate.

"If you want to take your shoes off, we can get under the sleeping bag."

"You thought of everything, didn't you?" Amber followed his command without any fuss.

He removed his boots. Set their shoes together side by side. Then he went to the small cooler he had packed. "Want a beer?"

She laughed. "Yes. Please."

He grabbed two bottles , then joined her at the far end, sliding underneath the sleeping bag beside her.

He handed her the bottle. "To another great rodeo." He clinked his bottle against hers.

"Yes. It's a lot of fun but a ton of work too." She sighed and took a drink.

"I also scored some of these." He withdrew a bag of chocolate chip cookies he'd bought at one of the vendors.

She laughed. "Beer and cookies. It's perfect." She took one, bit into it, and moaned. "Oh my god!"

"I know, right? Morgan and Kate have outdone themselves with the café." He took a bite of one of the cookies with a satisfied smile.

"I'm sorry you didn't win the riding contest."

"I'm not. You're out tonight with me, anyway. That's the only reason I challenged Brecken to that bet anyway."

She looked at him like she was attempting to divine all his secrets. It made him wonder what it was she saw when she looked at him. Did she see that he was completely gone over on her? Did she notice the invisible tarnish from his upbringing that he had never been able to scrape off entirely? Did she see how much she had him wrapped around her pinky? That if she asked him to lasso the moon, he would give it his best shot?

There was little he wouldn't do for her. "What?" He couldn't contain his curiosity any longer.

"Nothing. It's just, every time I think I have you figured out, you go and do something like this." She gestured to the spread in the truck bed.

"Likewise, babe. But then, a little mystery is good for a relationship."

She laughed. "Like you're that forthcoming."

"If you want to know something, ask."

"Why did it make you so angry when you found out who I was all those years ago? After our kiss in the Park Tavern parking lot?"

Of course she would go straight for the jugular. No beating around the bush for Amber. "The truth?"

She nodded. "Yes. Unvarnished."

"Because you made me feel things. I've always been fairly contained when it comes to emotions. It's a knee-jerk response to the way I grew up, the emotional protection I needed to survive my less than stellar upbringing. We connected that night. Really connected. And I thought here, finally, was someone I could let my guard down around and be myself and be accepted. And then I discovered that you were Colt's sister, that doing what I wanted to do with you that night could potentially get me fired. I panicked."

"I'm sorry. You don't know how many times I wished I had a different last name."

"Really? Because after the fact, on the ranch, you acted like you didn't know me. And I was still angry enough that I turned into an asshole."

"From my perspective, you were fine with me being some random girl. But the moment you learned I was an Anderson, you treated me the way men in this town have been treating me my whole life. Like I'm an untouchable, spoiled princess. Do you know I went through the majority of high school never being asked out on dates or to the school dances? Because guys have always been intimidated by my last name, when that's something I had no control over. People judge me because of my last name before they even know me. And when you reacted that way, to me it was just one more rejection because of who I am. It was humiliating. I pretended like I didn't know you because I didn't want anyone to know that the poor little rich girl had been rejected once more."

"Jesus. I'm so fucking sorry." He pulled her onto his lap. "What a pair we make, huh?"

"Yeah. You know there was a time throughout high school that I actually looked into legally changing my last name."

"Did you really?"

"Yep. Then my dad found out about it and read me the riot act about how I should be proud to be an Anderson. When to me, it was isolating and exhausting." She laid her head against his shoulder.

He'd been such an idiot. And butt hurt over something that wasn't her fault. "I'm sorry. Truly. I wish I would have had my shit together more back then."

"I think it all worked out in the end. Besides, I'm glad that I had the opportunity to go to college away from Winter Park and the ranch."

"You really liked Boston?"

"Of course I did. There was always so much going on. And the history was fantastic. There was this little café right around the corner from my dorm room with the best bagels. I would go there in the mornings before class."

"I've never been to Boston. But I'm not overly fond of my home state of New Jersey. Then again, it wasn't like I got to see much more than the small town where we lived."

"I think your upbringing has made you into the man you are today. And I'll let you in on a little secret."

"What's that?"

"I think you're one of the best men I know."

Touched, he took the empty beer bottle from her hands and set it off to the side. Then he cupped her face, rubbing his thumb over her bottom lip. With nothing but the stars as their witness, he lowered his mouth, brushing lightly, enjoying her tiny gasp as she leaned into him.

He kept the kiss light, brushing his lips over hers again and again. So much of their time together had been a race to the finish line, like they were storming the castle.

But he didn't want to rush it tonight. He wanted to seduce, to draw the pleasure out and show her what she made him feel.

As he traced his tongue along the seam of her lips, she moaned, opening to his seeking tongue, granting him access to the warm cavern of her mouth. She tasted like beer and chocolate chip cookies. It shouldn't be a good combination, but on her, it was intoxicating.

He explored her mouth with his tongue until he knew the interior by heart. Until she was sighing into him, surrendering so sweetly, he had to battle back the surge of lust that demanded he take her.

He wanted to love her tonight. Give her a taste of how good it could be.

He lowered them down so that she lay on her back and he was beside her, nudging her thighs apart with a knee. But he didn't make a move to get any closer just yet. He wanted to take his time with her.

She slid her hands up into his hair and held on tight, like she never wanted the kisses to end. Truthfully, he didn't either. Not when she tasted like his every erotic fantasy brought to life. Not when he felt himself slide under her spell. Not when he knew beyond a shadow of a doubt that there would never be another woman for him.

Even if she didn't choose him, in his heart and soul, he knew she was it.

A better man would send her on her way with the man who could give her everything. But he was a selfish bastard at heart. He had wanted her for far too long. And now that she was here with him, he never wanted to let her go.

He drew his hand down to the hem of her shirt and slipped it underneath. His fingers brushed over her taut belly and ribcage to her tits. He groaned at the silken bra cupping her breasts. Felt the nipple pebble beneath the material.

He needed to touch her, taste her. Hear her cry out his name in ecstasy.

He didn't break the kiss until he had her shirt up to her neck. Then he helped her remove it over her head. The moment it was off, he cupped her face in his hands and kissed her again, needing the connection. Loving the way she went pliant for him.

When they were like this, all the problems around them disappeared. None of it mattered but this, touching her, loving her, feeling her move with him.

In all his days, there had never been a woman who moved him like she did. He'd been with plenty of women in his time. Women he'd fucked just for the sake of companionship, a need to slake his lust. But the women never mattered. He couldn't recall a single one of their faces.

Amber was the only one he could see. He might be the Dominant, but it was her face and form and being that dominated him. She had no clue that she held all the power.

Lincoln finally left her mouth, trailing his lips down her slender neck. His hands located the clasp on her bra, removing the silky material as his mouth traveled down to the pale mounds. He cupped her tits, kneading them, circling the hard peaks with his thumbs until his mouth was hovering over one point.

He glanced up, caught the look of desire in her gaze, then took her nipple into his mouth. His tongue laved over the hard bud.

"Lincoln." She moaned. Her fingers threaded back into his hair. She arched her back, feeding him the mound.

"Mmmhmm," he murmured with her nipple in his mouth.

He switched back and forth again and again between the two. He didn't leave a part of her breasts untouched. And he even placed his mark upon one—on the underside, where they would be the only ones who would see it.

Then he undid her jeans, drawing them down her legs until she was in nothing but silk covering her mons.

"You're so goddamn beautiful."

He drew the panties down, setting them with the rest of her clothing, and spread her thighs. He caressed his way up over her calves and thighs to her crease.

Dragging the pad of his finger through her slit, he found her drenched, and groaned. "You're so wet. And it's all for me."

He laved his tongue through her folds, from her naughty back entrance to her clit. He circled her clit, flicking his tongue over it again and again until it swelled and poked from beneath her hood. Only then did he suck the nub into his mouth.

"Lincoln." Amber writhed.

He added his fingers, pushing two digits inside her sheath, thrusting them in and out. He located that one spot that drove her wild, curling his fingers up, hitting it each time.

Amber's cries of pleasure grew louder, echoing off the mountain. If someone came upon them, they would know exactly what they were doing.

He felt her ardor build. Watched her face transform as pleasure took hold. He could watch this woman with ecstasy riding her every day for the rest of his life, and it still wouldn't be enough. It would never be enough.

And no matter who she chose, he wanted her to remember this night, remember the way he'd made her feel.

Lincoln was relentless, driving her body up a steep cliff. Her cries spurred him on.

"Oh god," she keened. Her thighs clamped against his head as she quaked. He could feel her orgasm gripping his plunging fingers.

He kept pumping his fingers in her tight pussy, until her undulations ceased and her thighs fell open.

Lincoln lifted his face, licking his lips free of her cream. He withdrew his fingers and sucked the wetness off them. Then he almost ripped his shirt off over his head. His jeans and underwear followed.

He knelt between her thighs, stroking his shaft. She watched him with a small, satisfied smile.

"Are you just going to jack off and let me watch?"

"No. I'm going to make you come so hard that you scream my name, and it echoes throughout the valley."

He positioned himself between her thighs, rubbing his erection through her drenched slit.

"Lincoln." She sighed as he pushed his way inside her.

Her hands slid onto his back, sliding south to cup his ass. He took her mouth, claiming her there as they began to move. He kept their pace slow.

With all the rushing and hot hands, he hadn't taken the time to savor this woman, to love her properly. It shifted everything for him. This was the woman he wanted to come home to every night. This was the woman he wanted to wake up beside. She was everything to him, and then some.

Even when they were fighting and sniping at each other, there was no place he would rather be than here in her arms.

And she was right here with him, undulating and writhing beneath him, meeting him thrust for thrust. Her nails dug into his ass. He drank down her moans.

And he knew he was a goner.

Increasing his pace, he pistoned his hips. The truck rocked as they reached for that glistening peak, wrapped in one another.

He ripped his mouth from her lips, burying his face against her neck.

"Lincoln," she sobbed as she came. Her pussy clamped and spasmed around his dick.

It was the catalyst that sent him hurtling over the ledge into ecstasy. He came. Hard. Hard enough, he saw stars behind his closed lids as he poured ropes of semen into her fluttering pussy.

Amber's lips against his neck had him lifting up. He didn't want to crush her with his heavy weight.

The smile on her face was his undoing. He kissed her

gently, tenderly. Imparting without words what she meant to him.

Everything. She was everything.

Nothing else mattered if she wasn't a part of his world, even on the periphery. When he finally lifted his head, he withdrew, regretfully, and rolled onto his back, bringing her sweet little body up against his side.

He yanked the sleeping bag back up over their naked forms.

They lay that way for a while. Snuggled together. Sated. Comfortable even in silence, watching the stars.

She yawned against him.

"I should get you home. Let you get some sleep."

"Um, kay," she murmured sleepily.

Lincoln helped her dress first, before dressing himself. He carried her to the passenger door and deposited her inside. He started the truck to get the heat going for her. She had bird bones, and the temperatures had dipped into breath-misting territory.

He took care of the stuff in the truck bed, making sure it was all stowed safely for the drive back.

On the way home, she sat in the middle seat, snuggled up against him. And as he pulled into her driveway, he knew that if she didn't choose him, there was a part of him that would cease to exist.

She was light and beauty and everything good in this world. If she ever took that light and left, he'd wander in a barren desert for the rest of his life.

Lincoln helped her out of the truck and up the front porch steps. He even took her keys and unlocked the door.

"I'd invite you in but..." she began.

"I understand. Another time."

She leaned up and brushed her mouth over his.

"Thanks for understanding, and for tonight. I had a really great time."

"I did too. Get some sleep." He watched her walk inside, close the door and lock it, before he headed back down the steps.

He glanced up as her bedroom light flickered on. He wasn't entirely sure how or when it had happened. But he was head over heels in love with Amber Anderson.

23

*A*mber stared at the numbers on the feed count.

That can't be right.

She double checked again. Someone had ordered more than was necessary, significantly more. She went through the manifests on the computer, checking each order. And then found what she was looking for.

Order number seven-eight-five-nine-one for the horse feed. An additional twenty thousand units had been purchased. In the comments section, someone had entered that it was to replace damaged feed—which was news to her. The employee who'd put the order in was Harold.

That crotchety old cuss of a cowboy had pushed the envelope too far. She looked further down on the entry. Because ordering this much feed had to be signed off on by management.

Son of a bitch.

Colt had signed off on it, and forgotten to tell her that he had done it. It wasn't the need to replace the feed, or the money spent on the feed that irked her, although she did want to know what had happened to the other feed, and she would get to the bottom of it.

No, what rankled and had her seeing red was Harold's inability to treat her with even a modicum of respect for the office she held. And as for her brother—they were going to have words later, when she tracked him down.

But she could at least nip one end now. She called Maverick.

"Hey Amber, what can I do for you?"

"I need you to send Harold to my office immediately."

Maverick sighed. "What's he done now?"

"Went behind my back on a large order of feed. And I won't stand for it. This is going to be his last chance."

"I'll speak to him."

"No, you won't. Not until I speak with him first. I want him in my office in the next thirty minutes."

"You've got it. Let me know if he gives you a hard time."

"Thanks, Maverick." Like hell she was going to do that. She didn't need Maverick and all the others to protect her from dunderheads like Harold.

Harold made it to her office in twenty minutes.

"Have a seat." She cut her eyes to the empty chair in front of her desk.

Harold had a chip on his shoulder as large as the mountains. His face was grim, and mouth set in a firm line. He didn't want to be in her office. She could tell that he was pissed he had to be there.

She waited until he was seated and started to fidget under her hard glare.

"It came to my notice, as I was going through accounts today, that you failed to come to me about a large feed order, to have me sign off on it."

He shrugged. "I had Colt do it."

"Let's get one thing straight. For an order that large, it needs to be signed off on by the CEO, which is me, not my brother."

"You weren't here."

She lifted a brow. "I had a checkup, and was gone for maybe an hour on Monday. Now, you know from the past eighteen months of my being the head of Silver Springs Ranch that I rarely take any time off. That I can be found in this office at least six days a week, a good twelve hours a day."

"I didn't know when you were coming back."

"Let's be real, Harold. You've been difficult ever since there was a changing of the guard. I know it's not my work ethic or even the work I put in that bothers you. It's the fact that I'm a woman."

"That's—"

"I wasn't finished. If you ever think to undermine my position again by going behind my back for something you know the proper procedures for, it will be the last time. This is your final warning. You do it again, you might as well come collect your last check, because you will be done here. And I will be notifying Colt of the issue we've been having so there's no chance for you to continue backstabbing me. I don't care what your reasoning is, I don't care if you don't like that I'm a woman. I don't even care if this pisses you off. Ever since I took this office, you have been downright offensive toward me and the job I perform, and it stops today. I don't want any more bitching and moaning from you. If you don't like your job here because I'm in charge, then you can give me your notice today. Understood?"

"Yes, ma'am," he grumbled with a hard set to his face.

"Good. You can see yourself out." She jutted her chin toward the door.

Harold slunk to the door and walked out without closing the door behind him. The ass.

She rolled her eyes heavenward.

"Hey."

Amber jolted at Lincoln's deep voice as he entered her office, shutting the door behind him. His presence punched through her. The man oozed dark sensuality in his long-sleeved Henley, jeans, and lumberjack boots. If she didn't have a pile of work staring her in the face, she would play hooky with him.

"Hi, what's up?"

"What the hell was that all about?" He jerked his thumb over his shoulder.

"How much did you hear?" she asked, because it was a private personnel issue. The trouble she could get into if she discussed other employees with him, including disciplinary measures, could make things tricky fast.

"Enough. Look, whatever it is, you can talk to me, and it stays between us." He took a seat across from her.

With a sigh, she leaned back in her chair, needing to tell someone instead of letting it boil and stew in her brain. "My brother can't seem to help himself, is what it's about, because the little woman I am can't handle a ranch all by her lonesome. Harold went to Colt behind my back. And Colt being Colt, he stepped in and took charge, without even coming to me about it. Granted, it doesn't help that Harold's a petty jerk who can't stand that he has a woman for a boss."

"Harold's always been difficult."

"Well, this was his last warning. I can't have people undermining me simply because I have girl parts. Besides being archaic, it strips away any headway I've made with the rest of the hands. And it makes me not want to do this job anymore. Hell, I've had more thoughts about running away from home as an adult than I ever did as a kid."

Lincoln moved around the desk and hauled her into his arms. And what did she do? She leaned. His shoulders were strong enough to bear the burden, and gave her the freedom to be weak for a change.

"Have you told Colt this?" he mumbled against her forehead.

"Yes. Not in so many words. I don't know that it will matter. I've never been good enough or worthy enough to run things around here, and I don't know how much more I have in me to keep trying." She sighed heavily, wishing she could simply stay in the protective circle of his arms instead of dealing with the list of demands awaiting her.

Lincoln shifted and tilted her face up toward his. "Are you not happy here?"

"What do I have to be happy about, Lincoln? That I've had to work twice as hard as my brother for a modicum of respect around here? Yet I still have employees who go behind my back to my brother the moment he turns back up. I wake up every day prepared for another full day battling just to prove I'm worthy and smart enough to be at the helm of Silver Springs. Tell me, why I should be happy?" She disentangled herself from him. She was just so damn tired of fighting. And it was every single damn day.

She was wealthy enough that she didn't have to work. She could move somewhere else and live a life of ease if that was what she wanted. But no, she was a glutton for punishment, apparently.

"I didn't know things were that bad." Lincoln didn't try to pull her back into his arms. He just studied her solemnly.

She snorted and shook her head. "Please. You've given me a hard time since I returned from college, and it only amped up once I took over. Although, to be fair, that was for reasons not having anything to do with my being a woman and your boss."

There was that, at least.

"For what it's worth, I think you've done a remarkable job with the place. Better even than Colt."

Warmth speared through her at his compliment. "Um, thanks. I appreciate it. Was there something you needed, work related?"

"Yeah. The cabin is finished if you want to include it back in the rotation. I had to stop by to grab more parts for the next cabin's repairs, and figured I would tell you in person."

More like he wanted to see her for some nookie. She wished she had the time. She hid her smile. "Thanks for telling me. If you would check with Maverick—that whole to do with Harold was about some feed being spoiled. Apparently, the roof over one of the feed storage lockers has been leaking all winter long."

"Damn. That blows. I'll take a look. See if I can patch it up quick as a bandage measure until I can get it fixed properly. Depending on the extent of the damage, I might need to put the cabins on hold and take care of that."

"I trust your judgement on what you feel is most necessary. I'd really like to not have to reorder twenty thousand pounds of feed."

Lincoln winced. "Damn. I'm on it. Try to relax a bit."

The phone on her desk rang, and she sighed. "I'm sorry but I've got to take this, unless there was something else you needed?"

"No. I will leave you to it. And I'll see you tonight."

"If I can get a handle on these spreadsheets, you will."

She smiled as he left with a nod, before turning to her phone.

At least he seemed to be in her corner. She ignored the worry that he had given her that compliment because he was getting in her pants almost nightly. And then she could think of it no more as she immersed herself in her tasks.

24

*L*incoln felt like a goddamn heel as he strode out of Amber's office.

The surprise that had flickered across her face when he had complimented her arrowed straight through his chest. It was like she could hardly believe she was being given a compliment on a job well done. Had no one told her how well she was doing? Had everyone given her a difficult time since she'd been promoted, himself included?

Fuck. He felt like a heel.

Because it was damn well looking like it.

Lincoln headed to the stables. He might not be able to take Amber to fancy dinners or offer her stock options and fancy cars, but there were some things he could do to help her out.

He located Colt in Maverick's office. The two of them stopped talking when he entered.

"Problem?" Colt looked him over.

"Yeah. I do have a problem. The next time you decide to undermine Amber's authority on the ranch, don't do it, or you will have me to deal with."

"What are you talking about?" Colt frowned, appearing confused.

"You signed off on replacing the damaged feed."

"And?"

"Jesus. You're even worse than I am. No wonder Amber is miserable on the ranch. Harold and some of the other cowboys have not given Amber a fair shot. Not because she's not capable, but because she's a woman. And by signing off without making Harold go through the proper avenues, you completely undermined your sister's authority."

Understanding dawned on Colt's face. "Damn. I didn't realize that. I'll talk to her."

"Give her some time to calm down."

"How do you know all this, anyway? She shouldn't be talking to you about other employees."

"She wasn't. I just happened to be outside her office door when she was ripping Harold a new one. This isn't the first time he's pulled a stunt like this."

"Is that so?" Colt's eyes narrowed.

"Lincoln's not wrong. Harold and some of the older cowboys who are throwbacks to when your father was running the ranch have banded together to cause her trouble. Nothing too outlandish, or anything that actually hurts the ranch. Just making a nuisance of themselves," Maverick confirmed.

"I didn't know. She never told me," Colt admitted thoughtfully.

Perhaps this clearing of the air needed to happen to change things around here for the better for Amber. "Well, now you do, and you need to stop. You left, and forfeited the position of CEO. If the shoe was on the other foot and she had undermined your authority when you were in charge, you know that you would have called her out on it."

Colt nodded. "You're not wrong there. I'll talk to her tonight and apologize."

"Harold is on his last chance. One more eff up like that and he's done here. At least, that's what the email from your sister mentioned," Maverick added.

"Well, there is that, at least. As much as it pains me to do it, I will stay out of it."

"Good. That's all I ask." Lincoln felt like he had accomplished something that might tip Amber's choice in his favor. It wasn't why he'd done it in the first place, but adding another point in his favor couldn't hurt.

"Did you ever think for a second that our boy Lincoln would be playing knight for your sister? Defending her honor and being her champion?" Maverick said with a grin.

"Nope. Never saw this one coming. Granted, I haven't been on the ranch much in the last year and a half."

"You guys can laugh it up all you want. It's not like either of you are any different with your wives," Lincoln admonished with a blazing glare.

"He's got us there." Colt laughed.

"Yeah, he does. But at least we figured out that we should put a ring on it and not let some city slicker challenge us," Maverick said conspiratorially to Colt.

The offhand remark rubbed salt in a gaping wound. "Not everyone is marriage minded."

"Maybe you aren't but I can guarantee Amber is," Colt replied, studying him closely.

"Has she said as much?" Lincoln didn't like asking her brother for personal information like this. But sometimes, he wondered what was going on in the brilliant mind of hers.

"Nope. And I've chosen to stay out of it as much as possible. But I also know my sister. As much as she might act like she doesn't need or want it, she does. The real question becomes, is that a direction you are heading with her, or is it just a passing fancy? If it's the latter, you might want to consider letting her go."

"So I'm not good enough for her." Lincoln hated the insinuation. Hated that deep down, he knew he wasn't, and was reaching for her anyway.

"I didn't say that at all. You know I think highly of you. But if you're not going to step up and be what she needs, then let someone else step up and be that."

"And you think Brecken is the right kind of guy for her?"

Colt shrugged and sighed. "That remains to be seen."

"She might not even choose me." Lincoln spoke his deepest fear aloud—that at the end of the day, he would be found lacking. It pained him to even think that way. To even consider that there would come a point in the not too distant future where he would never be allowed to touch her again. Never be allowed to hold her again. The thought was unfathomable.

"That depends on you and what you're willing to sacrifice and compromise on. I know I did with Avery."

"And I did with Bianca. I was willing to go live in England to be with her, if you remember. Ask yourself what are you willing to do for her to ensure her happiness." Maverick added in his two cents.

Lincoln glanced between his buddies, men he considered his brothers from other mothers. "I'm not sure. I haven't thought about that part of it. I can't seem to move past whether she will choose me or not."

"You love her, don't you?" Colt asked with a small smile.

"I do. And I would appreciate if you kept that to yourself, as I haven't told her that. But yeah, I do."

"If you want Amber to choose you and stop this nonsense of dating you both, then you're going to have to step up and do what's best for her. Be the man she needs you to be. Otherwise, you're just spinning your wheels and wasting each other's time," Maverick said.

"I'll consider it. Now, if we're done talking about our feelings, mind showing me the feed locker with the damage that needs to be fixed?"

Colt and Maverick hollered with laughter like his response was the funniest thing they had heard all week.

"Boy, he's even more hard-headed than I was." Maverick chuckled.

"You're right about that," Colt said in total agreement.

Maverick rose at Lincoln's glower. "Don't get your panties in a twist. It's all good-natured fun."

"And if I remember correctly, you gave me a hard time over Avery," Colt stated.

Lincoln had, with them both. "Fair enough."

Lincoln followed Maverick and Colt to the feed locker in the stables. It was one near the back end, which was not visited as often.

"We've removed all the feed from the locker until we can get it fixed," Maverick stated, nodding to the empty pallets.

Lincoln surveyed the ceiling, spotting the water damage staining it. "I see where the leak is coming from but I'm going to have to get up on the roof to examine the full extent of the damage."

"I'll come up with you, help you out," Colt stated.

"Appreciate the help."

Lincoln worked with Colt through the rest of the day. They located where the roof had been damaged. It had likely happened during one of the winter storms.

Working in concert, they were able to remove the damaged section and replace that part of the roof to stop the leak. Lincoln would have much more to do tomorrow, on the interior. But at least they wouldn't need to worry about it continuing to leak.

On his way home, his thoughts churned over the situation with Amber, and really it had been in the back of his mind all day long. He loved her. He wanted her. He was a selfish bastard who didn't want to let her go.

But he couldn't help but wonder if that was the best thing for her. If his selfishness was hurting her. If continuing this charade was the best thing for her. Because deep down, a part of him understood that most likely the best course of action for Amber would be for him to bow out of the running.

Even though the thought of letting her go was a dagger through his chest, his buddies were right. He had to put her needs above his own, no matter the consequences to his own peace of mind, and heart.

---

25

*B*y Friday, Amber was ready to yank her hair out.

And for a change of pace, it had nothing to do with the job and everything to do with the men in her life.

Brecken would be at the ranch this evening to spend another weekend here on his quest to win her back. She had secured one of the guest cabins for him to stay in. Although he had protested over that, saying he would be fine in the guest bedroom again. Except, dating two men was rather awkward with one of them staying with her.

And then there was Brecken's proposal to consider. She hadn't told anyone about the ring he'd given her and told her to think about, mainly because she didn't know how she felt about it. Until she did, it was no one's business but her own.

A part of her wanted to tell Lincoln. But that was for a purely selfish reason. She wanted to see how he reacted to the news. Every time their relationship had leapt forward, it had been in large part because another man was interested.

She had even considered that she might be subconsciously keeping Brecken around because it fueled her relationship with Lincoln.

It was lunchtime. And even though she was eating in her office, her employees knew not to bother her unless it was an emergency.

She removed the blue Tiffany box from her desk drawer. She had been keeping it here in the locked drawer because at least here, no one else would see it. When she flipped the lid, the huge diamond shimmered. Lifting it out of the case, she slid the ring on because she wanted to see for the hundredth time, what she felt when she put it on. Did it make her happy or sad?

The four carat, princess-cut stone on the platinum band fit her ring finger to perfection. The diamond sparkled with unmatched clarity. She was hoping that putting it on would act as something of a divination tool, giving her insight into which man she wanted to be with, but all it did was make her more confused, not less.

And she knew it couldn't continue this way. She couldn't continue to ping pong back and forth between Lincoln and Brecken. She loved them both. Each guy fit her, but in different ways. Although perhaps the real reason she couldn't choose one over the other was because she hadn't made a clear decision about what she wanted for her life.

What she did know, was that she couldn't go on this way without losing her mind. Not to mention, she was hurting them. She could hear the hurt and disappoint in Brecken's voice when she put him in a cabin instead of her bedroom, and in Lincoln's when she told him that she would be with Brecken that night.

It wasn't fair to them. She knew that. She had no problem sleeping with Lincoln. But still couldn't bring herself to sleep with Brecken too. Not that she didn't want to have sex with him. She did want Brecken that way, didn't she?

Lincoln strode into her office without knocking. "You wanted to see me."

She didn't know why but the scowl on his face aroused her. The caustic man merely had to frown in her direction, his forehead all scrunched, and she turned into a gooey pile of need. Shoving the ring box in the desk drawer, she did her best to hide the ring on her finger.

"Yes. I wanted to thank you for speaking to Colt. You didn't have to do that, but I appreciate it just the same." His interference had been a catalyst for her and Colt to open discussions on a path forward for them both that would be satisfactory.

Colt was now going to be in charge of all the animals and their care, while still answering to her for additions and changes to the status quo. While she would remain CEO and maintain her focus on the hotel, cabins, and events. It was a win-win for them both. She preferred doing those, anyway. Plus, it meant she no longer had to deal with those cowboys.

"And that's the only reason you wanted to see me?" He flipped the lock on her office door and prowled her way.

Her sex went buttery at the blunt desire on his face. Everything inside her quivered in sweet anticipation. She pressed her thighs together in her chair to contain the throbbing. "Yes. Of course. Why else would I want to see you?"

"Why else indeed." He rounded her desk, yanked her to her feet, and crushed her lips with his.

This, right here, was why she was no closer to making a choice. She didn't know if she could give this up. The moment his lips touched hers, she lost all sense of self. She turned into a greedy wanton in need of the lovemaking that only he seemed capable of providing.

Their kiss rode the line of vicious in its scope and tenor. Lincoln angled her head in the direction of his choosing as he ravished her mouth like he couldn't get enough of her. It made her dizzy with longing.

Those large hands skimmed down her back to cup her butt, and squeeze. She moaned into his mouth. Amber gripped his chest, holding on for dear life as he towed her under into the erotic world where nothing but the two of them existed.

The truth was, she couldn't imagine living without this kind of passion now that she had tasted it. And it was partly why she hadn't been willing to go to bed with Brecken yet. What if she found him lacking by comparison?

Before Lincoln, she would have defined sex with Brecken when they'd been dating as great, fun, enjoyable. Yet since she had been with Lincoln, her memories paled by comparison.

She needed the smattering of domination. It made sex that much hotter for her.

And it might simply be Lincoln. That this was the way she responded to him.

He broke the kiss, turned her body around, and bent her over her desk. She moaned. "Lincoln."

He drew her skirt up, shoving it to bunch at her waist. "Are you wet for me?"

"Yes," she whimpered.

"Show me."

With her right hand, she reached back and drew her panties aside, exposing her pussy. The thought that anyone could walk in and find them like this had liquid flames lapping at her.

"Such a pretty little cunt." He drew a thick finger through her slit. "I've been thinking about it all day long since you left my bed this morning."

He pressed that finger inside her, thrusting it deep, leaving her moaning his name and tilting her hips up.

"Have you been thinking about this, about me fucking you in your office?"

"Yes." She'd be lying if she replied otherwise.

"And what if Brecken walked in to find us like this? Would you tell me to stop?"

"No." She needed him too damn badly. Was too on edge and needy.

"Never figured you had an exhibitionist's streak in you. But if it's something you'd like to explore, we can. And if you don't feel comfortable at Cabin X, Noah's sister belongs to a club in Denver that I'm sure we could try. Would you like that? Like to be put on display naked, your pussy dripping for me while strangers watch me fuck you?"

"Yes," she whispered at the erotic portrait he painted.

The delightful sound of his zipper being lowered had her quivering low in her belly. He notched the head of his cock at her entrance. She whimpered.

"Is this what you want?"

"Yes."

"Tell me what you want me to do with my dick."

"Fuck me with it. Hard and fast, and make me come."

"As you wish." He grabbed her hips, and thrust.

Lincoln thrust hard and deep until his cock hit her cervix. "Yes, just like that."

He withdrew and thrust brutally. It was like he was trying to drive his big cock through her. And she loved it. Moans spilled from her mouth.

She jerked at the hard swat to her butt.

"Hush. Unless you want everyone on in the offices around us to know I'm fucking you."

She clamped her mouth shut, then clamped her right hand over it to dull the sound.

Lincoln fucked her. There was no other word for it. He roughly pistoned his cock in long, deep, earth-shattering strokes that left her rocking her hips up, greedy for more. At this angle, he hit that bundle of nerves inside with every thrust, taking her pleasure and increasing it tenfold.

"I love how your tight little pussy grips my dick." He grunted as he pounded her channel again and again.

"Mmmm." She whimpered behind her hand as her eyes rolled into the back of her head.

Sex with Lincoln was on another level. His touch was akin to dropping a match on nitroglycerin. They clashed and fought one another but only because the passion, the need, went beyond what was normal.

She really was addicted to him, to the way he made her feel when he was touching her.

His hand snaked down and rubbed her clit as he rammed again and again. He pinched her clit, and it was game over. The caress launched her system over the edge.

She came hard, clenching around his thrusting member as he strained and followed her over. His deep rumbling growl of satisfaction as he joined her in ecstasy set off a secondary round of flutters in her pussy.

They moved until they had extracted every ounce of pleasure from their bodies.

She finally lowered her hand from her mouth and lay there, with his cock still embedded deep inside her. Her pounding, racing heart began to return to normal. He leaned against her back, shifted her face, and claimed her mouth in a torrid mingling of tongues and lips.

When he lifted his head, she murmured, "Well, that was the best lunch I've had in ages."

He chuckled darkly. "Yeah, it wasn't too shabby."

Then he stiffened. He gripped her left hand. "What the hell is that?"

She flinched at the snarl in his voice. "It's nothing." She didn't want to get into it with him right now.

He angrily withdrew from her body. She rose and turned, shoving her skirt down as he tucked himself back in his pants.

"That's an engagement ring. Don't deny it. I'm not stupid, Amber. I may not have gone to fancy schools, but I do know what an engagement ring looks like, for fuck's sake."

There was no denying it. "It is, but I haven't given him an answer."

"And when did you plan to tell me? On your wedding day?"

"No. I haven't decided anything. Yes, he asked me, and gave me the ring to think about it."

"What's there to think about? It's an awfully big ring." He finished putting his jeans on.

She laid a hand on his chest before he could storm out. "I haven't given him an answer. I'm sorry that this hurts you."

"What do you want, Amber?"

"I don't know."

"Really? Because you seemed to know a few minutes ago when you were begging me to fuck you."

"I know. And I'm sorry that I can't seem to figure it out."

He snorted. "Please. From my perspective, you're enjoying the back and forth, while leading us both around by our dicks. Make a decision."

"It's not that simple."

"Yeah, it is. Either you want to be with me, or with him, or you just want to continue to fuck us both. Either way, don't come to me again until you've made a decision. I'm done with the yo-yoing back and forth. If you want to be with me, want to be my submissive, have me train you in the art of submission, and have an exclusive relationship with me, then you know where to find me. Until then, stay away from me."

Lincoln strode out the door of her office, slamming it behind him.

She jolted, then put a hand over her mouth as tears sprang into her eyes.

She had fumbled with him. All this time, she had been so focused on what she needed and what she wanted that she had barely stopped to consider the impact this was having on them.

Lincoln wasn't wrong. She had a choice to make. And it was time that she made it.

26

On unsteady legs, Amber cleaned herself up in the personal bathroom connected to her office. Looking in the bathroom mirror, she didn't like what she saw. And what she was feeling? Major regret because she was going to hurt a man she cared deeply about.

Back at her desk, she removed the ring, storing it back in the box, but she put it in her purse instead of the desk drawer. On her desk, her cell phone rang.

Pleasure filled her when she spied the name that popped up. "Grace. How are you? How's little Jamie?"

"Good. Do you have a minute to talk? I received the results from your annual well woman check the other day." Grace's voice was calm but Amber knew her well. Her words were laced with concern.

Tensing, she asked, "Oh, is something wrong?"

"Well," Grace hemmed for a moment, "that depends on how you look at it."

"What is it? An abnormal pap? Cancer?" she asked, thinking of all the ways her life would change if that were the case. It would be good that Colt and Avery were back on the ranch. She'd likely need to go stay with her parents while receiving treatment.

"No, nothing like that. Amber, the result of your pregnancy test came back positive."

"Excuse me?" The room tilted. That couldn't be right. She was on birth control.

"You're pregnant. From the calculations on the test, I would say you're maybe three to four weeks along."

"But I'm on the pill." There was no way she could be pregnant. This had to be an elaborate prank.

"I realize that, and understand this news is likely coming as a bit of a shock."

"Do you think? A baby wasn't even on my radar." Her voice sounded panicked, even to her own ears.

Grace sighed heavily. "I know, and depending on who the father is—"

"Lincoln." The man who never wanted to have kids was the father of her baby. Jesus Christ, she was having a baby!

"Are you sure? You're seeing two men, and—"

"I'm sure. I haven't slept with Brecken."

"Oh, so Lincoln is your baby daddy," Grace said, laughing softly.

Amber was still in denial. "You're not being serious, right? This is all some elaborate prank to get a rise of out me. I'm being punked, aren't I?"

"Honey. I'm not joking with you. The test results are conclusive."

"Then run another test." Wasn't that what you did with medical results? Run them more than once, make sure that the test was accurate?

"I did. Because we're friends, and to make sure there was no error the first time. Now I want to schedule a time for you to come in for an ultrasound. I can get you in next week sometime."

A buzzing started in Amber's ears. The room spun and tilted. This couldn't be happening. Kids weren't on her radar for a few years yet.

"I've got to go. Something at the office. I'll call you back later." After she finished having the epic panic attack that was barreling toward her at lightspeed.

"All right. Call me back. Or I will come hunt you down," Grace warned.

"I will. Just please keep this to yourself. Not even Emmett can know."

"As your doctor, legally due to HIPPA laws, I can't say anything. And I wouldn't even without those legalities."

"Okay, good. That's good. Gotta go." Amber hung up without saying goodbye. As guilty as she might feel later after the shock wore off, she couldn't worry about that now.

She called her brother. "Hey, I have an important errand to run. Can you watch the office while I'm gone?"

"Sure. How long do you need me to cover for you?"

"The rest of today. I don't think I will make it back in time." She could feel the scream building in her chest. She had to get out of the office before she had a total meltdown.

"I've got it covered."

"I'm leaving now. Any questions, just text me."

"Got it."

"Thanks." She hung up, grabbed her jacket and purse, and headed out. She didn't say anything to the employees she passed. For once, she didn't give a damn what was happening on the ranch. Her life took precedence over it.

Amber made a beeline for her SUV. She needed to see for herself. There was no way she could possibly be pregnant. Because if she was, it meant that first night with

Lincoln in Vegas when they had used condoms, she had gotten pregnant. She drove into town much faster than was really safe. But it was the panic bubbling and boiling inside her, threatening to explode, that had her punching the gas.

She pulled into the drugstore parking lot, screeching to a halt in the first empty space she came across. She raced inside. Her only objective was the aisle with the pregnancy tests. She knew it didn't make any sense that she was going to get a pregnancy test when Grace, a Doctor of Medicine, had run tests already.

But she needed it confirmed.

There had to be a mistake. Maybe her urine sample got switched with someone else's by accident.

She raced toward the feminine product aisle in the store and came face to face with Daniel Barstow. He was the owner of Mountain Junction Ski Resort. It was a posh upscale resort on the other side of town that drew loads of tourists into Winter Park.

"Amber. Fancy meeting you here." Daniel smiled at her. He was an attractive man in his fifties, still trim and active. The smattering of gray in his black hair made him appear rather distinguished.

"Daniel. It's good to see you. How are things at the resort?" She kept herself from appearing in a hurry and tapping her foot as she returned a forced smile.

"It would be running better if you would accept my offer and come to work for us. You've done great things over at Silver Springs, and I think you would be an asset at Mountain Junction."

He couldn't know how much that warmed her. Even though she was staring at a possible unplanned pregnancy.

After everything she had been through lately, instead of

brushing him off, she replied, "You know what, Daniel? I'll consider it."

"Really? What's changed?" he asked. His eyes had turned into sharp blades.

He was a superb businessman. He had to be, to turn the underperforming resort he'd bought half a dozen years ago into the multimillion dollar a year enterprise that it was today.

From inside his coat pocket, he withdrew his business card, then scribbled on the back before handing it to her. "That's my cell number on the back. If you're serious, it doesn't matter, day or night, call me, and we'll get a meeting set up."

"Okay. I'll think about it," she said, because she was just so tired of everything, of having to prove herself again and again and coming up short no matter how tirelessly she worked.

"Good. I'm glad. It was fantastic running into you today." He nodded and walked off.

With her empty basket in hand, she headed into the feminine products aisle to the home pregnancy tests. There were too many on the shelf to make a decision with her frazzled brain, so she bought one of each.

On autopilot, she tried not to think what she would do if she was really pregnant. When she got home, she was thrilled to find the house empty. Avery must be out doing something—shopping, putting up telescopes to look at the stars. It didn't matter. Because it gave Amber a buffer.

She raced up to her room with her bag and purse, dumped the contents of the bag onto her bed, then went and read the instructions for each test. She took seven pregnancy tests in all. She had them lined up like toy soldiers on the bathroom counter as she waited for the results of each one.

One by one, the tests all told her the exact same thing.

She was pregnant with Lincoln's baby.

But he didn't want children. Which meant he wouldn't want their baby.

What the hell was she going to do now? Out of all the constructs and scenarios she had dreamed up over the past few weeks, this was the last thing she had expected. No one expects their birth control to fail.

Lincoln had been adamant about not having kids. What would his reaction be when he discovered she was pregnant?

He'd been so angry earlier because she hadn't made the decision. It was pretty solidly made now. She was having his kid.

Her phone buzzed with an incoming text from Brecken. *I made it. When can I see you?*

She promptly burst into tears. She curled in on herself on her bathroom floor. Her tears flowed fast and furiously.

She thumbed out. *I'm sorry but I'm not feeling well. Can we get together tomorrow?*

Not two seconds after she sent it, she received his reply. *Sure. Do you need anything? I can come make you some soup and make sure you're taken care of.*

His response only made her cry harder. She didn't deserve him. He was too good, and she was going to hurt him. *I'm sure. Thank you, Brecken. I'm just going to lie down. I should be good by morning.*

She stripped out of her work clothes and almost lost it when she spied some dried semen on her panties from earlier today with Lincoln. Needing warmth, she got in the shower, letting the water soothe her battered heart.

When she was finished in the shower, she dressed in her comfiest pajamas. Then she curled up in bed under the covers, and burrowed as she cried herself to sleep.

~

A hand shook her awake. She blinked as the face came into focus...

And felt her hopes dashed. Hope that Lincoln would be there even though he didn't know something was wrong. Hope that he cared for her even one tenth as much as she did for him.

But those hopes were smashed as she stared up at Brecken with bleary eyes.

"Brecken," she said, her voice thick with sleep and from her bout of crying.

He smiled down at her. "I just wanted to check on you. Avery let me in."

"I'm sorry about tonight. If you want to give me a little time, I can get ready, and we can go out."

"Don't worry about it. I'm more concerned about you. Tell me what's going on."

She winced. This was it. She was going to hurt him. There was no way around it. And that was why she had been drawing it out as long as she had.

"I drove out this weekend, and can only stay until Sunday morning. I know we had talked about my staying through Tuesday, but work is demanding I get back. With my upcoming schedule, I don't know when I will be able to get back up here. But before I leave, I want to ask you formally even though I already gave you the ring." He glanced down at her hand to find it empty. "The thing is I love you. I've loved you since we first met at that frat party all those years ago, and I never stopped. I think I can make you supremely happy. Marry me, Amber. Come to Denver with me, and leave all this behind. You've said that you're not happy here. Let me show you what it could be like for us in Denver. And now with your brother here, you could take time away. Come stay with me for a week, and let me show you how good it could be. You wouldn't even need to work if you didn't want to—"

Tears spilled down her cheeks at the enormity of her situation, and the truth spilled out. "Brecken, I'm pregnant."

His eyes widened at her admission. Consternation filtered over his features as he absorbed the news before he nodded. "And the father?"

He knew it was Lincoln. That while she had been holding him at arm's length, she hadn't been so circumspect where Lincoln was concerned. Feeling like she was being ripped in half, she shook her head. "I don't believe he will be in the picture at all. I don't know."

Her voice wavered. She looked down at her clasped hands, where she had been wearing Brecken's ring earlier. And all she could think was what a mess she had made of everything. Maybe she wasn't fit to run the ranch. Maybe she wasn't worthy of being in charge when she had caused such a debacle in her personal life. Because there was no way this was not going to spill over and affect the ranch.

Brecken cupped her face, lifting her gaze up to his. "I'll take you both, and raise the child as if it were my own. My parents will be thrilled to finally have a grandbaby to spoil rotten."

Amber lost it. She sobbed. Brecken's solid arms slid around her and held her close. He stroked a comforting hand down her back, whispering, "It will be all right. I swear to you, I will love the child too. Marry me, and I will make it all go away. I promise I will do right by both of you. You can leave all this heartache behind."

When her sobs finally subsided, she lifted her head off his shoulder. Studying him as he wiped the tears from her face, she said, "Can I give you my answer tomorrow morning?"

"Yes. What do you say we get you something to eat? And then we can watch some movies. I'm thinking some grilled cheese and tomato soup."

Just like when they were in college, and she needed a pick me up. He remembered her favorite comfort food.

He was a good man. No, he didn't stir her the way Lincoln did. But that didn't seem to matter when her entire world had shifted. The ground was still moving beneath her feet, and she knew that it wouldn't stop shifting until she faced Lincoln.

Still, she couldn't stop the sinking feeling in the pit of her stomach letting her know that they were headed for disaster. That there was no way to stop it. That all she could do was prepare to pick up the pieces after the impact.

27

The next morning, Amber rose feeling much older than twenty-six. And perhaps it was knowing she was pregnant, or it could be what she was about to face, but she experienced her first bout of morning sickness.

Looking in the mirror after she dressed, she pressed her palm against her flat belly. Her baby was nesting beneath the surface, warm and protected. Her baby. She blinked back the sudden onslaught of tears.

I will take care of you, no matter what, she swore to the tiny peanut.

Steeling her resolve, she headed out. Even though it was Saturday, she knew that Lincoln was working. Today he was working on the cabin he'd had to put aside the other day in favor of fixing the roof in the stables.

It was a gorgeous sunny day. The trees were blooming. Wildflowers dotted the landscape. She was ready for spring after the long hard winter.

The drive to the cabin was shorter than she had hoped, or maybe it was just that now that she was being confronted with making a final choice, she wanted to delay it some more. She parked behind Lincoln's truck. Old classic rock music was playing out of a boom box on the porch as she approached.

But her gaze wasn't on the porch, but on the man on top of the roof, looking finer than anyone had a right to. He'd removed his flannel shirt. He was working in jeans and a white tank top that clung to every ridge of his chest. His sweat-slicked skin glistened under the morning sun.

Before she could say anything, not even looking up from his work, Lincoln asked, "What can I do for you, Amber?"

His husky voice shivered through her. She clasped her hands before her to keep them from shaking. "We need to talk."

She was proud of how steady her voice had sounded. It had given away no hint of the turmoil roiling inside her.

Lincoln set his tools down and rose. He agilely climbed down from the roof. Drops of sweat glistened on his chest. It took everything inside her not to go to him and touch him. Her addiction to this man was so potent it made her tremble as he approached.

"So you want to talk or you wanna talk?" He cast her a sexy smirk, his hot gaze raking over her form.

She hated that her girly bits quivered at his husky suggestion. Especially when it drove home how he considered her his very own personal sex toy. Did he care that while his words might be making her body purr, they were breaking her heart?

Shifting back a step, needing a safe distance so that she didn't do something like reach for him, she said, "No. I wanted to let you know that Brecken wants to marry me. I know you saw the ring, but he asked me again last night. Before I give him an answer, I wanted to talk to you and see where things stand with us. Do you see this thing between us going anywhere?"

At her question, Lincoln stared, then his gaze shuttered and became unreadable. Gone was the sexy half smile and light of desire. In their place was the Lincoln who barely did more than grunt in response. "I think that would be the best thing for you, marrying Brecken."

His words punched a hole clear through her chest, shattering her heart. Crossing her arms protectively in front of her, she couldn't keep the venom out of her voice. "So this thing between us, all those *I want to be with you* and *choose me* quips were lines. This was simply the two of us fooling around? You don't feel anything?"

Lincoln shrugged nonchalantly. "It's been fun. But we both know there was no future here."

Every word was a dagger being shoved straight into her heart. She had played her hand with him time and time again... and lost. A surfeit of pain crashed into her like a tsunami. She dug her fingernails into her palms, refusing to cry in front of him. Not when he had made her feel like a live sex toy.

"I see," she said. But she didn't. She loved him. Loved him more than she had ever loved anyone else. And she had been nothing but a passing fancy. A willing female body to slake his lust upon.

"It's for the best. He can give you a great life."

Any of the warmth that had developed in the last few weeks was absent from his voice. He didn't reach for her, wasn't protesting that another man wanted to marry her or that she should pick him. It was like she was talking to a stranger. She stared at him, at the harsh lines of his face, for what she knew was the final time. "Goodbye, Lincoln."

"Take care, Amber. Be happy," Lincoln said solemnly.

Amber marched away. It was either that, or Lincoln would witness her epic meltdown. She choked back the sob lodged in her throat and all but vaulted into her vehicle. With a final look at Lincoln, she backed out of the driveway and sped away, not really paying attention to where she was driving as waves of pain bombarded her. She waited until she had driven down the road a bit before pulling off to the side and sobbing her heart out.

Deep down, she had known. Deep down, she hadn't trusted him. That was why she had held back from making a decision. Because she knew the moment she pressed the issue, it would be over between them. The truth was, she had been in love with Lincoln for years.

And at the end of the day, she wasn't anything more than another faceless woman to grace his bed. The sooner she accepted that truth, the better off she would be.

Once she had herself together, she did the only thing left to do. She called Brecken. He was everything she should want, anyway—rich, successful, kind, honest, and he was willing to step into the role of father with no questions asked.

"Amber, I'm glad you called. I need to leave earlier tomorrow and will be heading out first thing in the morning. There's a meeting that had to be rescheduled that I can't miss that I need to prepare for, and I have to head into the office to get my notes for it."

"Then it's providence that I have an answer for you now."

"And?"

If she didn't feel like her heart had been ripped from her chest, she would consider the hope in his voice charming. She could feel his excitement through the phone. Closing her eyes, she responded, "Yes. I'll marry you. If you're certain you're okay about the baby and raising it as your own. I would understand if you decided you didn't want me, that it was too much trouble."

"Amber, stop. I meant what I said last night. You and the baby will be well taken care of, I promise that you won't be sorry. I will love you both. We should celebrate, we should—"

She released her pent-up breath. "Brecken, we can celebrate later. If I'm going to be able to leave tomorrow morning, I need to pack. And I'll just follow you in my car. But I need to spend today talking things over with my brother, since I'm having him take over the ranch, and getting things ready so I can leave with you tomorrow."

"Right. Sorry, I didn't even think of that. I'm just thrilled that you said yes. You've made me the happiest man on the planet. Don't worry about packing everything. Just pack what you will need for the next few weeks. We can come back to get the rest later, or I can hire a moving company to do it for us."

"Sounds like a plan. I'm in the car but will call you later tonight, after I have a chance to speak with Colt."

"Looking forward to it."

"Uh huh." She hung up.

The first hurdle was taken care of. Now she just had to go deal with submitting her resignation as CEO of Silver Springs Ranch. And if she wanted to weep over her decision to marry Brecken instead of cheer, she convinced herself that it must be the baby hormones.

Yeah, that was it. And not that she was making the biggest mistake of her life.

∾

Lincoln watched her leave.

What else could he do? Go after her? Confess that he loved her?

He shook his head. No. He couldn't do any of that. It was because he loved her that he was letting her go. If he tried to keep her here with him, it would be the most selfish act of his existence. The only noble thing for him to do was to let her go. Colt and Maverick had been right. He had to put her needs before his own. And in the long run, he would never be enough for her.

He rubbed at the ache in his chest.

Surely, he had made the right choice. It was the right decision, the only choice really that he could make to ensure her happiness. She was miserable on the ranch, and he was tied to it.

Brecken could give her a life that Lincoln would never be able to give her. No matter how far he had run, he was still just the trailer park trash kid. And people like him didn't get to marry the princess in the castle. They might get the chance to touch them.

But she was never going to be his for the long haul.

Lincoln turned and stumbled to his knees. He put his head in his hands and did something he hadn't done since he was a child. He wept for the future they would never have.

28

*A*mber came through the front door of the Anderson family home. It had been home for her for so long. But even this no longer fit her. It hadn't fit her for some time, and she knew it.

"There you are. I've been worried ever since I got your text message," Colt said as she walked into the kitchen.

"Where's Avery?"

Colt smiled. "Having a bit of a lie down. She's not having a good time of it with morning sickness. Although, it's not just morning, it tends to strike morning, noon, and in the evenings too."

Her brother sounded frazzled because there was nothing he could do to fix his wife's ailment. Not when the ailment was pregnancy. "You're going to be a great dad, you know."

His lips quirked. "Thanks. I appreciate it. Time will tell."

"No. I know you will be. You helped raise me as much as Mom and Dad did, so I know a thing or two about it."

"And look how you turned out." He winced, replying in mock horror.

She looked at his coffee longingly as she made some tea. That was one of the things about pregnancy she could already tell she wasn't going to like. Living without coffee.

Colt waited for her to begin. He was good like that, giving a person the space they needed to bring up a topic. She joined him at the kitchen table, and sighed. "The reason I wanted to speak with you here and not in the office, is because while it's ranch business, it's also family business."

He nodded. "I get that. What's going on in that big brain of yours?"

She pasted a smile on her face. "Brecken asked me to marry him, and I said yes."

Shock filtered over Colt's face for a moment. "I thought you and Lincoln—"

She shook her head. "Whatever Lincoln and I had, it's done. I'm marrying Brecken."

"But do you love him?"

"Sure do." It was mostly the truth. She did love Brecken. If it felt like the love she had for a friend and not a lover, so be it.

"Then I guess congratulations are in order. Does this mean we'll be sharing a house with the two of you?"

She laughed at that imagery. "No. Far from it. I'm leaving the ranch, Colt. I'm tendering my resignation as CEO of Silver Springs. I think, since you and Avery are back, it's perfect timing. You can take up the reins once again, and everyone will be happy."

"You're leaving? When? Why? I'm going to need you to walk me through, starting with Lincoln. If he did something to hurt you, I will go talk to him."

She put her hand over her brother's. "Please don't be mad at him or give him a hard time. We're just not suited for the long haul together."

"But if you love him—"

"Colt, it doesn't matter what I feel. He doesn't want me that way. But Brecken does. This will be good for me. I'm going to be leaving with Brecken tomorrow morning. I'm going to pack what I will need for the next few weeks. Then I'll be back to get more later. I'm just moving to Denver, so I won't be that far away." She was proud that her voice didn't waver, and that she kept her smile in place.

"Are you sure that you want to give up your position on the ranch?"

She finally let the words that had been bottled up inside spill over. "The truth is, I'm tired of fighting. The men here don't want a woman in charge of operations. I've worked myself silly trying to be worthy of their respect, and nothing I've said or done has worked. And at the end of the day, I'm exhausted. I don't want to work here anymore. This was your dream, and Dad's, and I went along with it. But I just can't anymore because it was never *my* dream. And I think it's time I found out what is, don't you?"

"Sweetheart, you are more than worthy. And I'm sorry if I did anything to make you feel like this wasn't your place and that you haven't done an amazing job."

Colt was so earnest in his response, she did tear up a bit. "So, you'll take over?"

"Only if you're one hundred percent sure. I don't want you to regret it once it's done. And I don't want there to be any confusion with the staff."

"I am more than certain. I've been miserable here, trying to make it work and it's just not. No matter what, I'm done. I wash my hands of it. This place is your problem now."

"But marrying Brecken? Are you sure?"

She wished he would stop asking her that because he couldn't change her mind. No. No going back. She had made her choice. It would be good for her and the baby. "He loves me. What more do I need to know?"

Colt sighed. "If this is what you really want then I'm not going to stand in your way. I do wish you were staying. It's been nice having you here."

"I'll be a simple phone call away, and can be here in about two hours. Hell, if you're really pressed for time, you can send the jet to collect me."

"All right, let's head into our office here, do all the transfers, and you can catch me up to speed with everything on the ranch." Colt rose from his seat.

With a shaky breath, she stood and gave Colt a hug. "I love you."

"Love you too."

She blinked back the tears. Leaving the ranch really was the best thing for her. She would call Noelle and let her know too. And all her friends... damn, but leaving was going to be a lot harder than she thought it would.

But then, it had been the people she loved keeping her here in the first place. And it was no longer enough to cover the fact that she wasn't happy.

29

*S*unday morning dawned bright and early. Amber had already said goodbye to Noelle. She had called her best friend and given her the news. Noelle had come over last night and helped her pack, while simultaneously cursing Lincoln for being an idiot.

And Amber had finally spilled her secret—that in about eight months, she was going to be a mom—after swearing her best friend to secrecy, of course.

"You know you're always welcome." Colt tugged on her ponytail.

"I know."

She hugged him and then Avery. "Are you sure you don't want to change your mind?"

"No. It's the right thing for me. I'll let you know once I've made it to Denver. Keep me in the loop with Baby Anderson," she said, not mentioning that Baby Anderson would have a cousin roughly three months after they were born. She would tell them, but now was not the time.

If her brother knew that Lincoln had knocked her up, Amber would end up with a shotgun wedding. This way, if she was going to have Brecken claim the child as his, she needed to announce the news to her family in another month's time.

Brecken had left an hour before, wanting to give her time to say goodbye to her family. He was good like that. But once all her goodbyes were said and hugs given, there was nothing else for her to do but leave.

It was rather surreal driving off the ranch, realizing it was going to be a long time before she came back. And even then, it would only be for short visits.

But she was proud of herself. She didn't drive by Lincoln's place on her way out. She wasn't a masochist. She might be submissive in the bedroom, but she did have lines in the sand that she wouldn't cross.

The drive through the Rockies along interstate seventy was scenic, and picture perfect. During the winter, she would avoid it. Maybe she'd make the trip for Thanksgiving and Christmas but she would be in her final trimester by then. So travel might not be the best thing. She would have to find a new doctor and obstetrician.

Amber followed the directions on her navigation system all the way into Denver and through the suburbs. She pulled into the circular driveway at Brecken's house in Arvada. Except, it wasn't a house, it was a mansion. Knowing someone was wealthy and seeing the proof of it were two different things. The home was more modern than she would have gone with, but she was sure she would grow to love it over time.

Before she could emerge from the car, Brecken was there, opening her door. "There she is, my beautiful fiancée."

For a moment, Amber thought he was talking about

someone else. Then she realized that was her title now. She was Brecken's fiancée. "Yep, I'm here."

"How was your drive? Did you have any difficulties?"

"No, the roads were pretty clear."

Brecken drew her inside the large oak front door. "Let me give you a quick tour. And then, if you want to wait, I can help you with those boxes when I return from the office."

"Sure. I can't wait to see the house." She kept a smile on her face as he showed her everything.

The foyer opened up into a great room with a high vaulted ceiling, and plenty of hardwood floors. There was a baby grand piano near the stone fireplace. And plenty of places to comfortably sit.

Room after room, it was the same. Heavy, custom furniture in rooms that were expertly decorated. Dramatic modern art with splashes of color on the pale beige walls.

The kitchen looked like it belonged in a high end restaurant, and was large enough for wait staff to help serve meals at parties. "Now, there are some prepared meals in the fridge. My cook comes Monday through Friday. Francois will make sure you have whatever your heart desires. And if we need to implement a special diet for your pregnancy, we can get him a list of everything that are no-nos, or what your cravings are and the like. But he also precooks meals for me and stores them in the fridge with instructions for reheating on each one. So, if you get hungry, help yourself to whatever is there. The maid, Mariel, is also here Monday through Friday, so you won't need to worry about trying to keep this place clean. I left my office number on the fridge for you. And I hate to do this since you're finally here, but I have to run to the office. We can celebrate the engagement tonight when I get home." He kissed her.

That was her first indication that she'd made a mistake. The kiss was nice, pleasant even. But it didn't turn her inside out.

It was ridiculous to compare his kiss to Lincoln's. They were different people. Of course, it was different. She had kissed Brecken plenty. And just to prove it to herself, she put her all into the kiss. It had to be all the shocks and major life changes affecting how she responded to his kiss.

When Brecken finally tore his mouth away, he was breathing heavily, and lust filled his gaze. "Minx. I'll remember that, and be looking forward to tonight."

He kissed her quickly once more and then headed out.

Once he'd left, she conducted her own private tour of the house. Even if it was a bit modern for her tastes, it was gorgeous. Everything was state of the art. There was even a library full of both expensive first editions behind glass, and sections stuffed with paperbacks.

Brecken always did enjoy reading. The library was cozy, if a bit sanitized for her tastes.

As she went through each room slowly, she kept trying to picture herself here—in the living room, dining room, family room, in the home movie theater or in the home gym. In the kitchen or on the back patio, where of course there was an in-ground pool.

And she entered the bedroom she would be sharing with Brecken, trying to see herself in here getting ready for some event with him. See herself as her belly grew rounded with child. See herself in bed lying next to Brecken for the rest of her life.

In that moment, Amber knew without a doubt that she had made a major mistake in accepting his proposal. She might love him, but she wasn't *in* love with him. The man she was in love with didn't want her.

She swiped at the stray tear. This wasn't her place. But even though this wasn't her place that didn't mean she was heading back to the ranch. Because that wasn't her place either.

On her phone, she brought up the listing for Brown Palace Hotel and called their reservations line. "Yes, I would like to book a room if you have anything available today."

"For how many nights?"

"Seven. And if you have a suite available, I will take one of those."

"Let me check. I do have one of the presidential suites available. It's a little pricey but—"

"I'll take it. Let me just grab my credit card." A week in a hotel room without anyone bothering her would give her the space she needed to figure out what it was she did want.

~

Later that afternoon, she was waiting on a padded bench near the front door with her purse at her side when Brecken made it back.

"Hey, did you have any trouble getting all those boxes in?" Brecken held a bouquet of roses in his hand and had a wide grin on his face. But when he spied her sitting calmly by the front door, his face dropped.

"You're leaving," he stated in disbelief.

She winced as she rose and faced him. "Brecken, I'm sorry... I love you. You know that I do, but I'm not *in* love with you. And it wouldn't be right for me to marry you."

Brecken tossed the roses on the bench she had just vacated and gripped her arms. "And I think I can love you enough for the both of us. Now with Lincoln out of the way, there's a real chance for us."

No. There wasn't. For them, that ship had sailed years ago, but she'd only just realized that when she was about to get everything she thought she wanted. "No. It wouldn't be right for me to do that to you. You deserve a woman who is over the moon in love with you, who doesn't need time to decide whether to marry you or not, who says yes the moment you ask."

He searched her face and finally sighed with acceptance when he realized she was serious. "Are you sure I cannot convince you otherwise?"

"Yeah. I'm sure. And I hope one day you can forgive me for hurting you." She handed him back the ring.

"It's him, that Lincoln guy. He's the one you love," Brecken stated solemnly, only just now realizing that he'd never had a chance.

"It doesn't matter what I feel because he doesn't love me." She shrugged, because it was the truth. Lincoln didn't love her. And if she went home and told him about the baby, she would trap him. She loved him enough not to do that to him.

"And what are you going to do?"

"I don't know yet, other than have my baby. But I've got time to figure it out. I should let you enjoy your evening." She was ready for a nice, long, hot bath, and a good cry.

"You're not going to at least stay the night? You can sleep in one of the guest rooms."

She took his face in her hands and kissed his cheek. "I don't think that would be a good idea. I've got a hotel room booked for the next week. I promise, I will be fine."

"Call me if you need anything. Or even if you change your mind," he said, walking her out onto the front porch.

His gaze searched hers for any signs of regret or uncertainty in her decision. But there was none because she was more resolved than ever.

"Goodbye, Brecken. I wish you a lifetime of happiness. You deserve the best."

He hugged her. She spied the shimmer of moisture in his eyes as he let her go, and had to blink back her own tears. She left his house, and felt a weight suddenly lift from her shoulders.

She hated that she had hurt someone she considered a friend. It was a wound she had never intended to make. But that didn't absolve her in the slightest because she had made it, and would have to live with it.

Traffic was light that evening as she drove to the hotel and gave her car keys to the valet. She had them bring up her five suitcases since she didn't want them left in the car. After ordering room service, she pondered her next steps, and came across the business card in her purse.

Studying the name of the resort for a minute, she flipped it over to the back and dialed the number.

"Daniel, hi, this is Amber Anderson. Am I catching you at a bad time?" Now it was time for her to make a life she wanted, not just for herself, but for her little peanut.

30

*B*y Monday, Lincoln was beginning to wonder if he had made the biggest mistake of his life. He headed in to the hotel and the offices. He wanted to at least check on Amber, while acting like it was work he was coming to her door about.

But the sad truth was, he missed her. He had been second guessing himself for the last forty-eight hours. When he arrived at Amber's office door, he had to look at it more than once. Her name was no longer on the door. It now read, *Colt Anderson, CEO*.

What the hell?

He knocked on the door.

"Come in," Colt's voice said from the other side.

Lincoln pushed the door open and headed in. "Where's Amber?" he blurted out before he could stop himself.

"Shut the door. You and I need to talk."

On autopilot, Lincoln followed Colt's orders and took a seat across from his friend. His friend who looked like he wanted to throttle him. "Where is she?"

"Gone. She left the ranch yesterday after resigning from her position as CEO. She's marrying Brecken."

Lincoln knew that part, but he didn't think it would happen so fast, that she would up and leave the ranch like that. "I see."

Colt steepled his fingers. "That's all you fucking have to say for yourself? I told you that I was fine with you dating my sister as long as you didn't hurt her."

"She wanted to marry Brecken. He can give her a life I will never be able to. It's the best thing for her."

"You sure about that?"

No. "It doesn't matter what I want or how I feel. You and Maverick both said that, when it came to the women you loved, you had to make sacrifices in order to ensure their happiness."

"We did. But you're missing the point. It was sacrificing a part of our lives in order to be with the woman we loved, not so we could send them off to marry some other guy."

"And the best sacrifice I can make is giving her a fabulous life where she will want for nothing."

"You're officially a fucking idiot, and truly know nothing about Amber if you think that's what is important to her."

Lincoln jerked like Colt had punched him. Had he made a mistake in sending her off with Brecken?

"It doesn't matter now. She made her choice."

"Yeah, but she's not married to him yet."

Resolved, regardless of the fact he was slowly bleeding internally, Lincoln stood. "It's done. It's over. If you want to fire me over this, then do it. I don't really give a fuck. If not, I have cabins that need repairs that I need to see to."

"If you change your mind, here's Brecken's address.

You're dismissed." Colt waved him off with disappoint shrouding his features.

Lincoln snatched the address before storming out of the office. She'd left. That was good. It would make it easier if he didn't see her every day. It would help him pretend like he wasn't hemorrhaging out.

Lincoln buried himself in work that week. He worked himself to the bone every day so that by the time he made it home, he crashed into bed each night. It was easier that way. But the worry and fear that he'd made a mistake hounded his every waking moment. He physically ached, missing the feel of her cuddled up against him.

He told himself it was for the best. Repeated it as a mantra so that one day he would actually believe it. That Amber marrying Brecken was the best thing for her.

By week's end, he was downright miserable. He was questioning every part of his existence, right down to what he had assumed was a noble sacrifice. It finally dawned on him what Colt meant by his statement.

Lincoln could work anywhere. What he couldn't do was live without Amber. If she didn't want to live on the ranch and wanted to live in a city somewhere, he could find a job wherever they were living. He'd had this fixed idea of Silver Springs being his place in the world, when the truth was, Amber was his place in the world. If she wasn't in it, he didn't want to be there. He would make whatever concessions necessary to ensure her happiness.

He was in love with Amber. Deeply, truly, madly in love with her.

Colt had given him Brecken's address earlier in the week. So that was where he was headed. He called in and told Colt's assistant that an emergency had cropped up and he was taking the day off. Considering he rarely did it, he was more than entitled to take a personal day. On the drive to Denver, he played over in his mind everything he was going to say to Amber, starting with telling her that he loved her. That their time together meant the world to him. That he'd lied when he'd told her it had only been a fun time. She meant everything to him.

He pulled up to the house. The dude had a goddamn mansion. Lincoln wrestled with last minute doubts before he exited the car.

Brecken answered the door looking rumpled and hungover, not to mention startled to see him. "What the hell are you doing here?"

"I need to speak with Amber."

"She's not here," he replied with a halfhearted laugh.

Not that Lincoln knew what was so funny. The guy looked like a mess. Was living with Amber that bad? "When will she be back?"

"She's not coming back. I thought she was with you this whole time. Especially with the baby and all." Brecken shrugged, running a hand through his unkempt hair.

"The what?" *Baby?*

"Yeah, don't you know that Amber's pregnant?"

Amber was pregnant. Holy fuck! That changed everything. "And what, you think I'm the father?"

Brecken leveled a glare at him. "You were the only one sleeping with her, dude. My sperm might be of the finest pedigree but it's not *that* good."

"You mean... you two didn't... wait, what?" Lincoln nearly staggered on the guy's stoop. He had been the only one sleeping with Amber. But that meant if Amber was pregnant, she was pregnant with his child.

"No. We didn't sleep together. Not for the last three years or so, anyway. I wanted to marry her, was going to claim the child as mine, but she decided that she couldn't marry me."

"Where is she?" Lincoln's world tilted. Amber was pregnant, with his baby. When he thought about how callous he had been that day when she had come to him with hope in her eyes, he knew he should be whipped. He'd made so many assumptions. He'd thought he had been sharing her, that she had been going from his bed to Brecken's, and back again.

"Not sure. We texted the other day. I wanted to make sure she was doing okay."

Lincoln nodded. "Thanks. I need to find her."

"You really didn't know about the baby?"

"No. She never told me." Because like an idiot, he had told her he didn't want kids. He still didn't want one—or did he?

Fuck. What a mess. And it was all his own making. If he had just talked with her, been honest with her about his feelings, they wouldn't be in this boat.

In his truck, he brought up his contacts and dialed. "Where is she?"

"Well, hello to you too," Colt replied drolly.

"Don't play games with me. I need to know where she's at. Dude, she's pregnant with my child," Lincoln snapped at her brother.

"She's what? You mean to tell me you knocked my sister up and then dumped her? I'm going to—"

"I love her, and I'm going to marry her." If she would have him. If she would even speak to him. He would do whatever it took to win her back.

"She bought a place in Winter Park," Colt explained, like it wasn't huge news that might have come in handy before Lincoln made the drive to Denver.

"In Winter Park? Why the fuck didn't you tell me?" Lincoln roared. She was in Winter Park. She had come back to the area he was in. That gave him a fighting chance.

"I'm telling you now, aren't I? And I kept it from you because I wanted to make sure you were serious when you finally removed your head from your ass."

Lincoln barked out a shaky laugh. "Yeah, it would have been nice if you'd told me before I wasted an entire day driving to Denver, and I still need to make the drive back."

"Ah, well, it serves you right. I'll text you her new address. Don't make me regret giving it to you," Colt warned him.

"I won't," Lincoln said. Because he was getting Amber back.

31

By Friday night, Amber's new home had really begun to take shape. Oh, she still needed to put art up on the walls and had rooms that needed to be furnished, but she had time. She was going to get as much done as she could over the next week. She began her new position as CEO and part owner of the Mountain Junction Ski Resort in a week's time.

While she only had a forty-nine percent stake in the company, it still gave her leverage. Besides, her new partner and boss was intelligent enough to let her do what she did best.

This past Monday, on her way to meet with Daniel where they had come to terms, she had driven past this house. It was a huge, ten-bedroom chalet on the outskirts of Winter Park. It was far enough away from the main hub that it wouldn't be inundated with tourist traffic, but close enough to her new job that she could be there quickly. Especially once the baby was here.

Daniel even knew about her pregnancy, and was fine with it. She would just need to make sure she had the right managers in place when she took maternity leave. Managers who would implement her plans without question.

After she and Daniel made the deal and had the paperwork set up with attorneys, Amber had stopped by this house. The previous owners had already vacated the premises. It was a property in need of a short sale.

Thankfully, money greased wheels. She put in a generous offer with the caveat that she got to move in, even while it was in escrow. Since it was a cash offer, it was easy for the bank to accept and get this one off their books. Granted, she still felt like this house was missing something. She had more furniture being delivered over the next few days, and would likely figure out what it was.

The doorbell rang, dragging her out of her thoughts. Who could that be? Not many people knew where she was presently living.

It was probably Noelle. She had been threatening to stage an intervention and show up on Amber's doorstep. Knowing her best friend, she had likely gone and corralled the rest of their group. Now that she had a path forward for herself and the baby, one that felt right, that was hers, Amber could use a little girl time with her bast gal pals.

On her trek to the door, thoughts tumbled in her mind over the tasks left to complete on the house. Which was why she wasn't prepared when she found Lincoln standing outside on her porch, looking devilishly handsome and frantic. He was missing his cowboy hat. His hair looked like he had run his hands through it a million times. His beard was unkempt. She opened her mouth to say something about his haggard appearance and figure out just what he was doing on her doorstep.

But he didn't give her the chance. In three strides, he had her in his arms and was kissing her. For a moment, she allowed herself to slide into his kiss. Because it was Lincoln. And god, she had missed his mouth. Had missed him. Every part of her being had ached to feel his arms around her.

Somehow, she found the strength inside herself and tore her mouth off his, shoving him back. Not that it worked, because he was two hundred pounds of dominant alpha.

"What the hell, Lincoln?"

"I love you," he blurted, his hands running over her like he was checking to make sure that she was real.

"What?" She stared up at him and began trembling. Tears pricked the corners of her eyes. He loved her? Was this some kind of sick, twisted game?

"You heard me, but I will say it again. I love you, Amber. When you came and told me that Brecken had asked you to marry him, I thought I could do the honorable thing for once. I thought what was best for you was that I step aside and let him give you the life you deserve. I lied when I told you that our time together had simply been fun."

"I don't understand what you're saying." There he went again, with the love. Could it be that he was serious?

"I'm saying that I love you, Amber. I love you so much, I can barely make it through my days without you in my life. I don't want to be noble and let you go. I want to be with you in every way that matters. And I know about the baby, love. I will be here in whatever capacity you want me to be. I will be a good father for our child."

He knew about the baby, and he wasn't mad. "How? Who told you?"

"Brecken."

"You called Brecken?" She shoved away from him finally, shaking and unsure, and afraid to hope.

"No. I drove to Brecken's house today, only to discover that you were no longer there."

"You drove all the way to Denver. But why?"

Lincoln took her trembling hands in his, staring at her with a surfeit of emotions in his eyes. "What part of *I love you* are you not getting?"

"That you're saying it now because of the baby." That could be the only reason why he would say those words.

"I deserve that. But Amber, babe, if you don't believe me, call your brother. He knows that I'm in love with you because we talked about it. And that was weeks ago. I only found out about the baby today."

"I need to sit down." She felt lightheaded. Like she couldn't breathe, and was worried she was going to start hyperventilating.

"Here, let's get you inside. It's cold out tonight, and you don't have a jacket on."

She didn't fight as Lincoln ushered her back inside her home, or when he sat her down in the living room, his attention and focus completely on her.

He knelt before her, studying her, never taking his hands off her.

"I know I messed up, Amber. And I know that I could live a thousand years, doing a good deed every day, and still not be good enough for you. I thought I was doing the best thing for you, so that you would have the best life possible."

It finally dawned on her, what he was saying. He hadn't sent her off because he didn't care about her; he'd done it because he loved her. "You did it because you don't think you deserve me?"

"Babe, I grew up in a trailer park, and that stench will be with me for the rest of my life."

"And you think I think less of you because of it?" she asked, feeling her anger rise.

"I—"

Her temper rose to epic heights, and she jabbed him in the shoulder with her finger. "You think I'm some vapid trust fund princess, that I can't see what a good man you are, that I can't look at where you came from and what you've made out of yourself and be thoroughly impressed?"

"You are?" There was such naked vulnerability in his eyes.

Why hadn't she seen this vulnerability? If she had, she would have reassured him. It was her fault for not looking deeper, not seeing that he still had wounds that bled.

"Damn you, Lincoln Sinclair, you can be a hard-headed son of a bitch sometimes, but I need you to hear what I'm about to say. I don't think less of you because of your upbringing. I think more of you."

"I don't think you're a vapid trust fund princess. I think you're a hell of a woman. I think you're my woman—that is, if you'll have me. And it's okay if you don't love me or if I killed it with my callous fumbling, because I will spend every day of the next fifty years proving to you that I love you. If you'll have me. And not just to date, either, I want to marry you. You can have me sign whatever prenups you want. I don't give a shit about your bank accounts. I just want you, and our baby."

The truth was right in front of her. She cupped his face in her hands. "Do you know the real reason I didn't speak up or say anything back then, after that first time that you kissed me in Park Tavern's parking lot? It wasn't because I didn't care, but because it fucking terrified me."

"Why?"

"Because I kissed you, and I was home. For the first time

in my life. And it rocked me to my core. It still does. The thing is, you are my home. You always have been, and always will be. I've been in love with you since that first kiss."

"Amber." He leaned his forehead against hers. "I don't deserve you. But if by some miracle you can forgive me for being an idiot, for hurting you like I did, I can promise you that you will never have cause to doubt my love for you again."

"Are you sure you're okay about the baby? I know this pregnancy wasn't planned. And I know you said that you don't want kids. I don't want to trap you into something that you'll regret."

"The only regret I have is not telling you that I love you sooner, and that I hurt you. I'll admit the news took me by surprise. But the thought that we made a child together thrills me. I know I'm not my dad, and never will be. So what do you say? Think you can marry a delinquent from the wrong side of the tracks?"

"Yes. Oh my god, yes."

Joy burst in a cacophony inside her as her heart rejoiced. Lincoln cupped her nape tenderly. His love shone brightly in his dark eyes. And then his lips were on hers, kissing her lovingly and deeply, welcoming her home.

This was what she had been missing in the house. Lincoln.

He rose, never breaking the kiss, and lifted her into his arms, only to sit on the couch and settle her on his lap. When he finally lifted his mouth, she had melted against him. He stroked her back.

"Fuck, I love you. Thank you for giving me another chance," he said.

"What were you going to do if I said no?"

He shrugged. "I don't know. Beg. Go all dominant on your sweet ass until you caved."

"I wouldn't have minded that. There's a lot of that world you haven't shown me. You still haven't restrained me, or tried the flogger, or any of those things."

"We have all the time in the world to explore your submissive nature. And it would be my honor to guide you deeper into that world. But there are some things that might have to wait until after the baby's born. I wouldn't be comfortable flogging you with the baby." He traced a hand over her belly.

She put her palm on his and pressed his hand flat. "I can promise you that the Peanut is okay. All safe and warm inside me."

"Peanut?"

"Well, what else are we going to call it? I mean, that's about its size right now."

"I never thought of that. But I suppose Peanut will work for now. I don't want to wait to marry you. I know it takes time to plan a wedding, and I will give you as much time as you think you want. But I want to start that chapter with you as soon as possible."

"How does next Friday sound? It would work best for me, before I begin my new job. We'll have to do our honeymoon at a different time though."

Lincoln barked out a laugh. "You want to get married next Friday? I don't know if we can find a minister willing to perform the ceremony that quickly. I'll search for one, though, whatever you want—"

She put her finger over his lips. "I was thinking Vegas. We could get the group together and fly down. We can even get my parents and your sister there. What do you think? Or is that too soon?"

"Babe, when are you going to realize whatever you want, whenever you want it, I'm game and am all in. Let's get married next Friday in Vegas. Because then you're mine, forever."

"And you'll be mine too."

"Always, Amber. I've always been yours." And then he kissed her. Infused within his kiss was all his love and desire. His kiss was a promise of that love, and hope for their future.

Amber knew that all the struggles and conflict of the last month, and through the years, had all been directing her down one path, one road. And through every twist and turn, that road had always led to Lincoln. It had led her home.

HOW TO ROPE A NAKED COWBOY
SILVER SPRINGS RANCH, BOOK 7

All she wants is a simple day outdoors to clear her mind and figure out a game plan for her life. After months of being little more than a reclusive shut-in, Noelle Addams forces herself to spend the hot summer day on one of the trails at Silver Springs Ranch. Perhaps the time outside will help her begin to mend her broken soul.

And yet, she never expects to come across a naked Tanner Ellis emerging from a secluded pond. Or, for the first time in months, since the night of blood and screams, to feel something besides fear and malaise.

Tanner was simply trying to cool off from the suffocating heat of the day. Running into the sultry Noelle in nothing but his birthday suit wasn't in his plans.

But after a scorching afternoon in her arms, the scared beauty is in his blood. He makes it his mission to bring her out of her shell and help heal her battered soul. He craves her. Yearns to claim her.

Yet, when it matters most, will Noelle hightail it, or will she give them a chance at forever?

Read the next installment in the Silver Springs Ranch Series! Read it now!

MIDNIGHT HIGHLANDER
DUNGEON SINGLES NIGHT SERIES, BOOK 7

Xavier Campbell needs a miracle. If he doesn't want to lose the life he's worked so hard to build, he must get married, and quickly. Trouble is, there is no woman in his life. Not even a friend with benefits. As a regular Dom at Eternal Eros, he gets what he needs and goes home. And a wife? Hell, no. This Highlander is single for a reason. So when his entire existence threatens to come crashing down, he realizes he might have to make some adjustments...or a bargain with the she-devil who beguiles him, body and mind, from the first moment he touches her.

Emma Morton wants a man. To play with. Watch television with. Cuddle with. And yes, God help her, she wants him hard, naked, and in her bed. More than once. What she doesn't want is complications. Expectations. She is dedicated to her work, to building her business. She's worked too long and too hard to change her plans for something as fleeting as love. No matter how much she wishes otherwise, life has repeatedly proven that romance is a myth. Pure fairytale.

But passion? Yes. She could *definitely* go for a 'Single's Night' of play—and release—at the infamous Eternal Eros.

After one scorching night of pleasure, a reckless bargain is made. Marriage with an expiration date. A business arrangement. Nothing more.

But what starts as a farce becomes a bit too real and Xavier realizes this is no game. Telling Emma the truth would be dangerous...especially when he realizes he is playing for keeps.

Head to Eternal Eros! Read it now!

ALSO BY ANYA SUMMERS

Torn In Two

Redeemed By Love

Box Sets

Dungeon Singles Night Collection Part 1

How To Rope A Cowboy Box Set

The Man In The Mask: The Complete Manor Series Collection

ABOUT ANYA

Born in St. Louis, Missouri, Anya grew up listening to Cardinals baseball and reading anything she could get her hands on. She remembers her mother saying if only she would read the right type of books instead binging her way through the romance aisles at the bookstore, she'd have been a doctor. While Anya never did get that doctorate, she graduated cum laude from the University of Missouri-St. Louis with an M.A. in History.

Anya is a bestselling and award-winning author published in multiple fiction genres. She also writes urban fantasy, paranormal romance, and contemporary romance under the name Maggie Mae Gallagher. A total geek at her core, when she is not writing, she adores attending the latest comic con or spending time with her family. She currently lives in the Midwest with her two furry felines.

www.anyasummers.com
anya@anyasummers.com

Join Anya's mailing list to be the first to be notified of new releases, free books, exclusive content, special prizes and author giveaways!
https://anyasummers.com/newsletter/

Follow Anya on social media!

Facebook: facebook.com/AnyaSummersAuthor

Twitter: twitter.com/anyabsummers

Instagram: instagram.com/anyasummersauthor

Goodreads: goodreads.com/author/show/
15183606.Anya_Summers

BookBub: bookbub.com/authors/anya-summers

Made in the USA
Monee, IL
03 March 2022